THE DELIVERANCE OF DILAN

KATHY COOPMANS

Copyright @ 2016 by Kathy Coopmans

This is a work of fiction. Names, characters, places, organizations, and events portrayed in this novel either are the product of the author's imagination or are used fictitiously, and any resemblance to actual persons, living or dead, business establishments, events, or locales is entirely coincidental.
All rights reserved. In accordance with the U.S. Copyright Act of 1976.
First edition: May 2016

Editor: Julia Goda Editing Services
https://www.facebook.com/juliagodaeditingservices/?fref=ts

Formatting: Affordable Formatting
https://www.facebook.com/AffordableFormatting74135

Cover Model: Lance Jones
https://www.facebook.com/LanceJonesTattooFitnessModel/?fref=ts

Cover Designer: Sommer Stein
https://www.facebook.com/PPCCovers/?fref=ts

Photographer: Eric Battershell
https://www.facebook.com/ericbattershellphotography/?fref=ts

DEDICATION

This book is dedicated to every woman who has found her true Soulmate.

PROLOGUE

DILAN

This bitch sitting next to me in my new Chevy Silverado has all but ruined the sweet smell of the inside of my baby. I can no longer smell the leather or the fresh scent of new. All I can smell is her and the damn bottle of perfume she fucking bathed in. Christ.

Why am I bringing her to this wedding again? Because I need the bitch. That's why. I have plans for her and her family. Ones I'll keep to myself for now. Well, not to myself exactly. My uncle Salvatore is in on it. He wasn't happy when I told him what needed to be done; he understands though. It's all about revenge, and thank god he's prepared to help deliver it. Tonight is the beginning. I promised him no one would know. I lied. They will all know who this skank is. I have no intentions at all of ruining this wedding. I have to go though. Sure, I could have gone alone. That's not the plan. I need her to set this in motion, finish this, so I can move on with my life.

It's quite obvious Jazmin has plans of her own the way she's leaning into me over the console, her hand rubbing up and down my thigh. Her arms are like that of a damn daddy longlegs. Long and thin, while the inside of her skin is as poisonous as a flesh-eating spider's. Dangerous.

Either she desperately needs to get fucked, or she wants to kill me. Either way, I will make sure I achieve my plan first. That nasty hand with her well-groomed fingernails glides seductively up and down my leg, if that's what you want to call them; they look more like pointed blue talons. Like they'd drill a damn hole in your back, stab you in the back, and fuck you up. Poke your eyes out. Ugly as hell. And if she gets any closer to my dick with those fuckers, I may say to hell with my plan and break them off right along with her hand. Woman or not, she's just like her brother. Juan Felipe Carlos. The man who fucked me over. Set me up along with my now very dead cousin Royal Diamond. They say hell has no fury like a woman scorned. Fuck that shit. Hell has no fury like a man whose destiny was prearranged, a man who was set up and forced to spend a few years behind bars for a crime he didn't commit. That's what hell is. Hell on earth, that is. It won't be easy to bring them down. They have eyes everywhere. Seedy fuckers.

Jazmin Maria Carlos is a vile, self-loathing, vengeful, and hateful cunt. And when I look her in the face, you bet your sweet ass I will make those words count by shoving them down her nasty throat. She may have had nothing to do with what happened to me. But she is exactly like them. She's been after me for years. Claimed she always wanted me. The strange thing is, every time my ass was taken out while in prison, she was there to visit the very minute I recovered. How goddamn ironic.

I will get my revenge on them all. EVERY. LAST. ONE. OF. THEM.

This is the second time I've taken her out. The first time, all I did was take her to dinner. A get-to-know-you type of thing. I followed her from New York to Vail, Colorado. Saw her at the bar. Walked right up to her and nearly gagged on my own vomit when she damn near dry humped my ass right there. Even though we knew each other, there was no way I was taking her to my bed. She reeked of death just like she does now.

And God, Vail is absolutely breathtaking. She dirtied the place up though with her presence. She wanted me to go back to her room after I invited her to dinner. Visualize a man about ready to regurgitate his food right in the middle of the restaurant. That was me when she asked.

Granted, the woman is a knockout with her long, black hair. Her fake tits. Her long legs. But she is a born-to-be killer. She will fuck you and then shoot you right in the head before you have your dick back in your pants, or cut you up into unrecognizable pieces.

She poisons men with her date rape drug. That's how she is. I shut that shit right down. Lied. Told her it was a coincidence I bumped into her. I'm not the typical guy to just jump in bed with a woman. She pouted and then purred like a cat. Well, there are some pretty damn viscous cats in this world too. Besides, this bitch and her family don't deserve shit. Except what I'm about to throw at them all. Once I piss her the fuck off, they will get what's coming to them. Every goddamn one of them.

Her hands are nothing like the ones I wish were on me right now. Anna Drexler. The woman I needed to get away from. The woman who is way too good for me. Sweet, innocent, and so damn beautiful. The woman I need to protect.

I take my hand off the wheel, tell the bitch I love this song, and crank up the sweet, methodic rumble of Eminem rapping and carrying on about a Demon Inside. Fucking perfect song for me.

I have way too many demons inside of me. Too many for Anna to handle. That's one of the reasons why I took off after I got shot. I'd go through all of that pain again though, knowing that Anna survived and I played a part in saving her precious life. I plan on freeing myself of these demons, so I can go after the woman who utilizes every bit of my dreams. I'm crazy about her.

Fuck, that night I was shot and the weeks that followed sucked me right back into the hell I'd escaped from. I cannot allow my mind to go there. Not today. Not when I'm going to come face-to-face with sweetness for the first time in six months.

Whatever it is about Anna that lights up my world whenever she's around is a mystery. After my stint in prison, she's been the only female to put a genuine smile on my face. To make me feel like I'm worthy of her or some shit. I'm not. And fuck, the way she looked at me when she thought I didn't notice. She looked at me like I could save her, when in truth if I were to let her in, she would be the one to save me. I need to get her out of my head. At least until I get this night over with. Then, when I lay my head down on my pillow and close my eyes, only then I can think about her, like I do every other night. Dream about her and what could be if I didn't have this debt to settle.

Instead, I let my mind float to the conversation I overheard and the discussion Anna and I had when we went to get ice cream. A simple walk that should have taken us all of twenty minutes. A walk I should have never agreed to after I heard her tell Deidre she was a virgin. And a walk I should have asked her to stay home for. She wouldn't have been hurt if I had.

I knew she was innocent, suspected she was a virgin, but when your suspicions are confirmed from the woman you want more than anything you've wanted before, you tend to lose your damn mind. Her virginity wasn't nor is the issue. It's me. I'm so fucked up that there is no way I could take that away from her. She needs someone stable, and that's exactly what I told her that very same night. It gutted me to tell her what I did. Ironic as it was, five minutes later, trying to save her life, I was shot in the gut. Fuck. I should have died. The urge to give up pulling me in one direction and her screaming my name, telling me she needed me, in another. While that piece of shit beat her. Then took her. I would have given up and succumbed to death calling my name louder than her screams. I couldn't. Not until I knew she was safe.

When I came to in the hospital, the look on my parents faces gutted me. My mother Ginny with her thankful, red-rimmed eyes; my dad with his tired expression and the words, "Our son. Oh, thank god, my baby," coming from my mother. Damn it was tough to see them so battered and broken, not knowing if their only child was going to die. I knew I had to live, for them.

And now as Anna's words echo in my head from that night, the closer I get to this wedding, the more my gut fucking kills me again. Not from the pain of the gunshot wound. That's nearly healed. The pain I know I'm going to see on her face when she looks at me, or the one that's on mine if she's with someone else. I recall everything she said. Vividly.

"You heard me, didn't you?" Anna boldly stated the minute we walked out the door and descended the stairs leading into Deidre's apartment building. I stopped moving, not knowing what the hell to say. I went with the truth.

"Yes," I simply said.

"That's why I volunteered for us to go. I wanted to talk to you. Get whatever is happening between us out in the open. I'm not crazy, Dilan. I feel it when you look at me, and I know you feel it when I'm looking at you. There's something happening between us." She sighed, then kept on talking, while I was standing there thinking, 'Christ, you are so damn beautiful. I find it hard to breathe around you. You make me want to feel, but I can't feel anything for you. If I do, and you get caught up in my world, it will kill you.'

"I know it's not safe for us to even be out here right now, Dilan," she said as we started to walk to the store. "Somehow, I feel safe with you. Like you would do anything to save me. I want you to know I would do anything to save you too." And those words right there set me off and stripped me at the same goddamn time.

Shit. What the hell could I say? I've had this plan in motion since I was released from prison. I couldn't back down now. I needed to destroy the people who fucked me over. One of them was dead, while the others were still out here, breathing the same goddamn air as this beautiful woman walking silently now beside me. God. I was going to have to lie. I heard hope in her tone. Those things she told Deidre about me. She couldn't know I felt those things too. That I wished things could be different. That I could pull her into my arms right now and kiss her like my life depended on it, because it does. She's special. She's the only woman I've thought about having a future with. Dreamed of it even.

I've thought of everything about her. From how soft her hair would be to how smooth her toned legs would feel when I slid my hands up and down them, her muscles contracting, goose bumps forming on her skin. From my touch alone. No one else's, just mine.

How she would look at me with love, knowing I would keep her safe. Not only from the danger that would always lurk outside with the life I lead, but how I would keep her heart safe too, because it would belong to me, as much as mine would belong to her.

"Listen, Anna. I like you. Hell, who wouldn't? But whatever you think could, should, or would happen between us, will never happen. For one, all I want to do is fuck you. Fuck you until you're screaming my name. Fuck you raw. I fuck, Anna. I don't do love." I shrugged. She stopped.

I turned around and looked at her. She had a look of astonishment on her face. Disbelief.

"I don't believe you," she shouted. "Believe it, Anna. I was waiting until this shit was over to take you to my bed. And hey, if you still want that, then I'll be glad to take what you're offering, but that's all you get. You'll give up your virginity to a man who will gladly take it and give you nothing in return." Her mouth dropped open. My heart splattered all over the sidewalk.

Then I saw the shadow in the alley, close, ready to strike. I dove for her. Saved her that night. I'd do it all again, knowing she's safe. The pain from those gunshot wounds that are now in the past, I've dealt with, recovered from.

However, Anna is the type of woman a man like me—who's been secretly planning to destroy, kill, and take down the Mexican Cartel that helped put him in a hellhole for years—needs to stay away from. Very few people know what the fuck went down with me when I was in prison. My Uncle Salvatore and John Greer know. How he knows, he hasn't told me to this day. Someone inside those fucking walls of hell, I'm sure.

The rest of my family knows nothing. I've asked my uncle and John to keep the knowledge of the shit I endured to themselves. If Roan and Cain and the rest of my brothers knew, they would be out for blood. They're as loyal as I am. They would want to help, but no damn way am I risking any more of the people I care about getting hurt.

I sure as hell can't risk any of them knowing what I've been planning. They'll sure as shit be up my ass, demanding what the hell I'm doing with this bitch when they see me tonight though. I won't lie to them, but I will try like hell to tell them to stay out of it. Especially Roan. This is his wedding. Fuck. I hope he doesn't notice me until he's at least said 'I do.'

My only wish is that I could have a woman as pure as Anna. She thinks I can save her. She couldn't be more wrong. It's my heart that needed saved. Still does. I've fallen for a woman I may never have. A woman who could erase my tainted past. A woman I left behind, knowing that if she comes anywhere near me, this time I won't be able to save her. This war will end with more bloodshed than any war before this. This is my war. One that is going to go up in flames.

CHAPTER ONE

ANNA

"You look beautiful, honey." My mom, as biased as she is, stands behind me in my bathroom. I've never been one to care about my looks. I've never had a reason to, not until six months ago. But hey, who's counting, right? He's gone. Traveling the country, he said. Well, he told everyone but me. He refused to see me. That destroyed me more than the hurtful things he said before all of our lives did a nose dive, dangling on the upper ledge of pure damn hell. Liar. Coward. Prick.

"Thank you, mom. You look stunning yourself," I say truthfully. She does. Her blond hair is in a French twist, her makeup light on her gleaming, blue eyes I'm grateful to have inherited. And her dress. She's wearing a light blue, strapless dress with a sheer overlay that sits just below her knees. No one would believe she was forty-six years old. She's beautiful.

Right now, though, I want to be alone. I'm thankful she's become close to Beth and Charlotte. As a result of their friendship, along with the fact we both work for Deidre now, mom baked the cake for today, so she has to leave a little earlier, which also means her boyfriend of a few months will meet her there. I couldn't be happier for my mom. She deserves someone who is only devoted to her, and Ramsey is the guy. He adores her.

"I'll see you there, honey," she says happily.

"Be there soon." Following her down the hallway in our apartment, I help her put on her long wool coat and grab her clutch for her. The minute the door closes behind her, I prevent my shaky legs from collapsing from underneath me by bracing myself up against the door.

I'm not looking forward to today at all. And this is what pisses me off.

Filled with anger mixed with sadness, I make my way back to my room. I stop just inside the doorway, staring at the dress I bought for today. It's a sexy, short, royal blue dress with a lace overlay. One arm is draped to my wrist in lace, while the other shoulder is completely bare. It screams sophistication and confidence, which I've never had. I do now though. Thanks to Calla, Alina, and Deidre, and the many talks we've had. They boosted my confidence to levels I never even knew existed.

I no longer think of myself as the athletic tomboy. Even though I do everything to still stay in shape, to keep my body limber and toned, I no longer look in the mirror and see what I used to see before. Now, I see a woman who holds her head up. A lady who wants a man who doesn't deserve me. And yet, I still want him. The things he said to me are lies. I know they are. He is so full of shit. He's scared. Of what, I have no clue.

"Shit." I'm so mad for thinking of the one man who I desperately want to see me in this dress. I chose it for him.

I know he'll be there. I feel it in my gut. It's been six months since I've seen him. Six months since he helped save my life, only to destroy it the first chance he had. I hope he chokes on whatever the hell he's drinking tonight when he sees me. It may be childish of me to think that, but after what he said to me, it's the way I feel. Loser.

I sigh and sit down on the edge of my bed. I shouldn't be thinking about him at all. The ungrateful son of a bitch.

Over the past several months, whenever my mind would drift to him, wondering what he's doing, or better yet who, I tried focusing on anything else to try and get my mind off of him. It didn't matter what I did, whether I would work late, try and follow a new recipe, bake dozens of cookies or cupcakes, only to shove half of them in my mouth and watch those calories go straight to my ass, nothing helped to keep my mind off of him. I like my new curvy body, thanks to my sweet tooth. I can have my cake and eat it too as they say. Although, I would much rather eat him. Asshole man that he is.

I always think of him. The man with the dark brown hair and eyes just as brown, with the colorful tattoos on both of his arms, across his back and chest. Fucking asshole.

I bend down, retrieving the box that holds my five-inch strappy heels. Not the best shoes for winter, but hey, when you live in a place where there's a cab on every corner, or where you can call to have one pick you up and drive you wherever you need to go in this large city, then strappy high heels it is. On top of that, these heels show just how smooth and toned my short legs are. At five foot two, I need all the help I can get.

"Ouch." I grimace and place my hand through my robe over my now bare pussy. This morning, all of us women went down to the day spa on the third floor of our apartment building. We all got manis, pedis, waxing, and our hair done. My long, blond hair is curled into loose waves and swept to the side, where they drape over my shoulder. I love having the spa right here. I even made an appointment a few weeks ago and had my hair colored. It's darker underneath with a few slivers of dark threaded throughout the top and sides.

Mom and I are living in Aidan's old apartment. He immediately moved all his personal belongings over to Deidre's after the night I try to forget. Not only did Dilan almost lose his life that very same night, there were several others of us who thought we were going to die or wound up hurt worse than we actually did as well. I had several bruises and broken ribs to prove it.

I cringe, thinking of that night, all thoughts of my very first waxing gone. It's not like anyone will see it anyway. Why I let Deidre talk me into it, I will never know. That shit hurts, but it sure beats shaving, especially if the hairs stay gone for four to six weeks, like Monique, the wax specialist, said.

I move to my dresser. It's the one I had in our old home. A bedroom set my father bought for me when I graduated high school. The dresser and nightstands are black. My king size bed is black too. The headboard is made of leather. I've accessorized it with a cream-colored sheepskin-styled rug. The bedding is a deep burgundy, with a matching sheepskin comforter, in which I tend to drown my sorrows. Off-white lamps with their spiral design bases and square shades finish the style. I even dangled some crystal beads from them. I love this room. And the view of New York it gives me.

Tears spring to my eyes, thinking of my father. He was murdered by my half-brother. It was a nightmare. One I don't care to relive. Ryan Drexler Jr. is dead now. He can no longer hurt me, or my mom, or Aidan. My dad may have been a scammer, a cheat, and an evil man, but he was good to my mom and me. Always there when I needed him, even though he lead a double life, married to Ryan's mom, who is a bitch, while having an affair and then had me with my mom.

"God, Anna. Today is a happy day. Roan and Alina are getting married. Leave things in the past. Especially things you have no control of," I scold myself. I've been down this shit road of self-doubt, an uneasy mind, and heartbreak. Fuck them all. My so-called half-brother didn't win when he tried to destroy us, when he left my body broken and beaten. And my dad didn't break my mother's heart either, like I thought he would when we found out he was dead. I mean, it broke her heart when he died, especially the way he died, but she moved on. So did I the best I knew how.

I remember her words so clearly when I asked her how she was doing a few days after we found out about his death. "He was never mine to begin with, sweetheart. I loved him once and he loved me. We remained friends for you. That's what parents do when they love their child." That about knocked me off of my ass to hear my sweet mom say that, when all this time I thought she loved the man.

And we didn't find out until a week later when I tried to call him, only to have his son Ryan Jr. answer the phone. Abhorrent and disgusting terms flew out of his mouth. The names he called both my mom and me. He was out of control with rage, angry over the fact that my dad had left me money. Money I couldn't have cared less about. Hell, I didn't even know he died, let alone left me money. All I wanted to know, deserved to know, was where my dad was buried. The man was out of control, told me nothing. I didn't even attend my dad's funeral, didn't even know he was gone. I've learned to deal with it though. He loved me. This I know. He knew I loved him too. I don't feel sorry for myself. I'm only sad I wasn't able to say goodbye to him.

"Enough, Anna. Move your ass. Maybe some hot, single guy will catch your eye tonight." With my mood perking up, I move, pulling out my matching strapless bra. I ditch my panties. No way am I covering up down there. Not when it feels like it's on damn fire.

Thank god it's not bright red anymore. This causes me to laugh, out loud. Here I am with the top half of my body cold with insensitive memories, while my bottom half is hot and heated. Could make for a very interesting evening. Especially if Dilan does show up.

I slip my robe off and put my bra on, loving the way it makes my breasts look even bigger. I pick up my dress and moan when I step into it at the way the silk feels on my skin. Soft. With a little wiggle of my hips, I have it over them, then place my arm into the lace and feel like a woman.

"Oh, wow," I say when I look in the mirror. "Not too bad, Anna." I turn around, checking out my ass. Eat your heart out, Dilan. If you're there tonight, you watch how this ass can move.

I place a pair of silver diamond studded earrings in my ears—another gift from my dad when I turned sixteen. Then I spritz my favorite perfume on and strap on my sandals. I leave the confines of my room, pull my long wool coat out of the closet, and grab my matching clutch and my phone off the counter.

"Here we go," I say, grabbing my overnight bag to stay at The Rosalie Hotel overlooking Central Park, where the reception will be. I open the door and lock it behind me.

I make it to the lobby, my sandals letting everyone know I'm determined more than ever to have fun tonight, as they click across the tiled floor as if they have as much of a strong mind as I do. I'm determined to enjoy witnessing Alina and Roan pledge their love for another, to appreciate the fact that I'm resilient—despite the whole kit and caboodle so-to-speak shit I've dealt with over the past several months. Marty, the sixty-five year old doorman whom I adore, whistles when I stride up to him, greeting me in his pleasant voice. I love this man.

"You have a wonderful time tonight, Miss Anna." He opens the door and helps guide me into the waiting cab.

"I sure will. And you tell that wife of yours I said she's lucky to have you." He nods. Then chuckles. I tell him that every time I see him.

"You know I will." He winks then shuts the door behind me.

The snow is falling lightly as I stare out the window of the cab I called for earlier. I'm not one to drive much in this town. And my car isn't the best in the snow anyway. Another gift from my dad. A red Jaguar. I've had it in storage since moving here. One of these days, when the weather breaks, I'll take it out. Drive through the mountains. Who knows? Right now, though, I'm enjoy watching the people walking around in the middle of winter. Bundled up. Some hand in hand with a loved one, while others out looking for love. It's a town full of so many possibilities. People flock here for no reason, from all over the world.

The skyline at night is like nothing I've seen before. It's breathtaking, seeing the tall buildings lit up. This is a city in a world of its own.

We pull up to the quaint church on E. 61st Street. My nerves are probing away in every direction by the time I pay the driver and step out into the crisp winter air. I'm chilled the minute I climb the steps, my bare legs screaming for warmth.

"Hi, Ramsey." He's waiting inside the door like he said he would be.

"Hey, Anna. Let me take your bag and set it in the room with all the others." He takes my bag from my hand. Even though the wedding is small with family and close friends, I suspect it will be larger than expected with all the acquaintances the Diamond and Solokov families have combined.

"And your coat." He helps me guide it off. "Thank you," I say politely, while I wait for him to hang my coat and take my bag to the room where a staff member from the hotel is supposed to retrieve them from and leave them in our rooms.

"This is exquisite," I tell him when he returns.

"I've never seen anything more beautiful, except you and your mom, of course." I playfully tease him by saying, "I couldn't agree with you more. She is quite breathtaking, isn't she?"

"She is. So are you, Anna. Don't ever forget that," he answers bashfully. He's always saying sweet things to both mom and me. "And here she is." His eyes gleam when my mom approaches. So do hers as she walks our way, focused on him. Her gaze shifts to me when she stops in front of us.

"My little girl is all grown up. And quite the knockout. That dress looks heavenly on you, dear." She pulls me in for a hug.

"Thanks, mom."

"Well, let me escort two of the most gorgeous women in, shall I?" Each of us loop our arms through his. We find seats in the middle of the church. I find myself looking around for the one person I hope to see. When I don't find him, a ping of disappointment bellows through me. His loss, I suppose, if he doesn't show up. He better though. Not for me, but for Roan. I know how badly he wants him here.

I take the next few minutes to look around. It's simple, yet elegant. There are light-cream-colored ribbons at the end of each pew, adorned with dark green flowers. The same flowers and candles in every shape and size embellish the front of the church. It screams Alina. Rare, pure, and elegant.

More people trickle in and just as I expected, before long, the place is packed. Small and simple, they said. If this is small, then I wonder what big looks like. There are several hundred people here. I smile, knowing all of these people are here to witness a love like I've never seen before. Well, that's not entirely true. Cain and Calla along with Aidan and Deidre's love speak volumes too. As soon as the music starts, I remind myself that someday, I will be loved like that. I deserve to be.

It's in the moment I stand up when Alina begins to walk down the aisle with her father, that I see the man I was hoping to see. Only he doesn't look like the same man. No, this man has much longer hair, dark sunglasses on, and his arm around a tall, beautiful, long-haired brunette.

My heart stops. I can't breathe. I know he sees me through those glasses. And when he lifts his hands and takes them off, his eyes holding mine, I falter in my confidence, because he's not looking at me the same way he used to. No, he is most assuredly not. His mask is blank. Void, as if he doesn't even know me at all. He's full of shit. It may have been a while since we've seen each other, but he's a liar if I've ever known one. And I've known a few in my short years. He wants me as much as I want him. Nevertheless, he's here with someone else. And damn it, that hurts.

CHAPTER TWO

DILAN

Shit. Just my luck. The minute I walk through the door, my mom spots me. "Dilan." She looks me up and down. Her disapproval of my attire is written all over her. I know my appearance is different from the last time she saw me. My hair is longer. I haven't shaved in a week. At least I'm dressed up, a little. Black dress pants. Black button-up shirt. She hates black, unless it's black tie. Which in this case, it is. This is as close to black tie as I'm going to get. She'll have to deal with it.

I'm practically choking to death on my own guilt now that I'm here. I should have worn a suit jacket. No damn way am I wearing a tie though. I'd hang myself with the damn thing by the time this night is over. Especially with this greedy, money hungry, powerful, and dangerous woman by my side.

"It's so good to see you." She approaches, leans in for a hug. "I've missed you too, mom," I say truthfully, wrapping her in my arms. "You look like hell, boy. Are you doing okay?" she whispers in my ear. "I'm good, mom. Just tired. It's been a long drive," I lie through my teeth. Jazmin lives here, about an hour out of the city. After our dinner date, I invited her to the wedding. She stuttered her answer of yes. Shocked, I'm sure. I'm sure the minute my friends and Roan have the chance to talk to me, I'll get my ass chewed out. Like I said, they know where I've been. I'm surprised Roan hasn't demanded I get my ass back here before now. He wasn't happy when I told him I wouldn't stand up with him. It killed me to tell him that. But my plan was already set. All I needed to do was find Jazmin, and then it started rolling.

"Who do we have here?" She releases her hold on me and turns toward Jazmin. Fuck. Here we go. "Mom, this is Jazmin. Jazmin, my mom, Ginny Levy." I decide not to tell Jazmin's last name. Not yet anyway. The minute Roan, Cain, and Aiden see her, I may end up dead by the end of the night. Not to mention all the others who will more than likely be there. Each one of them will wonder what in the fuck I am doing.

"It's nice to meet you." Mom sticks her hand out for Jazmin to shake. "You too," Jazmin replies, taking a hold of mom's hand. I want so badly to tell her to sanitize the hell out of her hand. I don't. "You should really go take a seat, honey. We can talk at the reception." Mom releases her hand, scrutinizing me as she does so. Fuck, she knows. I can see it. Her eyes are sending me that what-in-the-fuck-do-you-think-you're-doing look. My mom normally speaks her mind. She's not one to hold a damn thing back. I'm thirty-one years old, and if she feels like she has to crack me upside my head, she will. Her cheeks twitch. This is killing her not to call me out. But it isn't the right place for her to say anything.

"Where's dad?" I ask, trying to lighten the disappointment coming from the only woman I've ever loved. Well, up until Anna walked into my life anyway.

Jazmin doesn't pick up on shit. She's scoping out the place, her eyes flitting all over. I give the bitch credit. Hell, she could be walking into a trap for all she knows. She most assuredly is though. I put my arm around her, my insides balking at me, trying to claw their way out of my body. Even they can't stand her. "He's already in there. I came out to grab these." She pulls out tissues from her hand.

"Weddings are a joyous occasion. Why we cry at them, I'll never know," Jazmin pipes in, leaning into me as if we're a couple. Yeah, we're a couple all right. A couple of people who would shoot the other one in the back if given the chance.

"This is true. But you see, this is my only nephew. I'm happy for him. He's been through a lot these past few years. So has his bride. I'll do everything to make sure the two of them stay happy and no one tries to ruin their happiness." I almost choke on my mom's insinuation. Again, Jazmin doesn't pick up on a thing. She smiles politely, showing her agreement.

"I'll let your dad know you're here," she says and strides away.

"Shall we?" I ask pleasantly.

"I'm excited. Never would I have guessed I would be attending this wedding. I mean, we all know how our families don't get along. Maybe with us seeing each other, we'll be able to call a treaty like The Diamonds and Solokovs did. I mean look, they hated each other once, and now their children are getting married. I think it's wonderful."

This bitch is good. I'd love to give her my honest answer to her dumb question. Two families who despise each other can make amends. Become friends. Not in our case though. When one family provides the drugs to help set another family member up to go down for shit they knew nothing about, then fuck no, we do not become friends. We kill to the death like male BETA fish do when they're dropped in a tank. Either kill or be killed. I'm not about to die. I'll seek revenge in the most excruciating form.

In my case, I'm killing them all. Wiping out the entire empire. With no misconceptions, no turning back, and no remorse.

She loops her arm through mine. My skin is screaming at me to take a shower. To wash her filth off of me.

"Two dates do not qualify as us dating. And if another marriage is what you're looking for, you won't find it in me, Jazmin. Ever. Let's find a seat." Her red-stained lips part open, a soft gasp of surprise escaping her soiled mouth. Everything about her is unclean. And the Oscar goes to? Her, not me. Dumb bitch.

We walk the rest of the way in. I guide her around the back of the last pew. I know I'll be spotted the moment the guys all stand up there.

I should be one of them. Up there with my cousin, my friend. I've fucked them all over with this personal vendetta I have.

I hate myself for it. I follow behind Jazmin, allowing her to sit first. The minute I sit, I spot her. Anna. Her hair color is different. One of her sexy as hell shoulders is bare, exposing skin my fingers curl up into a fist over, because all they want to do is touch her. She hasn't seen me yet. She's talking to her mom and an older man.

Her pheromones are invigorating. Sweet and innocent. Airborne to a degree that stimulates a stir to my cock. He hasn't awakened since the last time I saw her. Before she was taken from me.

The music starts and yet I still can't look away. The minute she stands, her tiny frame rotates in my direction, her gaze darting all over. My mind is wondering if she's searching for me. Hoping.

When her baby blues find me, I feel a hit of regret in my chest. She's hurting. I would give anything to not be the cause of her hurt. For her to see the real me. The man who wants her more than anything. I would walk through a burning fire with nails sticking of out my body for her to look at me the way she used to. She's not though. Instead, she looks defeated. Like she knows she's truly lost whatever connection we once had. The pull deflates in her eyes, and fuck if it doesn't puncture my gut worse than any gunshot ever did.

I observe her stance. It's assured, stronger, if at all possible. Her head is held high. Her shoulders are pulled back. Christ, how I wish I could jump over these pews and touch her. Hold her up against me, run my fingers down her bare arm. She's killing me with that sexy as fuck dress. I'm unable to see the whole thing from where I'm standing, but I know it's short, showcasing those legs.

Her eyes dart back and forth between me and the skunk-smelling bitch. I restrict the urge to go to her. Instead, I pull my glasses off. My stare changes from lust to disgust. Her gorgeous head snaps back. A line of confusion draws across her forehead. She needs to stay away from me. I do the one thing I hate to do. I sketch a mental picture of her in all her beauty. I need to try and forget about her, for now. I'm not good for her, not when I have a vendetta to end. Lives to take. I watch sadness overlap her hurt when I place my arms around Jazmin's stomach, tugging her gently against me.

Fuck. When Jazmin tilts her head back to look at me, her overly heavy made-up face is enough to make me want to vomit. As much as it kills me, I divert my gaze away from Anna. Fake a small smile and wink at Jazmin. She giggles lightly. That puke wants to unquestionably come up now. This bitch is sour. There isn't a damn thing sweet about her. Christ, I feel sick.

I am instantly aware that someone else is glaring at me. Logic has me shifting to the front of the church, where both Aidan and Cain move from watching the wedding party come down the aisle to finding me, while Roan watches his soon-to-be wife approach him. Anger is pouring out of them at the recognition of who I have with me. Questions demanding to be answered sear into my brain from them. I stare back, telling them not here, not tonight. Not ever. I will not allow any of them to be hurt or killed.

I glance at Anna one more time before the ceremony starts. Her back is to me now, her hands gripping the pew in front of her tightly. My heart drops to the damn floor when I see her lift a hand to swipe away a tear. Fuck, darling Anna, if you only knew how much I wish it were you standing next to me right now.

We take our seats the minute Alina reaches Roan. I feel a slight tug at my heart, knowing he's happy and found true love.

After that, I have no clue what is said during the ceremony. I am fixed to the back of the head of the woman I crave Not once does she turn back to look at me. Her spine is straight the entire time. Focused on the now happily married couple.

Jazmin and I leave, along with my mom and dad. We trek the short distance to the reception, Jazmin walking alongside my mom, who is doing a damn good job pretending she's paying attention to whatever the hell she's saying.

It's my dad, whose angry vibes hold my interest. "What the fuck do you think you're doing bringing that bitch here? Whatever the hell you have planned, you need to end this now. Dumbest thing you've ever done in your life, Dilan." He grabs me by the elbow to slow us down some.

"I'm going to destroy them, dad. Every single one of them. Uncle Salvatore knows. You keep out of it." I speak quietly as we continue to walk. "Keep out of it? What part of you're my son and I love you did you miss your entire life? I sure as hell will not keep out of it. Christ. This is your cousin's wedding and you bring the enemy here. That woman is viscous. You've lost your damn mind if she doesn't suspect you have something brewing. God, boy, you spent a few years in prison because of her family and Royal setting your ass up. Let that shit go."

He has no clue how badly I want to let it go. Fuck that shit. I will not let it go until they pay with their lives for putting me in that hellhole. For making me live in a cage for a couple of years. Locked away from my life.

"Roan will understand. And as far as that bitch goes, I know damn well she has an agenda of her own. She's made it perfectly clear for years she's wanted me. She's on the other side of fucking crazy. The sight of her makes me sick. She thinks I'm giving in to her." My skin actually starts to crawl. I may even be shivering, and it sure as hell isn't from the cold outside. Dad scoffs at my remark. "Of course he will, Dilan. He's also not stupid. He's going to know. So will she." He nods his head with a chin lift in Jazmin's direction. Good, let her. Let her get pissed and run to her brother.

I stop walking for a bit and shove my freezing hands into my coat pocket. "Let me handle it my way, dad. My goddamn way." He just stares at me. Like he has no clue who I am. Like he's lost his son. Right now, maybe he has. It doesn't matter what anyone thinks. This shit has to be done. I will deliver my revenge. I will seek justice in my own damn way.

"I can see you've made up your mind. You better have a plan, boy. You're my son. I love you more than anything, but don't you dare think you can take them down all by yourself. If you and Salvatore don't finish them soon, then by god, I will. Bringing that bitch here will arise suspicion. Did you think of that?" People walk around us. Glaring, wondering what the hell is going on out here.

"Calm down. Jesus. I'm not stupid. I know they'll have questions. Lots of them. Let me handle this, dad. I'm not backing down. This is something I have to do in order to have peace up here." I point to my head.

"Christ, son. I hate this shit. And your mother. It's killing her not to take that woman by her hair and beat her ass. You know she would do it if we were anywhere else but here." That comment gets a chuckle out of both of us. She would do it too.

He pulls me in for a hug then releases me to catch up with the women. I walk slowly in the same direction. My head is clear. I got this shit. I know what I'm doing.

The less my parents know, the better for them.

My uncle has provided me with the help I need. It's not from the ones I care about the most. Not that one life is more important than another. It's not. Never will be. But Roan, Cain, and Aidan have all been through enough. Their women too. I'm not about to inflict any more worry or heartache on any of them.

If they knew the shit I put up with while inside that damn hellhole from Juan Carlos' men, they would all be standing by my side.

I took many beatings from those fuckers. One of them being the notorious Miguel Angel Verdoza. One of the Mexican Cartel's hitmen. He claimed it was us who set him up when he was caught. It was his sloppy work. We had nothing to do with it. Our family doesn't work that way. We stay loyal to ourselves first. Loyal to other families second. Our paths never cross, unless you fuck with one of our own. They fucked with me in there. I will seek my own deliverance on those who broke the seal of treaties amongst our families. They will pay. My way.

No, they will never know how he left me for dead. The guards doing nothing but letting his men hold me, while he pounded his fist into my face until I lay bleeding out of every goddamn hole in my face. Orders from the outside. From none other than Jazmin's brother. The man I'm going to kill with my hands. I don't want anyone to stop me from killing him. This is where Jazmin comes in. Not only is she a killer herself, she's also the ex-wife of Miguel Angel Verdoza, who will spend the rest of his life ruling the inside of that prison. She divorced him shortly after he was sentenced, leaving him bitter. Angry. You would think he would want revenge on her, knowing she's out here, walking free. Doing his job by killing people. I guess they stay loyal no matter how much someone else fucks you over. It wouldn't surprise me one damn bit if they did set him up themselves. Not my problem. Thank fuck he never knew about her stupid visits to see me. Thank god the guards who were on my side were easily persuaded to keep their mouths shut. Another favor I need to return to my uncle. The woman was smart enough to hide her identity too. She knew the entire time what was going down in there. She wants me for herself all right. The conniving cunt. She had the power to stop it. To have the bastard killed in there. Like I said, she's on the other side of fucking crazy. I'd also be a man on a suicide mission if I didn't think she has an agenda of her own. It wouldn't surprise me one bit if it has everything to with my family and me. Nah. She's using me as much as I'm using her. Only this time when we play the game of hangman, I'll be prepared.

And her ex-husband, who tried everything he could to kill me. To disgrace me. To have his men beat me and try to rape me in prison. The key word here being try. Shortly, his life will come to an end.

Today, I'm here to congratulate my cousin and to make one more request from my uncle this evening. I need the help of the best hitman out there. Well, he's technically not anymore. He's retired. Still the best though. I know without a doubt he will help me take these fuckers out. I need the help of John Greer.

CHAPTER THREE

ANNA

I would give anything to not be stuck in my own head. To see him with someone else when it should be me by his side. It's obvious to me now I was wrong about him. Those bitter words he said to me were true. I should have believed him. Tried to move on the entire time he was gone. And yet I couldn't. Something was holding me back. The instant his eyes glared into mine like he hated me, sending that hatred straight to my heart. If he cared about me at all, he would have made some sort of effort to contact me these past months. I realize now he's not the man I thought he was. As much as it crushes me, it's true. Dilan Levy is not the man for me. Aidan tried to tell me not to wait for him to pull his head out of his ass. To live, have fun. I'm stupid for not listening to him. But how can you go on when your heart tells you to wait? To not give up, to hold on, because when the time comes, he will open his eyes and see that what he needs is standing right in front of him, postponing her life? I've been holding on to that flicker of fire I've seen in his eyes. I wasn't blind. It was there, but now that fire has smoldered. All that remains is a pile of ashes. Dust.

Right now, though, as I walk with my mom and the rest of the wedding party, including the bride and groom, over to the reception after pictures were taken, I'm angry with myself. Angry because I let him get to me. Angry because I had to try to concentrate on the beautiful wedding in front of me, when all I could focus on was him, with her. I'm an idiot. Jealous. Envious of that woman. She has the man I want. For me to even think that makes me sound pathetic.

He deserves nothing from me. And now as we enter the hotel with the bright lights, the black and white tiled floor, and the gold trim, I watch the love between two people I care about, and I hold my head up. It's time to let go of someone who was never mine. He doesn't want me like I want him. I can and will get through this night, not only for myself but for my family.

"Anna, you're quiet. What's going on?" Aidan asks quietly, his face serious.

One thing I'm not is a liar. Mom always told me I could never hide my feelings well anyway. So even though I don't want Aidan to worry, I tell him the truth. "Did you see Dilan?" I bite the side of my lip, palpably obvious in showing my defeat. Aidan's like a brother to me. We've become close. He knows how I feel. Hell, they all do. Especially the girls.

"I did. Come here." He pulls me off to the side. Deidre glances over her shoulder. A sad smile slowly dances across her face. Then her smile fades. Knowingly. She nods and walks into the room where the reception will be, leaving the two of us alone. We wait until the noise from inside from the whistles, the clapping, and the loud congratulations quiets down. He puts his arms around me, planting my face into his chest. I let out a strangled breath. The need to cry slides its way up my throat. My head is shaking back and forth. It hurts when the one who broke your heart is the only one who can put it back together.

"He's with someone else." His grip on me loosens. Strong fingers coax my chin, lifting my head until he has me looking at him.

"I love Dilan and I love you. But Anna, he's not worth it. Let him go. Enjoy your night. Don't let him or anyone take away the real you. I can't speak for him. But if I could, I would say he's a giant asshole. Now, I don't know about you, but I'm fucking starving. So come on. Let me see that beautiful smile." I smile, although it is hard. But it is real. As real as it can get.

"Thank you," I whisper. "You may not thank me tomorrow morning when you wake up with a big, fat hangover. Deidre can't drink. I need a drinking partner tonight. Come on. Plus, I know damn well she'll be on the phone with Evie every half hour, checking on Diesel." Evie is Beth and Stefano's housekeeper. She adores both Justice and Diesel. One of the few people Deidre trusts leaving her son with.

Aidan helps me guide off my coat and hands it to the gentleman standing outside the door. Then he opens the doors for me to enter. I gasp, right along with him, when we enter. "Jesus Christ. Small wedding, my ass," he mutters. This time when he talks, I smile and laugh right along with him. It's not hard at all. No. It is easy. Very easy. Until I look over to one of the bars. My laugh dies instantly. Dilan has a menace of a scowl on his face as he stands there, talking to Salvatore and John. The conversation appears to be heated. Fury is coming from the two men as they glare at Dilan, whispering quietly. Not my problem. I turn away from them, my expression blank. My mind saying 'Fuck him'.

"Two Jim Beam on the rocks. Please." I roll my eyes at Aidan when he asks the bartender for his famous drink. He has me liking it though. Especially tonight.

I sit my small clutch on top of the bar and turn to admire the room. Aidan is spot-on. There are more people here than there were at the church, sitting at round tables with the most intricate centerpiece in the middle I have seen. They're small trees with green and white lights. Candles in the same colors sit at the foot of them. Lights hang from the ceiling. I feel like I'm in a winter wedding wonderland.

"Fuck. Look at this place." Aidan hands me my drink. "It's beautiful," I say truthfully. "Yeah, it is." He sips his drink. When I look up to him, his stare isn't on the scenery in front of us. He's looking at Deidre, who's standing by the woman Dilan is with, along with Calla. They seem to be in an uncomfortable conversation. Both of them are tense, pretending to listen to whatever this woman is saying.

I sip my drink casually, my eyes staying on them. I lean in and whisper to Aidan.

"So, who is she?" He jeers his head down close to me, his eyes never leaving them at all.

"You really want to know?" I study this man I've become close to. His jaw is contracting, twitching in a way I've only seen once before. In the dead of the night, in the back of a dark van with only the headlights of oncoming cars shadowing across his face. He's nervous, upset, and something tells me it's all directed towards this woman.

"Yes," I tell him.

"She's... fuck. The idea of her even talking to them makes me want to rub my skin raw. She's poison. And whatever Dilan is doing with her, I don't believe for one damn minute it's because he likes her. In fact, I know damn well he doesn't." I have no idea what he's doing with her if no one seems to like her. I do know the impact it's having on me right now. I'm trembling. The glass in my hand shakes. The sound of the ice is rattling over the background music. What is he doing with her if he doesn't like her? What does Aidan mean?

"You need to elaborate, Aidan." I set my glass down on the bar and lean into him more.

"She's the enemy. That's what I fucking mean. Her brother and Royal had everything to do with why Dilan went to prison. He's up to something, and I don't fucking like it. If you see her, stay the hell away, do you get me?" That's it. He offers up nothing more. He places his hand on my elbow, nudging his head toward my drink. I pick it up along with my clutch. "Come on. I want her away from them." I follow quickly behind him, not understanding what the hell is going on. Confused. I make it halfway before I'm suddenly stopped by my mom and Ramsey.

"Go ahead without me," I say to Aidan, irritation clear in my phrase. "No problem there," he comments as he keeps on walking. We all stare at him. He's a man assuredly on a mission to save people he cares about from the clutches of someone he obviously despises.

"What's going on?" Ramsey asks. I clear my throat, my hands becoming clammy, sweaty, even though I'm holding a glass filled with ice. With my stomach in knots, I force my eyes away from them. "I'm not sure," I half lie. "He was looking for Deidre, and now I guess he found her." I shrug. My mind is whirling with information I'm not even sure what to do with.

I know Dilan went to prison. He told me during one of our many talks. He said he was set up. I had no reason not to believe him. With everything going on at the time in my own life, I just tucked it away. Forgot it, really. Until now. Until her. I wish now, I would have asked more questions when he told me. If I did, I would know what's going on, would know exactly who she is, maybe try and put some sense into why he would be with her. Dilan having been to prison doesn't matter to me. Even if he were guilty, it still wouldn't matter. He's a good man. Stupid as a damn squirrel running out into the middle of the road, but he's loyal.

I stand there for several minutes, pretending to listen while mom and Ramsey talk about how beautiful this place is. The wedding. The honeymoon. My gaze shifts back and forth between them and this woman, who is now standing alone. Aidan said something to them all, then guided the women away from her. Now, she's alone.

There's something about her that has my suspicions rising, the hair on my arms standing up, a cold chill racing up my spine.

Her head veers back and forth. I intently watch her every move. She picks up a drink, takes a sip, sets it back down. Then she picks up another one. My eyes bulge. What the hell is she doing? My brows shoot up in horror when her head drops, and her fingers dip inside of her silver clutch and pull something out. Her head shoots in Dilan's direction . I don't dare look away. Fear has to be etched across my face. She takes what I assume is a pill and drops it in the drink then pushes if off to the side of her on the table. Whoever she is, I do believe her intentions are to poison Dilan.

Oh my God. Aidan's words hit me. "She's poison," he said. A sick feeling seeps into my gut. I glance around the room. No sign of Aidan at all. I spot Cain, who is now standing with Dilan. I look back to her. She's smiling as she glances around the room, her eyes finding Dilan. She picks up both glasses and weaves her way through the crowd. I move too, my veins thick with anger.

My mom calls my name behind me. I may look like a complete fool doing this, but I really don't care. I slam into her just a few feet from the two of them, the clear liquid from the glasses spilling all over her dress and hands. Her eyes shoot me the look of death. "You careless bitch," she spews. "I'm so sorry," I say maliciously, my defiance obvious to everyone around us. All I want to do is claw her goddamn eyes out with her own fake nails.

"Anna, are you all right?" Cain and Dilan approach. It's Cain who asks. That thickness I have settles right in my throat as I watch Dilan step up by her side. That makes me even more furious with him. He won't even look at me, and it hurts. God, does it hurt. Aidan seems to think Dilan is up to something. Well, whatever it is, he can carry on with it. My job is almost done here.

I try and stay calm when all I want to do is ask him if he has lost his goddamn mind by bringing someone, who by the sounds of it, is not welcome here.

"This cunt ran into me. She spilled our drinks all over me. Look!" She's good. Playing the innocent victim. The way she regards his attention by showcasing her fake boobs with the span of her hand. Maybe Dilan is all over her, this perfect replica of a bitch. Not me. I know Cain well enough he's not either. I slowly step in between them all, planting my tiny self directly in front of her, my back to Dilan. That's all he deserves, my back to him. Fuck him.

"Cunt? You really did not just call me a cunt?" I lean into her. Before I say another word, I set my drink and clutch down on the table behind her, deliberately nudging her as I do. "I saw you," I whisper into her ear. I pull back. Her eyes challenge me. I won't back down. I don't care who she is. "You saw nothing," she spits back. 'Right,' I think to myself.

"Anna," Cain says.

"Cain. I'm not sure where Dilan found this cunt. My guess is some drug outlet or the corner of Division and 48th. Whoever she is, I watched her put something in one of those drinks." She sets both glasses down casually, grabs several of the cloth napkins from the table, and begins dabbing down the front of her dress. I know how to stand up to people. I've been doing it most of my life. To bullies in high school, who looked down on me because I was an athlete, never one to hang out with the girls, only the guys. My half-brother, who tried to kill me. I don't care who this so-called poisonous woman is. I want her out of here. Now.

"What the fuck, Jazmin?" Dilan's voice speaks roughly from behind me. His voice is clipped. Angry. It's still his voice though. That shiver is back, racing up and down my spine. It's been too long since I've heard the deep monotone of his voice. Even though he's directing them toward her, I feel it in my chest. I do my best to shove it aside. He's a fool. A stupid fool.

Suddenly, I'm lifted off of my feet and moved out of the way. I may have saved Dilan from this woman's poison, but my heart is breaking at the scene playing out in front of me. Not for her, but because she's cussing, causing a scene. "She's a liar. I did no such thing. You'll pay for this, you little bitch!" she screams. Roan is suddenly at our side. "Get her the fuck out of my wedding reception. She fucking stinks, reeks, and I want her gone. You can get the fuck out of here right along with her, Dilan." This is the first time I've heard the usually calm Roan lose his temper. I take a deep breath as I watch Aidan and Cain escort her out of the room. Dilan walks to where her purse sits tucked away on the chair and snatches it up, saying nothing to his cousin. He doesn't look back. Not once.

Me though, I feel as if everyone is staring at me. Well, not everyone. My mom and Ramsey. John and Salvatore, who are now standing around us too.

I bury my hands over my face. And cry. I feel so horrible. "Hey."

Strong arms wrap around my waist.

"Anna, are you all right? What on earth is going on here?" my mom demands. "She'll be fine, Grace. She had a slight confrontation with someone who shouldn't be here." It's Roan. I know I shouldn't feel bad. I know what I saw. And yet, I do.

"Anna. Look at me," Roan demands gently. "I'm sorry," I say through my tears. He guides me around. My hands are still covering my face. I pause momentarily, catching my breath before I drop them to look up. I must be a mess now. My perfect makeup ruined. And I did it all for him. A man who wouldn't even look at me, speak to me, or thank me. God. I'm the stupid fool.

"I'm not sure what happened, but I promise you we wanted her out of here. Please, don't feel bad. If anyone should feel anything, it should be him. Not you," he says calmly. "Thank you." I stare at him for a moment, trying to smile but failing miserably. "It's true, Anna. She doesn't belong here. He knows that." This now comes from Salvatore.

The music is still playing softly in the background. The lights are low. I'm shaking. Not from the conflict with her, it's more than that. I know the minute I turn around, everyone in here will be thinking I've done something wrong.

"Anna, sweetie. Come on. Let's go get you cleaned up. I promise no one saw anything," Deidre says. I didn't even notice her and Calla approaching us. Tearing my eyes away from Roan, I scan around for Alina. When I don't see her anywhere, I let out a thankful breath, feeling somewhat better. I have so many questions to ask about this mystery woman. Who is she? Why would Dilan bring her here, if he knew she would cause discomfort to his family? And lastly, what is he doing with her?

"Go. Get cleaned up. We all want you here to celebrate with us." Roan winks at me.

"I'll come with you," mom says, her gentle hand sliding up and down my back.

"I'm fine, mom, really. You stay here. I'll be right back," I say. My lips are trembling. She goes to rebuke my plea. "Let her go, honey," Ramsey declares. "Are you sure you're all right?" Her hand is still on my back.

"I'm fine. Let me get cleaned up. I'll be right back." I resist the urge to cry some more. I saved him. I know I did. Roan's words stay lodged in my head. I have no clue what I witnessed or why. All I know is, my gut tells me I did the right thing. Unfortunately, my gut also tells me I may have made an even worse enemy out of this woman than I had in my half-brother. There's not a damn thing funny about this at all. It's a paradox of contradictions. A jack in the box full of danger, never knowing when that lid is going to pop open; and when it finally does, it scares the living shit out of you.

It pounces. Attacks. Am I strong enough for more? God, this is too much. All I want to do is crawl into a bed and start this entire day over. Life doesn't work that way though. I grab my clutch, smile at my family, and once again hold my head up.

Then I overhear Salvatore tell John that obviously Dilan's plan went the way he wanted. To go take care of her. That can only mean one thing, especially when I hear John reply with. "My fucking pleasure." Something is going down. I will not be sheltered from this storm. Not this time. I know what I said earlier about giving up on Dilan. I won't though. I may not have him the way I want him, but if he needs me for anything, if anyone in this family needs me, I will do everything I can to help them, the same way they've helped me and my mom.

Because yes, I'm strong enough. I've been beaten down before and survived. If danger strikes me or anyone I care about again, nothing will stop me from doing the right thing, even if I have to kill someone.

"Who is she?" I ask Deidre, the very second we step into my room. I dare not say a word until I know we are alone. The lights immediately come on when we step inside. Well, that's nice. At least I don't have to skim my fingers along a wall to find a switch.

I don't bother to look around. I head straight for my suitcase, which is sitting unopened on a chaise lounge at the foot of the bed. I unzip it, retrieving my toiletry bag. I head straight for the bathroom, where Deidre is already running a washcloth under the sink.

"Thanks." I take it from her and wipe the dark streaks of mascara off of my face. God, I look hideous. Thank god the elevators are right down the hall from the reception. How embarrassing.

"Her name is Jazmin Carlos. She's an assassin for The Mexican Cartel."

CHAPTER FOUR

DILAN

"Shit," I muttered under my breath the minute Anna barged across the room in our direction. I knew she suspected something the way she flew across the room. My world damn near went from desperate to desolate not to touch her. Those eyes set deep on a mission to destroy the woman who has no damn soul.

Call me an asshole, but I couldn't help but convey every dream I've had of her in the few short seconds it took her to almost knock this bitch off of her feet.

I stood still, watching her firm breasts move as her chest heaved up and down. My cock has never wanted out of my pants as fast as he did then. My hands ached to bring her into my arms. To feel her pressed up against me. To wash the repugnance toxin from her body from Jazmin touching her.

There wasn't a damn thing I could do. I had to play like I didn't know her. That killed me more than not being able to touch her. I fucking hate it. I can lie to myself until I take my last breath about not wanting her. Christ, I'm a fucking idiot.

I felt her presence the moment she walked into the room with Aidan. She glanced over to where I was talking with John and my uncle. We were discussing our plan with John. I followed her out of the corner of my eye, until I couldn't see her anymore. It killed me not to go to her, to wrap my lips around hers, if only to feel if they're as soft as they look. To tell her I'm a liar.

My intentions to stay far away from her, to not drag her into this, have been shot to hell. She unknowingly brought herself into this. Now, she'll be right in the middle of it all. That's the gift Anna has. She's like the rest of us. She protects those she cares about whether there's danger involved or not. And now. Fuck. She'll demand to know what the hell is going on. They all will.

The corners of my mouth tip slightly. God, I hope she'll talk to me, let me explain everything to her. Let me look after her, in more ways than shielding her from all the contamination that surrounds our lives.

"Shut your trashy mouth," John spurts out to Jazmin. The urge to think about Anna is so deep, I'm not paying attention to what this bitch is saying as we sneak out of the back exit door of the reception.

I approached my uncle and John the minute I had a chance to get away from her. To say John was all in is an understatement. Not so much at the revenge I need to seek, to want it to the extent it's been the backbone so powerful to my life that I've shoved living a full life out of the way until I destroy those who deserve it. He wanted to make sure no one knew. That he was the one who caught her off-guard the minute they could be alone. He was going to slip her out the door, undetected, after he slipped a sleeping aide in her drink. She beat us to it though by trying to get to me.

I had no doubt she would try and poison me with her famous drug, though I didn't think she would try and do it here. She's been caught. I owe Anna, and I'm a dick for wanting to pay her back by worshipping her body, claiming her and showing her what she means to me. My brain is so fucking warped. Jesus Christ.

But this is how Jazmin kills her victims. She's like a spider. They bite you with both of their fangs, leaving two puncture wounds. The poisonous ones can kill you within minutes, while others eat away at your flesh. Jazmin chooses which way she wants to kill you. Then she strikes. Although, I didn't think she would do it this fast. It's apparent she had plans of her own. I underestimated the conniving bitch. "I've wanted you for a long time, Dilan." That right there should have set me off. The knowledge of how she strikes and kills her victims. Usually, they're ones who have crossed her family. The reason she poisons them is because she's too damn weak to capture them any other way. Once she slips her venom into their bodies, that's when her hunches drag them away. Most of them never to be heard of again. She's fucked up.

"You won't get away with this. My brother will kill you this time instead of sending you to prison, you fucker," she wails as she tries to get out of her restraints. The minute we were out of view, John clipped her hands behind her back, securing them with the zip ties I had in my pocket.

"Should I be scared?" I say with acrimony. My eyes barely dart over her man-eating flesh. "I want him to come after me, you bitch. All of them. In the meantime, my plan begins with you. For a woman who's known to be a killer, you sure did the dumbest act tonight, Jazmin. Did you really think drugging me in front of my entire family was going to work? You must be getting desperate." I swing her around to face me. My grip on her arm is painful. I watch her facial expression change to sheer panic when she realizes she's in a back alley with four men who would all give anything to put a bullet through her head.

"He knows where I am. He has men here," she confesses.

"Not anymore, he doesn't," John admits.

"What?" She tries to crank her head to look at John. I won't allow it. Not until I'm done saying what I have to say. Then he can take her.

"Seriously, woman." I place my hands around her neck, shove her up against the SUV waiting to take her where we will keep her until the time comes. I squeeze tightly, feeling her pulse speed up, fluttering in a tyranny of disarray as I pull as much oxygen out of her lungs as I fucking can. "Do you think two high-powered families would not have every bit of protection they can surrounding this wedding? Hell, there are people within a ten-mile radius of here. Every person was scanned the minute they stepped through the church. Then again the second they stepped into the hotel." Her eyes become as wide as if someone had lifted a hand to land that lethal blow. She's never been the victim before. Always the hunter. Not this time. Now, for the kick in the teeth. To not only her but my friends and family surrounding me. The ones I didn't want involved in this shit.

"I know everything, bitch. Part of this is for me. The other part is for Alexei Solokov. You do remember him, don't you? The man you helped Royal Diamond kill?" She gasps.

"What the fuck are you talking about, Dilan?" This is coming from Cain. I feel them all guarding my back. Their rendition of this known cunt gets better. They will want her family destroyed after they find out the truth and her part in how Alina's brother was taken.

"She spiked his drink. That's how Royal was able to catch him off-guard. Isn't that right, you fucking cunt?" I grip her throat tighter. I couldn't care less if I kill her. She reeks of her venomous poison. It's leaking out of her pores, polluting the fresh, crisp air.

"So you see, I haven't been off having the time of my life. No. I've been planning the demise of you and your entire empire. This is war, Jazmin. Not only with me, but with the Solokovs. I planned on having John kill you nice and quick tonight. But now I think you need to suffer. I say he sends one piece of your body to your brother at a time. Take her, John. Lock her up. Let her go crazier than she already is with worry. She knows damn well her life is coming to an end. She's all yours." I release my grip. She coughs, leaning forward to try and catch her breath. Her legs damn near give out. No one here will help her. The moment she gains control and tries to sputter her harsh words at me, I turn, ignoring her, nodding to my friends. Nothing more needs to be said, not until we get inside, away from the smell of her.

John tosses her into the back, or more like throws her like the trash she is. Once the taillights are out of view, reality hits. I have to tell my friends and family what the hell is going on. They deserve an explanation, and I deserve the shit they will give me for keeping all of this from them.

"Motherfucker. This is some fucked-up shit." Aidan places his hands around the back of his neck and paces the hallway just inside the door from where we came in. I see he still likes to swear up a storm. He could create his own dictionary. I'm not kidding.

"I didn't want any of you involved in this. I had every intention of taking them down without you all. It's fucked up." I lean my head against the wall, waiting to be scolded like an adolescent child.

"We're a family, man. You know better than that," Cain says. Their disappointment in me does not go unnoticed when they both plant themselves in front of me, weighing me down with a disappointed stare.

"I know. But fuck, don't you think you all have been through enough? And now this. And hell, you all have families. Kids, wives, and fiancées." I nod my head at Aidan, letting him know I know he's engaged.

"We chose this life. So did Calla and Deidre. However, this gets done with our help. And this gets done after Roan and Alina leave for their honeymoon. She doesn't need to know about this. Not until they return." Fine by me. I couldn't agree with Cain more. Now the problem is, what the hell do I tell Roan when I show my face back in there? I lie. That's what the fuck I do.

I loom in the hallway long after they're gone, my ass planted on the floor. Hell, John more than likely has returned by now. Fuck if I know how long I've been sitting out here with my head shoved up my own ass, contemplating my next move. I'm scared to go in there. It has nothing to do with the scene played out a while ago. It has everything to do with her. Her response to seeing me again, her questions. All of it. And Roan. How in the hell do I explain this to him? He knows by now, I'm sure of it. He needs to hear from me. The first thing I need to do is apologize to both him and Alina. It wasn't supposed to go down like this.

I half chuckle, knowing Anna must have had her eyes on her. Was she jealous? Or bitterly angry? There's only one way to find out. I need to seek them all out. Starting with my cousin.

By that time I've come to the conclusion that it's not going to matter what I want to do. Once Salvatore lets Ivan Solokov in on the information I know about Alexei, they will decide how and when this plays out. What our next moves will be. How long we will keep Jazmin locked up. It wouldn't surprise me at all if Ivan has her killed right away. My plan was to send her brother one of her deathly hands, in a gift box. The same damn way they sent Alexei to Calla. To let the fucker know I know he played a part in his death. Ivan will want her dead. Her body thrown at the gates of the mansion of Juan's home. Hell, he may even know by now. These two powerful men may be at their children's wedding , but that does not mean their jobs go on hold. Not in the underworld. There are always secret rituals, complex procedures on the way things are done. This is one of the reasons I came to my uncle in the first place. He would have my ass if he knew I was out to bring another family down without telling him. I know damn well I would never be able to achieve this on my own. But fuck me if my loyalty in this tangled web is not to the men I care about the most. The need to protect them from this. Hell, maybe I need protection from myself.

They're involved now. Not a damn thing I can do about it. What I need to do is get my ass in there and face my cousin. I'm leaving out the part about Alexei's death . He's one of those need-to-know basis. He'll leave it be, until he returns. If he decides to go, that is.

Heaving my body off of the floor, I take the few steps down the hall toward the reception. The music gets louder with each step I take. Images of Anna hit me, dancing, swaying her sexy as hell little body to the beat of the music. Her lush ass is taunting me as it rules my damn mind as well as my cock. Fuck, I need to talk to her too. If she'll talk to me, that is. I'll make her, damn it. She will listen. Jazmin is no threat to her. It's her brother and his throne of treacherous men who will come after anyone involved once this war begins. A family is about to be brought down. I'll take my last lungful of air protecting her, keeping her away from this shit. She may not like it, but it looks like Anna Drexler will be stuck with me again.

"I should beat your ass for bringing that bitch here." Roan takes a seat next to me at the corner end of the bar. "I'd like to see you try," I tell him jokingly. I take a long sip of my beer, never taking my gaze away from him.

"I wanted to, until Dad told me the reason behind why you did it. We all knew Royal set you up. Hell, you and I talked about it more times than I can count. I never expected the Carlos family had shit to do with it. That fucker was more disloyal than I thought." I look for signs of betrayal on Roan's behavior, with Royal being his brother. I find none.

"Yeah, he was." I put emphasis on the word was. I know my uncle well enough that he hasn't mentioned anything about the other issue at hand. I leave it be. This is his wedding night. I've fucked it up already. No way am I throwing a match and watch the entire night go up in flames.

"I'm sorry, man. The last thing I wanted was to ruin this night for you. Congrats by the way," I tell him sincerely.

"You didn't ruin shit. Alina's fine. Everyone's good." He takes a sip of his expensive shit. How in the hell my friends can drink that crap is beyond me. Give me a damn beer over that nasty ass whiskey any goddamn day.

"Well, for what it's worth, I'll apologize to her." My gaze leaves him. I haven't seen Anna since I've been back in here. I've spoken to John, who was back in no time. My uncle caught me the minute he saw me. He's already set up a meeting for the day after tomorrow. Just like I knew he would, he'll have a plan in motion by the time we all arrive.

"I'll be gone ten days. Once I'm back, I'm with you on this, Dilan. We will bring them down."

Guilt suffocates me more, while pride hits me. I'm a damn lucky man to have these men by my side. This shit will get ugly. More blood will be shed than anyone of us have seen before. I keep that shit tucked away too. Roan is a smart man. Hell, they all are. He knows this without me having to define it.

"I better not hear from you for ten days, fucker. You enjoy yourself." He scoffs then turns around and finds his wife.

"Have you taken a look at my wife? There isn't a damn thing that will make me want to call your ass." I throw my head back and laugh. "I sure the hell hope not."

"You and I will talk when I get back. Keep your shit about you until I return." I pull him in for a hug, this hug taking on things that have no business being said here. He knows things will get out of hand while he's gone. Especially when Jazmin doesn't show up anywhere. They'll never find her. The tracking device I'm sure she has on her phone is in my pocket. I'll destroy the fucker the minute I step out of this room.

Everyone else will be on high alert. Laying low. It won't take those fuckers long to pin her back to me. "Go get your wife." I lift my chin in her direction. "I intend to. Take it easy, man. It's good to have you back." I watch him until he snakes his arm around Alina, who's dancing with a few of her sister-in-laws. Lucky bastard.

I study the entire room. The reception is still packed. People are dancing, drinking, and socializing. Anna is nowhere to be found. Fuck.

"She went to her room." Deidre strolls up alongside of me, rubbing her pregnant stomach. She's cute. I couldn't be happier for her.

"That obvious, huh?" I tip back the last of my beer.

"You hurt her, Dilan. I'll cut your dick off if you do it again. She's in room 821." That's all she says to me. Fucking hell, I love my family. Protective. Loyal to the god damn hub of our existence. We all have different blood flowing through our veins, were raised differently. Some were brought up with scruples, such as Calla, while others pretty much raised themselves. Like Cain and Aidan. Roan and Alina know this life better than most of us. They've lived it, breathed it. Alina wanted out of it. And here every single one of us stands, preparing for the biggest battle of our lives. But nothing will prepare any of us for what's in store. I'm not stupid. I know an empire is about to crash. It's going to be tough. There isn't any room for failure.

As I take in the likes of my family and friends around me tonight, one thing is for damn sure: these women are as badass as their men. And I'm about to go get my own woman.

I say goodnight to my parents. They look at me with emotions galore. Love, respect, and support. I nod in the direction of Aidan and Cain then walk out of the room, shutting my phone off as well as the bitch's, who won't have fingers to even dial the motherfucker by the time we're through with her.

It takes me one minute to stomp the phone into pieces. I yank out the device before I pick up what's left of it and shove the shiny, cracked pieces into the garbage. For tonight, they can think she's here. Tomorrow, this fucker will be buried at the muddy bottom of the Hudson River.

Right now, though, I'm heading to the room of the woman I need to protect. We may all be caught up in this shit, but Anna has no idea the good and the bad that will come out of what she did tonight. She not only saved me, she made it possible for me to be with her. Whether she likes it or not, Anna now has a bodyguard.

CHAPTER FIVE

ANNA

"You've hardly touched your food, sweetheart," mom whispers in my ear. "I know." I've been pushing it around my plate, taking small bites here and there, hoping no one will notice. After that entire scene happened, I lost my appetite along with wanting to be here. I'm bitter, hurt, and angry. Dilan never said a word to me, acted as if he didn't know me at all. A part of me wants to believe he did it to protect me from her. But why? And now he's gone. Cain and Aidan came back in shortly after, but no Dilan and no John.

An instinct in my stomach I cannot ignore, weighs heavily on me. Something I cannot explain. Dilan is in trouble, or he's about to be. I'm angry, because I want to help him when I shouldn't care at all. I'm bitter, because no one will tell me what the hell is going on. I'm stuck in my own head. It's inhabited by him, and I'm tired of it. I've been hesitating at the approaching yellow light for too long, deciding if I should stop or go. Every time I make the decision to go, I'm hit by a big truck. It's maddening. How many times do I have to remind myself he doesn't want me?

"I'm going to my room for a bit. Give me a little time," I tell my mom as I toss my napkin on the table, excusing myself. "Anna," she calls out, gently placing her hand over the top of mine when I stand. "Please come back. Don't let this ruin your night." Her expression showcases how worried she is. "Just a little time, mom. Don't worry." I grab my clutch and head for the door. I sigh the minute I escape. Guilt washes over me for leaving. I have no intentions of returning. All I want to do is lie in bed and cry myself to sleep. It's weak of me to do so. Especially when that's all I did for months after he left.

My feet carry me to the elevator, my heart dropping the minute the doors shut and I'm finally alone. Pressing the button for the eighth floor, I sag against the wall. The need to strip out of this dress burns away at me. I hate this. All of this was for him. And he didn't even notice. Bastard.

I step off of the elevator. No need to hold my head up any longer. I feel defeated. Angry. Bitter. And so damn mad at myself. By the time I make it down the hall to my room, retrieve my key card out of my clutch and slide it in, the tears hit full force. I open the door, closing it behind me, and I cry as I sink my ass down on the cold tile floor. This makes me even angrier. I cry for what was never mine in the first place. I cry for leaving my friend's wedding reception. God, I hate this. Stupid woman that I am.

I stare at the bed that seems to be calling my name. Leaning forward, I undo the straps of my heels, flinging the damn things across the room. Who cares where they land? Those were a waste too. If I weren't so exhausted, I could go on a laughing fit for even thinking he would notice me. He's an asshole, that's what he is.

I stand and pad to the chair in the corner, snatch my phone out of my clutch, then toss it onto the chair. I know my mom will text me. Hurriedly, I drag the dress off of my body, dropping it into the chair too. I leave my bra on and take the few steps to my suitcase. I unzip it and grab my white sleep shorts. It takes a few seconds to slip them on. Then I move to the bed, not even bothering to turn off the lights, pull the covers back, climb in, and curl up into a ball. Anger sets in, more deviant now. I hate crying. Especially over him.

I startle, flying straight up, when there's a knock at the door. I know it's my mom or one of the girls checking in. There's no doubt in my mind that whoever it is, is going to try and drag me back out. All I want is to be left alone.

I don't want to answer it. If I don't though, whoever it is will be calling me. I flip the covers off, mumbling for everyone to leave me be as I make my way to the door.

"I told you I needed some time," I say with annoyance. I unlock the door then swing it open. My eyes go wide when I see who it is. "Dilan," I manage to crook out, giving him an icy stare. His eyes leave my face, and I watch them dilate, turning from brown to black as he starts at my neck, then slowly travels the length of my body. Oh shit. I'm half naked. I quickly gather control of my mind that could easily become inebriated on him. I drop my hand from the doorknob, ready to slam it in his face, when he gently grips my arm. He pushes his way inside while coaxing my body backwards. The door shuts automatically behind him before I can tell him to get out. He swings me around, trapping me between him and the door.

My chest heaves up and down. I swallow nervously when his fingers ever so slightly skim up my arms. I feel the goosebumps forming in every spot he touches, leaving a firing trail of heat that makes them disappear the minute his touch roams higher, my blood forming into a liquid fire. He's never touched me like this before. Softly. Delicately. I love it and hate it at the same time.

"I knew you would feel like silk running through my fingers. Soft. So beautiful," he whispers softly.

"What are you doing here?" My hands go to his chest, trying to push him away from me. Of course, he doesn't move backwards. No, he moves forward, his firm body unrelenting against mine. My palms flatten against his chest. Oh hell. A fire begins to smolder in my core. I feel like a hundred different flames are igniting everywhere.

"We need to talk about a lot of things, Anna. My god, you're beautiful." His words are confusing. He's switching from one thing to the next. I swallow. Not from fear, but from the way his eyes are now glued to my mouth. I can't speak. I feel… I'm not sure what I feel. All I know is if he doesn't step back and take his hands off of me, I may melt like snow in the blazing, hot sun, or boil like hot water. My body is scrambling at the moment, trying to decide which way of the spectrum it wants to head to.

"Dilan. Please." He must sense the anxiety in my voice, because before I know it, his hands are gone. He steps away. I move around him and walk to my suitcase, grab a sweatshirt, and yank it over my head. My nipples are straining against my bra from his touch. I need to be the one in control here, not my damn body.

"Nothing is what it seems. Tonight isn't what you think," he divulges.

"You have no idea what I'm thinking, Dilan. How could you? I haven't talked to you in months." Dilan's pained face does not go unnoticed. He has to understand, even though I want him. *No, I don't. Yes, I do.*

He's here, in the flesh. Oh god. I cover my face, ignoring every impulse I have not to run into his arms. I turn away from him. When I place my hands down, I'm enthralled at the sight in front of me. This is the first time I really get a look at this room. This isn't an ordinary room. It's a damn suite. I knew Alina's family was paying for all of us to stay here, but I was under the assumption I would be staying in a normal room. Not a room with a small kitchen, a dining room table for two with a bottle of wine, fruit, and a card nestled in the basket. I continue to spin around, taking it all in. There's a small living room with a fireplace. Good heavens. I've been preoccupied, it's obvious. This looks more like a damn apartment than a hotel room, and because of him, I can't even enjoy this place.

"Can we talk? I'll tell you everything and promise to answer all your questions, Anna. I had my reasons for staying away from you. But, sweet girl, you have to believe me when I say it was the hardest thing I had to do." I hear the pleading desperation in his voice without even looking at him. I'm also losing that small ounce of control I've tried to gain back. His words slash right through my chest.

I move to the couch, my legs rickety like I'm old. I'm shaking so bad, I can barely stand up. He's by my side in an instant, guiding me down on the plush, deep brown couch across from the fireplace. Then he sits down beside me. I grab the blanket that's folded neatly on the back, bringing it over my exposed legs. I'm not sure what to think right now. All I do know is, I'm all of a sudden extremely uncomfortable being halfway dressed in front of Dilan. I'm sure I look like hell too. My makeup is ruined from crying, and I'm sure my hair is a wild mess.

I find enough courage to speak. "I'm listening," I say curtly. I still don't want to look at him. If I do, I will cave, crumble, because he's so God-given handsome. He's perfect in my eyes, and I hate feeling this way about a man who has hurt me.

Those first words out of his mouth after he clears his throat would have brought me to my knees if I were still standing up. "The first thing I need to tell you is how guilty I feel for running out on you, leaving you behind all those months ago. I should have had the balls to say goodbye. I just couldn't. One look from you, and I would have stayed. Will you look at me, please?" His request has me breaking down. I look at him. The truth is written all over his face. He's exposing his feelings for me without verbalizing them.

"Everything you said to me before…" his eyes close as if he's struggling with that night too, "before I was shot and they took you away from me. It's all true. I feel the same way about you. I have since the first time I saw you. Even when I was gone, Anna, I felt drawn to you. The things I said to you are unforgivable." His words come out unsteadily. Begging for my forgiveness.

"You hurt me," I say on a whim. Not to strike back at him. I need him to know that what he said and his disappearance after what we all went through shattered me. I refuse to listen to any more until he knows that.

"I know. I hurt myself too, Anna. There wasn't a day that went by when I didn't feel both of us hurting, in here." He places his hand over his heart.

Oh, dear god. I feel his hurt now. Right in the place where his hand is. But I'm scared he will do it again. I can't let that happen. My guard goes back up. I become brave. The need to know why he left is itching away at me.

"Then why? Why would you walk away from me? Leave me after what I told you. After what happened to all of us. I needed you, Dilan, and you weren't there." He leans back, resting his head against the back of the couch and pinching his eyes closed.

"No, I wasn't there. I've been hatching out a plan for months, even before I knew you. Like I said, I couldn't see you. I knew if I did, I would have tossed all those months of hard work away. I needed to stay away from you, for your own safety. No matter how much it killed me." A tear escapes his eye. I watch it fall, not being able to move. I feel tears prick my eyes too. I swipe them away before I try to speak again. What's so bad in his life that he feels the need to protect me? To hurt us both?

"What plans do you have? Revenge?" My declaration snaps his eyes wide open, his head turning toward me. "Yes," he simply says.

"I see. And this woman, Jazmin, how does she fit in?" I grind down on my teeth. If he says he's with her, I will die right here. But his next words stop me from thinking about him and her together. Completely.

"She's part of my revenge. I feel nothing for her. Except hatred. She's evil. Her entire family is. I'm going to destroy them all, Anna. Every last one of them."

I have no idea how long the two of us sit there, staring at each other. Our eyes slide down to each other's mouth. I listen as he speaks, absorbing every word.

He tells me everything. My brain is trying to absorb it all. Dilan is back to watch over me. The last time I checked the time on my phone was the second time my phone rang. The first time, it was my mom checking on me, wondering if I was coming back. The second time was Deidre; seems she was the one who told Dilan my room number, which saved me from asking him how he found out. I told both of them no.

Deidre knew Dilan was with me. Although she didn't pry, I could tell she was worried. My mom on the other hand started yelling, demanding me to ask him to leave. I had to quietly and calmly tell her to stay out of it. To let me deal with it. That didn't sit well with her either. Therefore, we hung up with me explaining to her I would fill her in tomorrow.

I'm no spiritualist. I believe there is a god and there is truth to the meaning behind the fact he doesn't give anyone more than they can handle. I can handle this. However, like Dilan, I worry about everyone else we both care about.

And Jazmin. She really is poison. Aidan wasn't bullshitting when he used that word to describe her. She may be a killer, but I saw the fear in her tonight when she was being escorted out of here. I won't ask what they've done to her, nor will they divulge the information.

"Are you cold? Hungry or anything?" Dilan stands and stretches, his black shirt riding up enough for me to see a peak of the tattoo he has across the bottom of his stomach. I swallow so hard, I swear he heard it by the way he chuckles.

"Maybe a little cold," I say truthfully.

"I'll turn the fireplace on." His arms drop, making me whine on the inside. I watch him as he moves then seems to study the buttons on the wall. He presses a few of them and the fireplace kicks to life. It's warm and cozy. God, his back is heavily loaded with muscles that seem to be peaking at me through his shirt to touch them. To graze my teeth all over them. To taste. To stroke and feel them flex under my touch. My pussy aches. My skin sparks, begging for him to touch me.

His phone rings. I push my eyeballs back into my head. He pulls it out of his pocket and turns my way, his brow furrowing when he looks at the screen.

He answers with a short, "Yes, sir," which leads me to believe it's his uncle. I stand, feeling his eyes on my back as I make my way to the bathroom. My vision is screaming 'wow' when I take a look at this room as well. "God, Anna, how could you miss this?" I ask my reflection in the mirror. *I can answer that for you. All you've thought about all day was the man standing in your hotel room. That would be why. Get a hold of yourself.* You know, I've talked to myself nonstop for months. Trying to answer my own questions about Dilan. Not a damn one of them prepared me for this. Just when you start to get your life back on track, when the demons are gone, another one surfaces. I'm graced once again with my inner thoughts talking to me as if I will listen and obey her every word. *So tell me, Anna, what are you going to do now that he's here? Now that he's told you everything?* "I don't know what the hell I'm going to do," I tell her rather rudely.

Then I look around briefly. I couldn't care less about the cream countertop or the long double sink vanity. It's the giant tub directly behind me that catches my thoughts. It's up against the wall, separating me from Dilan. Only, we're not really separated. The outdoor-shutter-like partition is open. His eyes are glued to mine while he continues to talk quietly on the phone. This man has me tied up in knots. I hear him say, "Thank you," and, "This is a safe place for all of us to stay, for now." My mind is whirling. We're staying here longer than tonight? Does that mean he's staying in this room with me? How long? My entire body tightens thinking about sharing this space alone with him. I feel aroused. My throat is thick while my pussy instantly clenches tighter than any other part of my body. When he speaks into the phone, I all but shrivel up like a god darn grape turning into a raisin.

Then I hear the single word, "War." Dilan used that word several times when he was explaining his entire plan of bringing down the Carlos family for what they have done to him.

This is war, Anna. War I tried to keep you safe from. War I tried to keep everyone I care about safe from. A war I intended on taking care of without involving any of you.

Yeah, well, I have questions of my own. Ones that could start a war in here. I want to know what his feelings are for me. He's apologized for the things he said. For the way he acted. He said he was drawn to me. Now that he's explained his whereabouts for the past six months—

the first few he lay low, recuperating, building back his strength; after he felt strong enough, he traveled a bit, putting his plan deeper in motion—Dilan needs to open up and tell me exactly what his plans are for my heart.

CHAPTER SIX

DILAN

I'm half listening to my uncle tell me how those involved will be staying here for a few nights, how plans have changed and we will meet in a conference room tomorrow at noon to derive a plan to get us all home safely.

His home. He wants all of us there, under one roof. No safer place to be in my opinion. But I'm not going to his home. The minute we can leave here, I'm seeking my revenge. Unless something has changed. Christ. I should ask him what the hell is going on, but I'm not about to give Anna anything more to think about tonight.

Hell is about to break lose. I know this, and yet I cannot take my eyes off of her, or my mind. The first word that pops into my mind when I think of Anna Drexler is lethal. And fuck if I don't mean that in a damn good way.

Her beauty and bravery make one hell of a lethal combination, and if she doesn't stop holding my gaze, I may not be able to control what comes next. I'm hanging by the tips of my fingers now. Ready to let go, to fall off the edge with her. What scares me the most is, I have no god-blessed clue how or what to say. I want her so damn bad my chest aches.

When she opened her door and I was greeted with a half-naked body, a body I have dreamed about touching for months, my dick instantly turned hard. She has me, if she still wants me. By the way she's looking at me right now with questions in her eyes, I know telling her everything before was the hard part of the inevitable conversation we were destined to have. Letting her know how I feel about her will be easy. I've fallen for her. And yet, those feelings frighten me more than this war that will break out. How crazy is that shit? I've spent time locked away from this world, beaten, and none of it compares to what I feel right now. The last thing I want to do is hurt her any more than I already have. Fuck, I could float on a cloud with how stunning she is. Even with her hair all wild and her makeup smeared on her face. My hands need to be in that hair, tugging it, so I can claim her neck with my lips. Her mouth with mine. Own her.

She's scared. I hate it. I understand her hesitancy. It was hard as fuck living the damn lie that I don't need her. But the fear to protect her was so deep I forced myself to see past the fact I broke her heart in the process. That the fear of being without her is a hell of a lot stronger than any other fear I've had.

"I'll be there," I say to my uncle and hang up. I shove my phone back into my pocket, not once pulling my eyes off of her. I haven't been this close to her in months and fuck, now that she's right here in this room with me, looking at me like she can't decide if she wants to swallow me in one bite or take her time and savor me, I'm unable to move. She's never looked at me like that before. Frightened, vulnerable, and sexy as fucking sin. Fuck me.

We stand there, staring at each other, for longer than I want. All I want to do is go to her. Kiss her and tell her everything she wants to know with that kiss. That given the chance, I will savor her, sampling everything she has and ordering enough to last me a lifetime.

"How long are we staying here?" she tries to boldly ask. Up till now, her voice has been strong, and now even though she's still trying to be, there is no denying the shakiness in her tone.

"A few days. Does that bother you, Anna? Knowing you're here in a room with me by yourself?" I prod, silently praying she says what I want her to say. I would gladly stay here forever, swear to Christ I would, if it were to seal the safety of her and those we both care about.

Fuck. How the hell I even got those words out of my mouth is beyond me. My goddamn palms are sweaty. I'm just as nervous as she is. My stare just as determined.

"No. I'm not afraid of being alone with you, Dilan. I'm afraid of my feelings for you. They haven't changed at all." Now, she's confident. She doesn't even have to speak; her eyes are speaking for her. I choose my next words carefully. I have a damn good idea the same thing is running through her beautiful head as it is through mine. Where does this leave her and me? Will I run from her again? Hell, no. I'm not running anymore. I need her. I care about her, trust her, and want her. I need a yes from her. One word is all it will take.

"Can I ask you a question?" I raise my brow to challenge her, let her know I'm serious.

"Of course," she replies.

"When you asked me if I overheard you telling Deidre how you felt about me, is all of that still true? Do you still feel the same? Do you still want me, Anna? Do you still want me to kiss you? To touch you?" I slowly walk her way. For months, she's lived inside my head and soul. I'm claiming her. She's already claimed me.

Her eyes follow me until I break between the small wall separating the bathroom and the doorway. Her eyes are right there when I step under and through the entrance to the bathroom. They're still on me when I stop just inches from her. Her breath catches. Her chest moves up and down. Frantically. Rapidly.

"That was five questions," she says smugly.

"Well, then I want five answers, Anna," I challenge once again. I move in closer. My hands are craving to dig into her hair. My mouth is aching to touch hers. She steps back until her sexy little ass is up against the counter. I have no answer to why my nerves are gone. Maybe because I know this is right. I've wanted this for so long, never thinking I could have it. What I've wanted is right here in front of me, and fuck me if it doesn't feel like it was meant to be.

"Yes to all five, but..." she whispers.

"But what, Anna?" I bring my hand up, brushing my fingers down her cheek until I'm cupping her chin in my hand. She shivers and Christ, if that one shiver doesn't make whatever last bit of nerves evaporate into the thick, sexual severity in this room.

"I need to know how you feel about me?" Her voice is wobbly.

I coil my other hand around her waist, dip my head down to within a mere fraction of hers. I don't speak. Instead, I brush my lips across hers delicately. She gasps, her mouth opening slightly. And I take what I've been dying to taste. I'm not going to fuck this kiss up with her. No goddamn way.

My tongue sweeps out to taste her bottom lip. It's sweet, innocent like I know she is. I crash then. Shatter. My tongue touches the tip of hers, and that's all it takes for me to dive in and taste her pure, little mouth. Our tongues collide. I see the beauty that lies beyond in her eyes until she closes them and her arms go up and around my neck. She pulls me in as close as she can get me, breathing in the same air as me. And Christ, I take her mouth in a ravishing tangle of lips and tongue. Circling. Consuming. Communicating how I feel about her. She's more than a dream come true. She is every damn thing I've ever wanted. I let go of her chin, tangle my hand in her hair, and lift her up onto the vanity with my other hand. I kiss her until I can't see straight. I taste her until she's all I ever want to taste again. I can't stop. My tongue explores her mouth. Every bit of it. I'm relishing and demolishing at the same time.

I need more of her. I drop my mouth from hers, my breathing uncontrollable. Her moaning shoots straight to my dick.

I trail up her neck to behind her ear with my lips. Slowly. Deliberate to drive her wild. Starting behind her ear, I move back downward. I tip her head back by tugging on her hair. Her neck is begging for my mouth. It's intoxicating when I get there. I suck and nibble until she's damn near panting under my touch.

"Oh, thank god," she moans.

"I'm thanking god right now for bringing you back to me, Anna." I bury my head in her hair and sniff, not giving a shit if I sound or look like an asshole. I've smelled nothing but skank for the past few hours, never thinking I would have the opportunity again to smell Anna. Again, I savor. Her smell is appealing, unique, and comforting.

"I have nothing to compare that kiss to, but if anyone asks me to tell them about my first kiss, I'm going to tell them it was indescribable. I've dreamed for so long of you kissing me." I close my eyes, thanking god once again for her not kissing anyone since I've been gone.

"Christ, Anna. I've missed you so much. I wouldn't be able to describe it either. So let's not. It's our first of many things. I promise," I murmur into her hair. I can't seem to let her go; that and I don't want to. She breaks away from me first, her dainty hands tugging on my hair to untangle me from within hers.

Her eyes are meaningful when they catch mine, showcasing another question. She's timid at first, struggling to release whatever it is she wants to ask. She can ask me whatever she wants. I'm here for the long haul. I plan on never leaving her again. I wait, feasting on her beauty until she speaks, her question nearly knocking me on my ass.

"I want a man whose heart belongs to me, Dilan. I can't share him with anyone else. I may look like my mom, but I'm not built like her. I want him to only want me. That's one of the reasons why I've waited to give myself to anyone. Please, don't hurt me again. Like you, I'm loyal. I will never betray you. I'll also do everything I can to help you bring down those who wronged you." She's damn near breathless by the time she releases all I've known to be true about her. Her words zapped right to my chest.

She doesn't have an ounce of pity for the things I've been through. It's sincerity I see. It's truth and honestly, if I weren't already captivated by her, I fucking would be now. And now I get it, one of the reasons why Cain, Roan, and Aidan have fallen for their women. They're just as strong as we are, if not stronger. They have to be to live lives like we do, to walk hand in hand with us. To stand by our sides. It's been hell for me these past few years. Worse even, if that's possible. However, with her by my side, knowing she'll be there, waiting and wanting, I'm confident and compelled to set my demons free, so I can be the man she sees in me. She will stay out of this though. These people are not amateurs who play well with each other. Fuck, they don't play with anyone. But that's a talk for another time. This night is ours, and I plan on spending it finding out what desires Anna has. What her skin feels like up against mine. I want her primed, ready, and begging me to do things to her beautiful body she has only dreamed about.

"I belong to you, Anna. I need you to understand that. I have since the first time I met you. Like I said before, this revenge I have is something I have to do. I need it, but I need you more. I don't think I realized that until just now. There might be hurt, pain, and even anger, but my sweet Anna, I will never betray you. First of many things, baby." I brush my lips across hers. Fuck, she is like a delicate flower that once it blooms, its scent is strong. Sweet, yet strong behind the way it blossoms, showing it's not delicate at all. It's strong. A wildflower.

"I know we have many things to talk about. But not tonight. I have a fire out there, and we're stuck in this room for a few days. I want to hold you, to touch you, to kiss you, and I want you to tell me when you're ready for more." I nod to the other room. I've never had a damn passionate bone in my body for a woman. I'm not a dick to them; I've just hadn't found the right one. Until six months ago when a petite blonde walked into my life. Now I want it all. I want to give her everything. Even my heart, that for the first time in years I feel beating so hard, it feels like it's dancing inside of my chest.

"I'm ready for more, Dilan. It's you who needs to catch up. I've been standing across that finish line for six months, hoping you would cross over it. Now that you have, I say let's start running this race together. Winning a race is never rewarding unless you have someone to share it with." Shit. She's wise.

"My sweet Anna. You may wish you never said that. I've caught up, baby. In fact, now that I have, you're about to be spun around, facing me while I take full advantage of tumbling you to the ground, spreading those legs wide, and drinking every bit of you. I've been thirsty for months." Her eyes flare. She gulps. It's insanely sexy. She's aroused. Her smell annihilates my senses. Fuck, I need to taste her.

I take hold of her hand, her words replaying in my head about catching up. I'm not going to take her tonight. Not with all that's been said and done today. When I do, it will be a day when it's all about us. When I can focus on her. I am going to play though, taste more of her, watch her completely lose it with my touch. I am going to worship, adore, and watch her fall apart under my hands. My mouth. My fingers.

I also know what I want, and I want that damn sweatshirt off of her. Dropping my hand from hers once we've walked out to the other room and stand in front of the fire, I place both of them on her waist and tug her into me. The flames from the fire are mirrored in the intensity of her heated gaze. Fuck. She is going to have me coming undone.

"Take off your sweatshirt," I say at the same time I begin to undo the buttons of my shirt. She doesn't hesitate at all. Her fingers grab hold of the hem, and she slowly lifts it over her head. My dick gets harder when her flawless, mouthwatering skin exposes itself. Her stomach ripples. Sweet Jesus, when she pulls it over her head and drops it on the floor, my fingers stop moving. I take her in. I haven't been with a woman in eight months, and not a single one of them before her compare. This is a first for me as well as for her, the desire to please a woman. To let her know she's wanted in more ways than I can describe. She's right about our kiss being indescribable. Everything about the relationship we're beginning to build fits into that one word.

She steps into me and places her hands over mine, shocking me when she undoes the rest of the buttons herself. Her hands run up my stomach until she has my shirt off and I let it drop to the floor.

"Do you remember hearing me say how I wanted to lick these tattoos?" Her head dips to the center of my chest, where she runs her tongue right down the middle of my chest piece. Her touch alone reaches me somewhere deep. I feel alive. Her movements stop right above the scar from being shot on the right side of my stomach. Her fingers replace her mouth. The scar is visible. Cut through my tattooed scripture. "Does it still hurt?" She peaks up from where she is bent at the knees. "Not anymore," I say truthfully. "What about this one?" Standing, she kisses the one on my left shoulder. "No." Our eyes exchange memories of that dreadful night. I don't want to discuss it with her. It's over. I'm here. She's here. That's all that matters. When this beautiful woman leans forward and kisses the scar on my shoulder, then bends at her waist, kissing the other scar again, that snug ass taunts me. That's all it takes for me to lose control.

Grabbing her by her waist, I hoist her up, turn and take the few steps to the bed, then toss her on top of it. My body crashes down on hers. The fire illuminates her bright smile. That smile needs to come off of her lips. I want her panting and moaning underneath me. I take her mouth, entangling it with mine. No more savoring. I need to devour.

She moans into my mouth, while I let out an animalistic growl. My limit is passed, buried in the goddamn snow. Anna Drexler never gave up on me; she's forgiven me. I'm going to show her that waiting for me was so worth it.

CHAPTER SEVEN

ANNA

Oh my god. I'm gasping. My breathing is becoming quicker, harder, and I suddenly have the urge to come. If I'm this wet, this aroused by kissing, I cannot imagine what having him inside of me will do. Or his hands on me. He has me on my back. The warmth of his skin against mine has my head fuzzy. My mind is dangling. My pussy is burning with flames scorching higher than the one in the fireplace, spreading throughout my entire body.

There is no denying he wants me. I could tell the way he held me in the bathroom. And I definitely can tell by how hard he is. God, I want him.

I don't care if this isn't a first for him. He's here with me now, told me I am his and he is mine. Everything from here on out will be the first for both of us, because we're doing it together.

"I need to touch you, Anna. Taste you everywhere." Those powerful, sensual lips of his linger above mine. I'm dazed, and yet I want to scream for him to do whatever he wants. I hesitate, figuring out what to say, while I try to read his thoughts. I really wish I could speak. I would tell him to fuck me senseless. Dilan won't though. He's too gentle. At least for now. I'm destined to fall apart. To let him swallow me whole. To learn from him. To please him.

His head lifts and he smirks down at me. Sexually. Wanting.

Needing. "As long as I can touch and taste back," I say. I may have pulled that out of my ass. I'm not sure, but when he grinds his heavy dick into me, I have my answer.

I'm tugged upward. Strong hands come around my back, unclasping my bra. It falls in between us. I'm not nervous at all. Not one damn bit. I've waited way too long for his touch, and now that I have it and him, I'm giving, taking, and never letting this memory go.

"Fuck, Anna, these breasts were always a mystery to me. The way they would peak out of the top of your tank top. The way I would look at them, dream about them, wondering if they would fit perfectly in my hands." Those are his words to me when he travels down from my face to my breasts. Erotically.

His large hands palm them both. He groans then discards my bra. My back arches when he flicks my nipples, releases them, and brings one arm around my lower back to support me. I may be saying something, I'm not sure, when his mouth wraps around one of my nipples and sucks it hard into his mouth. I know my hands shoot up into his hair, drawing him closer. He sucks more of me in. Then bites gently before he moves over and repeats the same thing on the other nipple.

My head has misted over. Like the outdoor temperature when cold meets hot. It's clouded. I can barely see. My breathing is uncontrollable now. I begin to grind into him. My hips, my core, my entire body is in a frenzy to find its release. The friction in and around my pussy is so enflamed, heated, that if I don't come soon, I'm going to scream.

"Let me give you what you need, baby." Dilan's voice is rough, raw, and real. He lays me back down. The ache between my legs is nothing like I've felt before. I need him. God almighty, I'm there, right on the edge. I watch through my clouded, hazy head as he shifts himself lower on the bed, and with one yank, he has my sleep shorts off. "Fucking hell, Anna," he says, not once taking his blazing gaze off of my bare pussy. I will thank Deidre later. Right now, all I want is him. I want him to touch me, to taste me, to show me what he likes, his desires and needs. I just want him.

"I need you to touch me," I say with no embarrassment at all. I've wanted him for so long, I'm without doubt sure of this. He questions me with a look of doubt. "Please, Dilan," I say pleadingly. Then his hand grazes over the top of my core. His movements are enticing, sexual. I want to call him god, because he's making me feel like a goddess the way he parts my pussy with his fingers, stroking through my wetness.

"Anna. Please tell me no one has touched you like this." He presses against my clit. "No one has, Dilan. It's all for you. Every piece of me is for you." Somehow, I manage to lift my head. I watch him as he stares at my flesh. My legs spread as far as they can go. "Christ," he whispers, pressing harder and then dipping one long finger inside. My body transcends the exact moment his finger sinks inside of me. It's a delicious, exhilarating feeling, and I come screaming his name. He moves that finger in and out of me while I ride out my orgasm, a beautiful smirk on his face. My hips begin to move with his hand. Then he stops, drops his head, and all I see is a mass of dark hair buried between my legs. My hands grip the hell out of the sheets when his tongue takes over where his thumb was. He tugs, licks, swirls his tongue. My ass lifts, my pussy clenches. "Fucking hell," he states.

I'm being licked, sucked, and finger fucked. He's ruthless when I thought he'd be gentle, taking what I'm offering and my god, this is both gratifying and tormenting at the same time. I've wanted nothing more than to have Dilan. Not only sexually, but any way. Any other way right now can bury itself in the snow, because of the way his tongue is darting in and out, taking me to an unknown, distinct place. I feel another orgasm building, rippling straight to my toes, clouding my head even more. When it tears through me like a memory that will never be forgotten, I scream his name once again, only to be rewarded with a chuckle and the sexiest man climbing his way up my body. His mouth leaves a trail up my stomach, my chest, the dip in the center of my neck. He even kisses my shoulders. My shoulders, for god's sake. I'm somewhere between heaven and hell. Heaven because he's here, and hell because I want more. My body needs it.

My body is shaking like a leaf in the wind. My insides are rattling around as if they're unattached and I'm rolling in a pool of sweat.

"You taste like warm, sweet candy. And fuck me. If it's possible, you are even more beautiful after you come." I can smell myself on him. It turns me on even more. My arms wrap around his neck, dragging him closer. The feeling of his warm chest pressed against mine thrills me, entices me to be bolder. This animalistic creature inside of me wants to taste myself mixed with the carnal taste of Dilan. I'm hungry.

"Kiss me," I plea. His brows shoot up in a sexy way. "My pleasure," he complies.

The first swipe of his tongue across my lips has me breathing more unsteadily. The heady combination turns me on. I take his tongue and suck it into my mouth. He groans, taking control and crashing his lips to mine. Our mouths blend together like we never want to break away. The warmth of his mouth sends a current coursing through my body. It's unexplainable. I feel greedy. He has no idea how greedy I am when it comes to him. Or maybe he does, I don't know. All I do know is, Dilan Hughes is caged in my heart, and I'm never letting him out.

I protest with a whimper when he climbs off of me and feel the loss of his muscular body on top of mine. "I'm not going anywhere, sweet girl. Just ditching my pants." He stands. I watch him in fascination. His ass is tight and perfect when he shrugs them off. I need it in my hands. I watch him, ensnared by his body. I'm thoroughly exhausted, happy, and sexually satisfied. For now.

I would give anything for him to make love to me. But I'll take what I can get for now, as stingy as that may sound. There's too much hanging over our heads. I want nothing between us when I give myself to him for the first time. He's stressed and worried. We shared something with one another tonight. His mind may have been latched on to me, but until he derives a plan with his family and friends tomorrow, his past and those who haunt him are still in this room with us.

If we're going to be stuck here in this hotel, one that has everything humanly needed at our disposal, then I'm going to make the best of it. Take advantage. I decide right there that during his meeting, I'm going to roam around. Make plans to take his mind off of his worries. Yes. Dilan can expect the unexpected tomorrow, and I know just the person to help me.

Dilan moves to the fireplace, pushing the buttons to shut it off. The only light on now is coming from the bathroom. He strides in confidence, shutting that off too, leaving me cringing at the loss of admiring his body with all those tattoos and muscles sculpted beyond belief. My mouth goes dry at the sight of him. Those black boxer briefs are the luckiest piece of clothing. I hate them because they're touching his ass. His cock. Snuggly, I might add. And I love them if for no other reason than that they have my imagination running wild.

The bed slopes when he climbs in next to me. He pulls up the covers around us and then tugs me close, his arm wrapping around me, my head lying on his chest.

I swing my leg around him, nudging his still hard erection. My fingers glide down until I firmly have his long dick in my hand, gripping it through his boxers. He's so hard. I need to relieve him.

He stops me when I start to stroke him through his boxers, his hand resting over the top of mine. "I'm good, baby. We have the next couple of days to play. Right now, all I want to do is hold you. Fall asleep knowing you're sleeping peacefully next to me, waking up knowing you're real and you're here with me."

Well, shit then, okay. I would be crazy not to take him up on holding me all night, especially when I've wanted him to hold me like this for so long. But I feel guilty that he's so hard. I know it has to be painful. Men and women are different, but god, a man who has a hard-on like that has got to be in pain. This unselfish man pleased me, took care of me, and showed me how he's putting me before him. Right before I fall asleep, I vow to make it up to him the first chance I get. His pleasure comes before mine too.

"I'm not going anywhere," I say through a sleepy yawn. "Neither am I. Not ever again." Those are the last words I hear before I fall into a dreamless sleep with a smile on my face. I wake up to warmth next to me, flesh against flesh, the exact same smile on my face, with the exact same man I've wanted beside me since my eyes first stumbled upon him.

"Good morning," Dilan rumbles, his voice husky from sleep. "Hey." I curl closer to him.

It's obvious I rolled over during the night. My butt is up against a very hard, throbbing dick. His arm snakes up, grabbing a handful of one of my breasts. I arch back more, my ass digging into his erection. "Best sleep I've had in months," he whispers into my hair. "Me too," I say, smiling so wide my face may crack. I'm ready to play some more. I want him in my mouth. I'm taking charge here. While he's playing with my breast, squeezing, I slide my hand behind my back, find the top of his boxers, then slide my hand in until I have a firm grip. My fingers barely circle his thickness. "Jesus Christ." He jerks in my hand.

"No, it's sweet Anna Mother of God to you. " I lift my body, lose his hand on my breast, and flip him onto his back without letting go of his dick. He titters on the edge of taking control. I tsk him. "I see we're going to have issues here with who's in control, Anna." Those darks brows shoot up in a challenging way.

"Oh, Dilan Levy," I verbalize mockingly. "You have no idea how controlling I can be. Especially when what I want is literally in the palm of my hands."

"Is that so?" He grinds his dick harder into my hand. "Very much so." My long, blond hair drapes across his chest as I descend. I'm dying here. A slow agonizing death from deprivation. I need to lick these tats. To taste his skin. I want him relaxed, to concentrate on the things he needs to do. Like shut up and let me explore. Then go to his family and get us the hell out of here.

I don't want whatever is building between us to start out with us not being able to go anywhere. I love being secluded with him, but I want this war over with. I want everything with him, and by god, I refuse to submit to the confinement of four walls like our friends had to. Or to not be able to do a damn thing for fear the enemy will strike at any time.

I need to see him, to feel his bare, thick shaft in my mouth. My tongue raids his smooth skin, licking across one of his nipples. He groans. His dick twitches. "Shit, Anna," he barks out, encouraging me more. I release my hold on him and slide my fingers to the band of his boxers, the tips teasing around the smooth hair. The instant they dip inside and I feel the silkiness of him, we both let out a rumbling curse. I grip him tight. God, he's big. My fingers explore him, moving up and down in a rhythm of their own, while my mouth continues to explore his chest. It tastes salty, tangy, and hard.

He continues to swear up a storm the farther my tongue travels down his stomach, the more vigorous my strokes become. I've never had the desire to take a man in my mouth before. No one has touched my soul the way he has.

He grabs my hair, pulling it into a makeshift ponytail. My eyes meet his, my tongue hanging out, dripping with more desire than before when I see how dark and glazed over they are. There's adoration there too.

My bare pussy scrapes across his thighs, wet and hot. I miss his taste the instant my mouth leaves his skin to explore his glorious dick. I shouldn't. His dick is going to taste just as good, if not better. His hips lift when I tug down his boxers until his dick is staring me in the face. Again, my boldness surfaces. Christ, I'm in blessed heaven. One lick up the center of his dick and the words, "Fucking hell" escaping from his mouth drive me to the point of wanting to undo him.

My mouth wraps around his head, my tongue swiping across the tip. I watch him as he watches me take him further into my mouth with my body half straddling his legs.

I fall away then, into the unknown. By the way he's moaning, I know I'm pleasing him. My free hand scratches down his thigh. I'm taking my damn time with this, slowly working his beautiful dick until it explodes. I want to feel, discover everything he likes.

Keeping a firm grip on the base of his dick, I begin to alternate, using my whole hand then my fingers as I pump him, my mouth moving up and down slowly, deliberately. "That's it, Anna. Like that. Christ, your mouth is a weapon, woman." His speech is slurred as if he's struggling to perform a sentence. I'm so into this. Even though I haven't had sex before, this is as much of a turn-on to me as it is to him.

I look up at him when he tugs my hair tighter, holding his gaze while I take his dick into my mouth, sucking him hard as I go down, licking under his shaft as I go up.

My breasts ache right along with my pussy. I need to touch one of them. I take my hand and pinch my nipple, causing me to hum. "Son of a bitch, you're a naughty girl, aren't you?"

"Only for you," I say through a mouthful of his big dick. Coherent or not, he has to know by the way I'm tugging at my own nipple, making it harder. I could come and I might. The thrill of this has me right there on the edge of coming all over his leg. I'm rejoicing in this carnal connection. I feel him grow more into my mouth. His breathing increases. Not once do we lose eye contact. Him telling me to continue, me telling him I don't ever want to stop.

When the first spurt of his come hits the back of my throat, I release his dick with my hand, cusp his balls, and I suck him harder, taking every drop he has to offer, letting it glide down my throat. I come with him, my wetness coating his leg. He smirks. I feel like a damn champ. I've pleased him. Taken charge and fucking shit, I cannot wait until his dick is inside of me, making love to me for the first time.

"Get up here." He drags me up his chest, making my mouth let go of him. I almost pout. I could do that again. "You, my naughty girl, have a very wicked mouth." He flips me over onto my back. I feel him kicking his boxers off the rest of the way. I also feel his dick up against my pussy. I whimper and squirm underneath him, pressing my hips up. Am I a naughty girl? I want to be, only for him.

"Soon, baby," he says. Then he takes my mouth ravenously, while I take his hungrily, all the while forgetting the outside world. The danger. The evil. The icy storm brewing outside. The one I don't find out until later has absolutely nothing to do with the weather.

CHAPTER EIGHT

DILAN

"I have never seen someone so beautiful, both inside and out," I say honestly. I look deep into Anna's eyes. Her hair is splayed across the pillow like an angelic halo. She's astounding, genuine, and I have never wanted to get my shit together more than I do right now.

"Right back at ya, big boy." She presses her slick pussy into my raging cock. Where I'm getting the willpower from to not make love to her is beyond me. I know she's the one. The one I can see myself spending the rest of my life with, pleasing her in the way she deserves. Sexually and emotionally.

It's impossible to describe my overflowing passion for her. I'm flooded with it. The last thing I want to do is leave this bed. We've been messing around for two hours. I've licked every inch of her body, gorged on her sweet pussy until she screamed so loud I swear whoever is next door to us heard her cries of pleasure when she came in my mouth.

Her stomach growls beneath me, which has her giggling like crazy.

"I need to make a phone call. Why don't you order us some room service? Then we can shower together before I go meet everyone," I tell her as I force myself to climb off of her. Her eyes shoot straight to my cock when I stand beside the bed. She sinks back into the pillows further, and her bottom lip pokes out. Christ.

"Okay. I'll call Deidre and Calla too. We can figure something out while you meet." Lifting herself up, she reaches for the menu on the nightstand. I retrieve my boxers and I slip them on then take my phone out of my pants. I need to get some clothes here. I had no damn idea my night would turn into one I never thought possible. Thank god it did. Swiping the screen, I scroll until I find my neighbor Micah's number. I place the phone to my ear. He answers on the first ring. Without hesitation, he tells me he will get everything I need and take it to the front desk of our apartment building, where I will call someone to pick it up. I hang up then dial my dad.

"Son?" He asks more like a one-worded question. There's worry in his tone. "Everything's great, dad. I need a small favor, is all." I ask him to call his friend Chase, who owns half of the damn cab companies in Manhattan, to see if he will send one of them to pick up my bag. It's the only way I can think of to deter any suspicion in case Juan suspects anything.

"What's mom doing?" I ask casually before hanging up. I would love nothing more than for Anna to get to know the other woman in my life. "Bitching because she isn't aloud at the meeting." I can see him now, rolling his eyes. "She's worried," I say in her defense.

"Of course she is. She's worried out of her goddamn mind about this shit, Dilan," he half scolds me. "I know she is," I say without even having to talk to her. I'm sure she will chew me several new holes in my ass the minute she can. "I love you, son. I'll see you soon." His words strike me in the chest. My parents have never held back on telling me they love me. And now, I'm putting them through more hell than when I went to prison. They have to understand that this is something I have to do.

I place my phone back into my pants, turn and wink at Anna, then stretch my arm out to help her off the bed. She takes it. Her naked body is trailing behind me into the bathroom. I'll crumble to the damn floor and spread her legs wide, licking her sweet pussy for my lunch, if I even look at her. God, I shouldn't have said I'd take a shower with her. I need a damn cold one. My dick has been hard for two hours. I don't see him coming down for a very long time. Maybe never.

I hated parting with Anna after our shower. I've never held back my restraint like I did when she ran her soapy hands over my cock. Christ almighty. Now after giving him a damn talk, I'm headed from heaven to hell. I want this done. Over with, for all our safety and piece of minds. This shit is getting old.

"What the hell is that cheeky ass smile on your face?" Cain grumbles. Someone's in a shit mood. Can't say I blame him. It seems every damn one of us thinks we find happiness, and before it even gets started, the fucking earth shifts in the wrong direction, leaving a gaping hole that swallows us up. Only this time, it's my damn hole everyone has fallen into.

"Anna and I worked things out. We're giving it a shot," I say casually, even though I want to beat on my chest, pretend I'm Tarzan, and swing from the damn chandeliers in this place. Yeah. Not going to fucking happen.

"It's about damn time you pulled your own dick out of your ass." He carries on like he knows what the hell I've been through. In a way, he does, only it was worse. It was bullshit that made him choose between his wife and her life, basically. Cut him deep from what I remember when I would visit. I'm happy for them both. He was a miserable fucking dick to be around.

"How the fuck do you know my dick is big enough to reach my ass?" I nudge his shoulder. Thank Christ I get a small tug of his lips out of him. We all need to loosen up. This meeting is going to be fucking hell. I know it. Shit's going down.

"You hurt her and I'll fucking cut that dick off." Aidan joins us as we stroll down the hallway toward the Bellamissio room, where my uncle has lunch waiting. I pray he has some booze for these guys and beer for me. I know damn well we're going to need it by the time this meeting is done.

"I'm not going to hurt her, fuckface. Back off." I swear he's more protective of her than I am. Can't say I blame the fucker though. She's worth protecting.

"I know you won't. Just had to throw it out there. Thanks for taking care of getting the kids here. Deidre was going out of her mind without having Diesel here." Aidan nods toward Cain. "My wife too. Now we're all here. Ready to throw this shit down. We're going home after this meeting though. As nice as this place is, I want my daughter sleeping in her own bed," Cain says as he pushes the door open to the room.

"We are too," Aidan pipes in. "No one will be going anywhere." My uncle stands from the head of the table, addressing the three of us. We stand stock still. Fuck me. "Bullshit. I'm not keeping my family here." Cain plants his hands on his hips. "You will and you are. End of discussion. Some shit went down last night after we all went to bed. It seems we've underestimated Jazmin. I should have killed the bitch, instead of thinking I could outsmart the conniving cunt. She killed Doug, Keith, and Austin. The bitch had a goddamn knife on her. How the fuck she managed to escape is beyond me." He runs his hand through his gray hair. Fucking hell. This is all my fault. He's right. We should have fucking killed her. Goddamn it.

"Fuck." I slump down in the closest chair.

"Dilan. Were a family. We take care of our own. Their death is on my hands, not yours. I should have killed her myself. This is my fault. Hell, boy, I've killed more people than I can count. I knew better than to leave a trained killer alone with those men. Don't you fucking dare take this guilt away from me. It's my burden to bear. Now we plan. I'm not living through this shit any longer. They won't come after us here, but the minute one of us walks out of this goddamn building, they will. Now, all three of you sit the fuck down and listen." Jesus. John is right about them more than likely being out there already, but he is wrong about the guilt. The blame. If I weren't so set on making these people pay, then those men would still be alive and everyone could go about their business.

I watch my uncle pour himself a shot of whiskey, then passing the bottle around the table. When it gets to me, I take the shot glass already in front of me and pour one. I down it and have another poured before the first one even starts to burn going down my throat. I take that one too then pass the bottle to Aidan. Fuck, I hate that shit. And yet, it will numb me quicker than any cold beer will.

"You didn't start without me, fuckers, did you?" We all turn to the door. I can't say I'm shocked, but I become more pissed off at myself when I see Roan enter. Goddamn him.

"Damn. I'm fucking sorry, man. Shit." I stand and go to him.

"For what?" He has a cocky look on his face. "For needing me?" he questions.

"So my honeymoon is delayed by a few days. So what?" He shrugs, strides over to my dad, pats him on the shoulder, leans in to pick up the damn gasoline that's burning my throat, and pulls a big swig of the whiskey right from the bottle.

"Sit your ass down. My wife is getting a massage with your woman. She's good. Are you?" I pause briefly to let what he's saying sink in, roaming around the table, searching for any sign from these men who are here for me. Every single one of them shows me the loyalty they have to this family, to me. Even Ivan Solokov. The head of the Russian clan. "I'm good. Let's get this done." I nod toward my uncle. However, if I didn't love this crazy fucker, I would smash his head in for being here and for his smart mouth. I tuck my guilt away. No one will know. Not Anna, not anyone. It will stay in my head. I will deal with it on my own. If I were honest, I'd admit it's taking this huge boulder off of my shoulder I've been carrying around for years, knowing this revenge is now in the hands of more than just me.

For two hours, we all listen and eat as my uncle and John tell us their plan. Both of them have been up all night, disposing of our vehicles and setting our own security in place. One of the big issues we have is that the Carlos family has just as many cops in their back pocket as we do, which leaves us no choice but to not call ours in for help, or at least to try and get us out of here. We don't have them kill for us, like some do.

We use them for protection, killing only if they have to, while we pad their wallets with a shit ton of money. Corruption is every fucking where. It doesn't matter with whom or why. It's there.

"I have no qualms about taking them out. They started this war. We'll finish it. Now, for the next few days, we will enjoy the amenities this fine establishment has to offer. No one does a thing. And Dilan," my uncle addresses me, "when that bitch contacts you, and trust me, she will, you tell her to pass a message to her brother." I raise my brows, waiting diligently for what this particular message will be.

"You tell her he's a dead fucking man for every mark, every punch, and every bit of harm he caused you. And then you tell her to expect a phone call from the prison where her beloved ex resides." He tilts his head in Ivan's direction. Then nods and folds his hands neatly on the table in front of him.

"Miguel will be dead by this evening," Ivan proclaims. I'm not shocked at all by his words, not from either one of these notorious leaders. I nod once again to both of them, my gratitude of thanks marking them with my expression.

"What the fuck?" Roan stands as if he's holding all the power in this meeting.

"Roan," my uncle warns. "No, dad. Don't 'Roan' me." He leans in, placing his palms flat on the table. I can feel the blood boiling in his veins. There's no need for him to glare at me like he wants to shoot that hot red family blood we have running through our bodies all over this damn table. I feel his pain. If the tables were turned, and thank god they aren't, I know damn well I'd be standing over the top of him, ready to kick his ass for keeping shit from me too.

"You forget to tell me something?" His aim is planted directly at me.

"Didn't forget, man. I didn't want to tell you." I stand and meet his gaze.

"That's a bunch of shit, goddamn it. If my intuition works correctly—and trust me, brother, it does—that motherfucker should have been dead a long time ago. Fucking hell, Dilan. What the fuck did they do to you in there?" He closes his pained eyes and inhales deeply. When he opens them, I see a storm, more like a hurricane, in his glare. A mixture of pain, anger, and frustration.

"I survived, that's all we should care about. So he roughed me up a bit. Now he dies." I toss my hand out, letting them all know I'm good. And I hope the piece of shit suffers before he draws in his last breath.

"Motherfucker." My dad stands, voicing his rights as my father.

Then Cain and Aidan join in. If this shit weren't so important to me, if I didn't want to begin a life with the woman I care deeply about, I may laugh at these brothers of mine. How each one of them is standing here with clenched fists and a troubled appearance, ready to fight for me. There's no pity though. I might have to knock them on their asses if they show pity. And the steam hammering out of Aidan would be downright fucking funny if our situation weren't deadly. It's as if he swallowed down a cloud of smoke the way it's dispensing out of his mouth and ears. He's worried about Anna caught up in this mess as much as he is about everyone else. Aren't we fucking all?

"Mom doesn't need to know. It's in the past, dad. You get me?" I direct my attention at him first. Hell, the way my mom can lose her temper with a flick of a wrist, she will stand out there with a machine gun bigger than her and try to shoot every one of those assholes. Even when I was a kid, she came unglued when someone tried to mess with me. I love her more than anything, but hell, she's a mom, and mothers can be deadly when it comes to their child. Doesn't't' matter if you're old enough to take care of yourself. She reminds me of that fact every chance she can get.

"She'll never know. I, however, do. And no one puts their hands on my son. Do you get me?" He comes around to stand in front of me, his hands gripping my shoulders. "I get you." He says no more, but pulls me in for a hug. "I love you, son, and I'm damn proud of you too. Always have been." He releases me then turns toward Ivan. His words are wicked. Hell, I didn't think my dad had this lifestyle in him, but his words prove otherwise. "I don't want to know how you're going to have that piece of shit killed. What I do want is his hands cut off, and one of them stuffed in his mouth, while the other is shoved up his ass," he says seriously.

"Your request will be fulfilled," Ivan returns.

"Well then, I'm going to go spend time with my wife." My uncle stands. "Are we all clear here?"

"Crystal," Roan expresses, never taking his regard away from me. He's not done with me yet. I know him too well.

I'm left in the room then, with three pissed off men. Each of them glaring at me.

"Jesus Christ. Come on," I speak in my defense.

"I'm so fucking mad at you and at myself. I should have been there for you." Roan and his sense of logic. He doesn't have to be there for everyone. Where he needs to be right now is with his new bride. The way I see it, if anyone should be pissed off right now, it should be me. I sigh then address these fuckers how I see fit. I'm done here. My phone vibrates in my pocket, but I choose to ignore it until I say what needs to be said.

"For fuck's sake. I'm not getting into this with any of you. Leave it. You're here for me now. This," I slam my hands down on the table, "means more to me than anything you could have tried to do back then. I took those beatings from him to survive in there. I chose not to fight back, because I wanted to get the fuck out of there. I chose not to tell you, because it would have started a war out here. And just like all of you, I would have died in that shithole and not from that fucker's hands. I would have died, because I wouldn't have been out here to fight alongside of you." I mean what I say when I stare down each one of them. I know damn well they would all do and feel the same way.

"I'm still kicking your ass when this is all over." Aidan and his damn smart mouth with the steam rolling out of it. He may be a big fucker, but he's as much of a pussy on the inside as the rest of us. He isn't kicking anyone's ass, and he knows it. Asshole.

"No one's kicking my ass again, fucker, so bring it. Now, I don't know about any of you, but hell, I have one beautiful woman around here somewhere. Like Salvatore said, let's enjoy the amenities." I hear Aidan growl, Cain laugh, and Roan say shit I don't even want to repeat when I walk out of the door and head toward the front desk.

I tip the concierge when he hands me my bag then make my way to the elevators with one hell of a smile on my face as I visualize the stoic expression on Miguel's face when whoever Ivan has on the inside surprises that fucker. I hope they fuck him with his own dick. The sick asshole. One down and a few more to go.

As I step off the elevator, I use the key card to Anna's room she gave me before I left. I have a beaming ass smile on my face. That is, until I pull my phone out of my pocket, noticing a voicemail.

I toss my bag on the bed and hover over the button. The number is unfamiliar, but yet I know damn well whose it is. I knew the minute I looked at my phone.

It's not Jazmin. It's her brother. I know damn well it is. Making my way to the couch, I sit down and place the phone on the coffee table, then hit the listen icon along with speaker. I thank god Anna isn't in here when his threats swarm out of my phone.

"Dilan Levy," Juan speaks in his heavy accent. "There's an old tale about weddings. Certain days of the week, and certain months of the year, are better than others for a wedding. It seems your family did not choose the right day. You see, Mondays you marry for health, which up until now, your family is healthy. Tuesdays are for wealth, which I could care less about at the moment. Wednesdays are for best of all, that one fits. See, I wish you all the best in this war you have started. Thursdays are for losses, which you will have plenty. Fridays are for crosses. I will make sure several of them are tossed on top of your graves. And Saturdays, this one is my favorite of all, especially since that was the day your piece of shit cousin was married. You see, they mean no luck at all. You've crossed me, Dilan Levy. Stay and enjoy your last few days on this earth. Your luck has run out." I lean forward and save his voicemail, chuckling at the stupidity of the way he has delivered his threat.

"You forgot the best tale of them all, asshole. This one could give a shit what day, year, or goddamn decade it is." *Dogs howling in the dark of night howl for death before daylight.*

CHAPTER NINE

ANNA

The muscles in my body feel like a piece of sponge cake after being massaged for an hour and a half. They're springy, pliable, and yielding to my own body. I'm refreshed.

All the ladies went to lunch together, including Dilan's mother, Ginny. I fell in love with her immediately. She adores her son. Even though she carries her worry and fear well, you could still tell by the dark circles under her eyes she's frightened for his safety as well as everyone else's . None of us know what's happening behind those doors the men are gathered, what plans are being derived. We won't find out either. They will keep it to themselves, tell us what they feel we need to know. But no damn way will I be left in the dark. The dark sucks. I will not let anyone attempt to destroy, hurt, or destruct anyone in this family.

I want to look at it as the beginning of Dilan and I, and the end of them.

Ginny, it seems, had no idea about the feelings Dilan and I have for each other, or anything at all about our past, until my mother cornered me the first chance she got. A spark immediately framed Ginny's dreary eyes when she overheard.

And my mom. God, I love her, but she needs to back off. Worrying is one thing, telling me what to do is another. I mean, she knows what kind of woman I am. I have more respect for myself than I do for anyone else. It's all because of her and the way she raised me.

When she told me how worried she was about me, I tried to set her at ease. I explained how Dilan and I talked, that we're working it out, leaving out the private details. I understand that she's concerned for me. She's my mother. But she needs to let me go, let me take care of myself. The minute I told her as calmly as I could that Dilan had his reasons for doing what he did, she wanted to know more, but I cut her off at that point. She does not need to know more than that. That's when Ginny stepped into our conversation. Maybe she wanted to calm my mom down before she went into hysterics or became irrational like she often does when it comes to protecting me. I don't know. But whatever the two of them talked about seemed to set my mom at ease, and I'm grateful for that.

After that, we diligently talked about our jobs, while mom talked about Ramsey. Then Ginny directed her attention to me. She's graceful, caring, and I'm so happy Dilan has a supportive family. He's going to need them. We're all going to need each other when it comes down to it.

She's a delightful woman, and I'm thankful my mom and her hit it off so well. She's taken her mind off of me, distracted her in ways I couldn't. I'll never be able to express my gratitude enough.

Guilt strikes me hardcore for thinking the way I do. My mom witnessed my downward spiral more than anyone after Dilan left. She's seen me at my lowest. I'm desperate now to find him.

The three of have been standing in the hallway for the past half hour, but I excuse myself, leaving the two of them to discuss whatever dinner plans they are making for the evening.

I begin to search around the hotel until I find all the girls. When I approach them, I see they're shopping online, all of them sprawled across the couch like they own the place, with their feet up on the glass table and their heads huddled together. Alina studies the screen with brightness in her eyes. Her demeanor is sweet. Not one shred of bitterness whatsoever shows in her appearance. I listen intently as they laugh and talk about whatever it is they are looking to buy. Family. Love. Those are the words popping in my head right now as I make my way to where they are.

My mind also goes right to Dilan. I know he is going to beat himself up about them still being here. By the way Alina is laughing at something Deidre points out on the computer though, I'm guessing Roan and her are here by choice, not because of the fact that something dreadful has happened.

"Anna." Alina looks up from the computer. Her calling out my name has the others looking up as well. Both Deidre and Calla have their adorable children on their laps, who are wiggling desperately to be let down. I'm assuming they needed to have their children here with them again, needed to know they are safe. I'm in love with this new family of mine. Right down to these little children, who steal your heart the minute they look at you with their mouths half full of teeth and their eyes full of mischief. Adorable.

"Did you have fun last night?" Deidre's eyebrows shoot up, a knowing smirk on her face. "Did you?" I retort back. "Oh, you know I did." She rubs the bump on her belly. "Deidre, mind your own business. I swear you need to walk around with a gag in your mouth at times," Alina says then rolls her eyes. "Oh, listen to you talk, Mrs. Diamond. The minute you let your husband inside of your super-glued vajayjay, you couldn't wait to tell me. And I like being gagged with my man's big co—" Calla reaches up and slams her hand across Deidre's mouth. She finishes her sentence through her muffled mouth. The four of us burst out laughing so hard, we have people staring at us like the crazy women we are.

"We talked," I say then wink. I'm not giving her any more, that nosy little busy body with no filter in her mouth. She probably lost even more of her filter the moment she fell for Aidan. He lets words roll off of his tongue and doesn't care who's around to hear them. I love how we all accept each other for the way we are, not giving a crap how you act or what you do.

"Whatever. Don't tell us all about the sexy, tatted-up Dilan Levy then. Come and shop with us. Alina has all her sexy honeymoon lingerie with her. Calla and I are shopping. Figured we may as well make the best of our stay here." Her eyes go back to the screen. "Why I spend money on this stuff I will never know. Cain just rips it off of me anyway." Calla hikes Justice back onto her lap.

"Well, I for one cannot afford it, I'm sure." Although, the thought of Dilan ripping anything off of me and having him take me hard and fast sends a streak of heat through me that spikes up my temperature to damn near boiling.. I'm ready to be fucked.

I peak over the top of their heads to see the site they are shopping at, and damn near gasp when I see some of the prices. Agent Provocateur. Definitely not in my price range.

"He rips it off of you, because it turns him the hell on," Deidre addresses Calla then turns to me. "And you, Little Miss Thing, will be buying something too. I've already found the perfect thing for you." I look at her knowingly. My friends all know I'm a virgin. Well, they may think I lost it last night, but I'm not telling them. Especially the mouth from the south here. Knowing her, she would broadcast it in the middle of Times Square with her big mouth. I love her though.

"All right, let me see it," I give in curiously.

She clicks a few times until the screen pops up. "Oh, wow. It's..." "So you, Anna. Yes, I know," she agrees delightfully.

"It's beautiful, Anna. Dilan would love it," Alina chimes in.

I love it. It's simple but sexy. A lavender silk bra with black lace and a matching thong.

"I just need your bra size, then we can call the order in. They'll bring our things to us." They all look so hopeful and happy. "How much is it?" I ask.

"Worth every penny you spend." Deidre's answer has us all laughing. I imagine what Dilan's expression would be when he saw me in this. That rush of desire spreading in between my legs boils over. I want him in ways I'm sure all three of my friends, who are so happily in love, desire their men. I exhale. I hate to spend the money, but I also know I would give my last dollar to do anything to make Dilan happy. Lingerie it is. He did tell me I was naughty after all. This ensemble screams naughty, seductive, and dangerous. I give Deirdre my bra size. Her brows lift when I expose it. "This bra is going to have his eyeballs bouncing off the walls, especially with tits like yours." I roll my eyes. I swear to god all this woman has on her mind is sex. Even when she's trying to help me out, pushing me to do things I've never done before. Like spending money I don't really have on lingerie. She then hands Diesel to Alina, picks up her phone, and places our order as she clicks away and rattles off everything, charging it to her account of course. The devious bitch.

"They'll be here in an hour," she declares after she hangs up. "Great. Let's find something for these two little cuties to do while we wait," Alina says.

"I'm happy for you." Deidre laces her arm through mine as we trail behind Alina and Calla down the long hallway, watching them chase after Justice and Diesel. This place has everything. We're headed to the gift shop, because Deidre claimed she needs a snack.

"I'm happy too. This place is beautiful, but I know Dilan wants out of here. We've all been through enough, don't you think?" I change the subject. Even though my friends seem to not be bothered by us having to be here, trapped once again, I need to know for my own peace of mind they're not angry about it. This isn't what Dilan had planned. He never wanted to put anyone in danger. He told me so before he left the room, his guilt written all over his face. And now with Roan here, he's going to feel like absolute shit.

"We have. Remember though, we're a family. A family that sticks together. We have each other's backs, Anna. Besides, a few days in this place... Who can complain?" She spreads her arms out wide. This place is beautiful; it's not home though. Nor is it normal. Our lives will never be normal. We will always try and protect ourselves in some sort of bubble. It's the day that bubble pops that scares the living shit out of me. Why do I feel that day is approaching rapidly? Will any of us be able to handle it when it does?

Deidre starts to talk again, bringing my thoughts out of the darkness that has taken over my mind. "Our lives are all coming together. You and Dilan are perfect for each other. And I know you're going to come out of this stronger. Yes, it's bullshit we cannot go home. But hell, if your room is anything like ours, then consider this a mini vacation. Take advantage of it." She signals with her hand once again. She's so right. Everyone loves the comfort of their own home. This place however, does feel like a vacation. Besides, it's cold outside. Freezing. I smile, thinking the possibilities here are endless. I know that Dilan and I are not where the rest of our family and friends are in their relationships. But that doesn't mean we don't know each other. We do. I remember everything he's told me about himself, and I want to know more. I want it all with him. The happy and the sad. The ups and downs, and all of the in-betweens. I want to know I have someone who cares and accepts me for who I am. My heart and soul. The pit that grows from nothing and shields you from destruction. I want the contentment.

I grip my fingers around hers as we walk into the gift shop, my mood upturned. I'm ready to face life and those who wish to destroy this family head-on.

"Finally." I slump up against the door when I enter my room, my pink Provocateur bag in hand.

"Finally what?" Dilan startles me when he comes around the corner.

"Those women can shop," I say, exhausted. The minute I see him, all exhaustion is gone, like the wind blowing from one place to the next. He thrills me.

I was hoping to beat him here, to be lying in bed when he comes in. The way he looked at me last night, like he wanted to have me for all three meals with just a simple black, strapless bra on, will be nothing compared to the look he's going to give me when I'm wearing nothing but the sexy little items I have now. That bra barely holds my breasts in, and I don't even want to think about how little that scrap of panties covers my ass. I'm turning myself on just thinking about it. My nipples are hard. My pussy is having a Dilan attack. I'm addicted. I want to be fucked in the hardest way possible.

I stuff the bag he's glaring at behind my back. His look is hazardous. Oh, yes. I am undoubtedly turned on. Wet. Aching. Wanting.

"Seems you do too. What's in the bag, Anna?" He approaches me slowly.

Dangerously.

"You'll see," I tease. "Oh, I most assuredly will. See. It. On. You," he emphasizes dramatically as his steps grow closer. While I become braver. How the hell does he know I bought something for him to see on me? Who cares? I'm in the mood to tease. Then please.

"Hmm. We shall see." I drop the bag on the floor. The plea to touch him is granted when I snail my fingers slowly up his massive chest, around his neck, and delve into his thick, dark hair. I pull him the rest of the way to me. All my control is gone when I swipe my tongue up the side of his neck and nip gently on his ear. "Fuck," he thunders out, grips my arms, and pins them over my head. His hard body is scorching mine when we connect. He grinds his hips, thrusting his hard cock against my body. Our chests mold against each other. He lifts me, and I wrap my legs around his hips. By the time he drops us on the bed and his body crashes down on top of mine, I'm a winded mess from his touch.

I'm desperate to feel his skin. I tug and pull his navy blue, long-sleeved shirt out of his pants, and run my hands up and down his back, indulging in the way he feels. Those muscles, those tattoos, and his heated skin have my insides crackling. Splintering.

"God help me when it comes to you, my beautiful Anna." I'm not sure what he means by that. But if the way he looks at me is any indication at all, I'm about to get what I've been aching for. All of him.

I lose his skin when he pulls me up and practically rips my shirt off of me, then tosses it behind his back. "Jesus, Anna. You are fucking beautiful. All of you. Your breasts are tempting me. Do you have any idea how bad I want to fuck you right now? " Those brown eyes flare when he looks at my chest. I changed in the public bathroom. I'm wearing my sexy, little new bra and very skimpy thong.

"Did you still want to know what's in the bag?" I joke. He shakes his head, his nostrils flaring. His gaze is heated as it travels from my chest to my mouth to my eyes. I grab hold of his shirt and guide it over his head. I need it gone. I'm salivating, damn near foaming at the mouth from the sight of him. He describes sex with his body alone. He's a woman's dream, a man who will fulfill your every fantasy, and I'm withering inside for him to touch me. And for me to touch those tattoos that are begging me to trace, bite, and tease them. "If this," I stroke his very hard and thick cock through the outside of his pants, "is any indication of how hard you want to fuck me, then do it."

"I plan to. I'm going to fuck this pussy. Make you squirm. Beg. Bury my dick deep inside of you. Then start all over again. Can you handle that? You're the first woman in my life who I want it all with. I mean everything, Anna." If I had any inhibitions or doubts before, I assuredly don't now. I'm mesmerized, enchanted by this man. His lifestyle is rough and dangerous. But when he's with me, he's passionate, protective, and caring. Even when he talks dirty.

"The question is, can you handle it, Dilan?" I whisper. Our eyes are searching. Our breathing is meshing. "Don't tease me, baby. I'll flip you over and slam my dick into you now. Be sure, Anna, you're stuck with me, baby. I won't let you go."

"I don't want you to let me go, Dilan." Not ever.

He shoots up off of the bed then, his fingers reaching for his sweat pants. Obviously, he received his clothes. I watch his hands hike them down, my eyes growing wide when his cock springs deliciously free. Oh, Christ. I swallow. Not from being nervous; it's more from the fact that I've dreamed about him fucking me for so long. Last night was perfect. But this. God, I want this.

"Take your jeans off, Anna," he orders, bringing me out of my daze.

My legs swing around the bed. I stand directly in front of him while I undo and shimmy my jeans down my legs until I'm standing so close to him, I swear I hear his heart thumping.

"You have no idea how stunning you are. I love this lingerie, but it has to go." Well, at least he's not going to rip it off, although the thought does entice me. *Maybe next time*, my little dandy planner in my head screams.

His voice is husky. I'm hauled into him, his hands gripping my ass. One finger is tediously toying with the silky straps on each side of my hips. He drags them down my legs. I step out of them, his hands lingering on my calves, slowly gliding up my legs until once again he's standing and undoing the hooks of my bra. Slowly, he takes a step back, his eyes never leaving mine until the bra is gone. Then they move to my chest. My nipples harden from his stare.

"You're sure?" he asks once again, gulping slowly, his Adams apple bobbling nervously. "Yes," I mumble breathlessly. He lifts me up and cradles me in his arms, then places me in the center of the bed. His gaze moves up and down my body. I feel chilled and warm at the same time, exquisitely cherished from his adoring mark as he takes in my naked frame.

"Don't move." Like I would ever. No chance in hell. He walks to the end of the bed and pulls his wallet out from the bag I didn't even notice was there, and retrieves a condom packet. "Oh, no. No condom. I'm on birth control. I have been for years," I say, sitting up. His eyes close. I know what he's thinking. He may be my first, but I know I'm not his.

"Anna," he says while shaking his head. "I trust you, Dilan. I do. I know you," I whisper softly.

He drops the condom back in the bag. His heavy cock comes back into view when he climbs on the bed. "I haven't been with anyone since I laid my eyes on you. No one. And I've never done it without one of those before either. I wouldn't be here with you if I didn't know for a fact I'm healthy." I breathe a sigh of relief, knowing he wasn't with anyone while he was gone. "I know you wouldn't." My breathing is coming in small gasps now. My desire for him has turned into a need to be able to breathe air into my lungs. I've waited so long for this, for him.

I lie back, spread my legs, and lift my arms to him. I have no idea what I'm doing. But I don't care. No one has a damn clue when they make love for the first time. I have no worries. I can see by the way he looks at me, touches my legs as he works his way up to my throbbing pussy, that I'm all Dilan wants.

"I need to taste you again. One taste of this has me wanting to slip my tongue inside of you multiple times in one damn day. Do you have any idea how delicious you smell, taste, and feel, Anna?" Oh god. My lungs have collapsed. I close my eyes when I feel his tongue swirl my clit. I want to ask him if he has any idea how good he makes me feel, yet I can't. The words are stuck in the back of my throat.

"Christ almighty. This pussy is fucking wet. You taste so damn divine. You're undoing me, baby." He strokes me with one of his fingers, while his tongue plunges inside of me. Licking, sucking until I'm on the edge, dangling, ready to fall.

"We're doing this right, naughty girl." My eyes startle open. My pussy is having a conniption.

"Wh...what?" I say, dazed and confused. He moves like a panther up my body, cupping my face in his hands. "Taste," he demands. His lips are wet when they meet mine. The erotic euphoria zings through me when his tongue caresses along mine. "You taste good. Better than anything." He lightly traces my lips with his tongue, the overpowering desire to taste myself again taking over at this point. Darting my tongue out, I follow and taste the tang he left, causing his eyes to turn the deepest shade of black. My pussy is still clenching, screaming for more. Those tasteful lips of his travel down my chin, my neck, gripping my breast as he leaves traces of my desire all over my chest.

"You tell me if I hurt you." He stops kissing my neck and stares down at me. I cup his face. I want him to see me when I speak these words.

"Dilan, I want you so bad I ache. You will never hurt me, unless you stop." I love it when he lifts his head and looks down to where we are so close to being connected. I love it even more when he brings his hand in between the two of us, gripping his cock that has been weighing heavily on my core, and centers it at my entrance.

"I'll never stop. Not with you." The tone in his voice is ragged. My pussy stretches and stings with every small thrust he makes that drives him in deeper. Then he stops, his eyes flashing wide. "Are you—" I place my finger across his lips to silence him. "I'm perfect," I say truthfully. Does it hurt? Yes, it does. But the mix of the pain with the pleasure of knowing we're finally connected eases it all away.

He pushes in harder, breaking past that barrier. I gasp from the shock, my back bowing slightly. The pain is gone as fast as it started. "You are so sexy. This," he looks down to where he's nestled inside of me, "is good, baby. So damn good." He starts to move slowly, while his eyes are searching mine. My hips are yelling at me to move with his. The burning discomfort eases with every stroke. It's impossible not to arch my back, explore my own breasts as the flares from my desire turn explosive. "Dilan," I moan when my orgasm crests. He moves faster, hitting places inside of me I knew existed, but never knew would overpower my entire body once they came to life. I'm being pushed to the unknown by the newness of finally feeling Dilan inside of me, thrusting, stroking, claiming one another. However, the feeling of having him there, slowly teasing me, breathing heavily above me, makes my hips jerk up to meet every one of those deep, driving strokes and the outstanding fullness his cock makes me feel.

I moan when I pinch my nipples. He hisses. I stare into his eyes, remove my hands, and scale them down his back, digging them deep into his tight ass, pulling him into me even more if possible. "A perfect vision. Nothing has ever felt so damn good," he groans, dropping his head to the crook of my neck. His pace is picking up speed. "I agree," I say with the last bit of breath I have. My body has never felt so alive, so tender and yet exhilarating, invigorating, and on the verge of an orgasm that nothing in my life will compare to. I feel it. I know it, and

Dilan holds it.

I bring my legs up around his ass. I want him to lose control, to let go. He pumps harder, faster to the point his hot breath on my neck has me craving to feel him come inside of me.

I'm delirious, knowing I'm losing my virginity to the man who controls the daily beating of my heart. The man who had me the minute I felt his stare. The man who glides his cock in and out of me like he owns me. Wants me. Needs me.

When his head bolts up, his hips stop moving and he stills, buried deep. I feel it. The warmth impaling me. Dilan coming is the most beautiful thing I've ever seen. His eyes bore into mine like I'm his everything. I leap over the edge to another tantalizing release of my own. Our eyes meet, and I get my first glimpse of the man's soul. "Anna," he whispers with respect and admiration. So much awaits us outside of this room. Because of this and the deep feelings I have for him, I'm going to do everything I can to let him know he is mine and I am his.

CHAPTER TEN

DILAN

I've never wanted to keep my cock inside of a woman like I do with Anna. The touch of her tightness up against my flesh is like nothing I've felt before. I'm a man who fucks, but what we did was far from fucking. It was as close to making love as you can get. It felt right. Real.

She makes me feel. All I want to do is return those feelings. To let her know she means more to me than words can say. Words have nothing on the way she makes me want to go all in for her. She brings out a part of me I've been too numb to admit I needed. One taste of her, and she's become a weakness that has brought this man down. She's shaken me up, made me want to be a man worthy of her. A lucky one at that. Heaven help me, because I will never give her up. Never treat her less than she deserves. I've claimed her, and it has nothing to do with the fact she gave her virginity to me. It has everything to do with the fact she's connected to my soul. A part of me that's been hidden for so damn long I forgot it existed. Until her.

Not in a million fucking years did I think I would be cuddling a woman after sex. With her, it is more than sex. It's damn near love. I know it is. I'm turning into my cousin, and Cain, and Aidan. A man out of sorts over a woman. And I don't give a shit. I knew it the minute I drove away from here, the whole time I was gone, and then the minute I saw her at the church. I was too blinded by my bullshit to put her first.

Not anymore. Her beauty has undone me. I knew it would. It's not just the sex, it's every damn thing about her all wrapped up in one tiny little sexy as hell package. Full of life, vibrant, and I'm a lucky as fuck man.

I've lived so damn long in a deep hole of revenge. In nothing but fucking shadows of a past that have my head so torn, it expended every particle of my life to the extent I haven't been living. Anna's changed me. I feel as if I'm full of life for the first time in I don't know how long, and I will not let the revenge these sick assholes deserve strip her. Me either. Fuck that shit. I deserve to be happy. And she is my happiness. We deserve each other.

I'm in deep with her. Thank fucking god she feels the same and understands what I need to do. That's who she is. Thoughtful. Wicked and dangerous in her own way. Downright sexy. Her giant heart beating inside of her is the sexiest part about her. It's big. Strong. Compatible with mine. She's tough. The shit we have to wade through shouldn't even be a part of us. But goddamn, it is.

I've waited, watched, and baited these sick people. But in this moment, none of the shit that lies past this room matters, it's all right here, curled up beside me, stroking my chest. The need to protect her from my shit is driving so deep inside, it's liable to burn a hole right through my chest. And I know damn well she won't have any part of me keeping what she needs to know from her.

Anna has given me a gift. Not just her body; she's giving me the gift of hope. Hope that I never knew was out there. I know she's tender. The way she flinched when I pulled out of her nearly broke me. I'm selfish for wanting to sink inside of her again, if only to see the look on her beautiful face when she comes. Christ almighty, there will be nothing in my life as memorable as this. I've opened a book in my brain. A book to savor, to remember this moment and every one that comes after with her.

"Can we just stay here all night? Order some dinner in?" her sweet-sounding voice asks. I take that back, her voice is husky as fuck. Sexy like a woman who's been sexually satisfied. Christ. The dirty things I want do to her and her body. Fuck. I could have both her and I indulging in acts in this room or at my place that would be considered a felony. *She just gave you her virginity, you fuckwit. Now you're thinking about tying her up and playing with her pretty pussy, while she has your cock in her mouth.* What the hell is wrong with me?

I have no problem staying here with her and enjoying every bit of privacy we can have. The storm waiting outside for us is cold, colder than the freezing temperatures. "I don't think anyone could drag me out of here if they tried. Are you okay?" I stroke her long hair. The urge to grab a fistful of it while I drive into her from behind is overwhelming. Her perfect little ass red from my hand. Fuck. I want to do so many things with this woman. Here's the thing. I have a feeling Anna has been holding out on me. I meant it when I said she's naughty. She has a streak to her, dying to get out. To explore.

"Well, I can definitely feel I've had a big cock inside of me. But yes, Dilan, I'm good." Those lips and tongue of hers are going to have my cock inside of them in about 2.5 seconds if she keeps her taunting ways about her. Mischievous little thing.

"Yeah, you're good all right." My words insinuate a double suggestion. My dick is still hard. I need more. Much more. "I'm only good because of you." Aw fuck. She's out of her damn mind.

"I think you have it backwards, baby. Women make men better, and I meant sex. My dick is still hard." I trace the delicate skin above the curve of her ass, the tips of my fingers aching to go further. To sink one into her tight hole, while my cock sinks into the other.

"I know what you meant, you ass. I'm not sure how to respond. What I am going to do is take a bath. When I get out, I'd like to hear as much as you're willing to tell me about the meeting today." How the hell can we be talking about sex, and then she changes the subject to the last thing I want to discuss with her right now? Her naked breasts keep my dick hard though, while her words have him wanting to lie flaccid against my stomach. Her ass wins this battle of her body parts as I catch sight of her perky backside.

Oh, the things I want to do with you, my naughty Anna, I think to myself. My cock may want to drive hard and deep into her tight, silky pussy, but fuck, those tits. Yeah, he wants those too. I'm taming down all control by a tight, thin shred. My mind is flittering back and forth from making love to her to downright fucking the hell out of her, or better yet, having her ride my cock and fucking the hell out of me, with her tits bouncing and her pussy gripping me skintight, while she glides her wetness up and down me. Fuck me. I'm a goner.

I reach for her before she has the chance to completely escape, dragging her up and over me. Her brows quirk up when she feels how hard I am, those luscious tits pressing up against my chest. I'm definitely fucking those sweet babies.

"Take your time in there. Just know though, I'm far from done with you. I'm going to fuck those sweet tits of yours, Anna, while I have your wrists tied above your head." What I presume is eagerness spreads across her face as her eyes light up with anticipation. I know there's a naughty, kinky side suppressed inside of her. I sense it. It drives me out of my goddamn mind.

"You can do anything you want to me, Dilan. Just know I will be doing the same." Fuck, yes, she will. "Challenge accepted." To say she doesn't look tempted would be an understatement. Her facial expression turns devious. My cock twitches as all kinds of seductive ideas run like a herd of wild animals through my head. I swat her on her ass, roll us over, and grind my cock up against her pussy. I know damn well she's sore, even though I took it easy on her when all I wanted to do was pound her sweet little body into the mattress.

"You're beautiful. Now, go take your bath. I'll order some dinner, turn on the fireplace, and then I'm going to explore every enticing inch of this body. Then we'll talk." But first, I need her mouth on mine. I take it hard, biting her lower lip, sucking it deep into my mouth, then grab a hold of her tongue like it's my lifeline to salvation, sucking it deep into my mouth. She moans as she duels her dainty, little tongue, her lively lips with mine. She squirms beneath me. My cock can't take any more, and I may have become the most lethal man on this planet. I want out of this place to explore life with her, and I'll kill anyone who tries to stop me.

"Go, baby." I knife up off of her, watch her saunter off the bed, her ass inviting me to take it the way it sways when she walks into the bathroom. I wait until I hear the water running then pull the comforter off of the bed when I notice small specs of blood from her innocence. A purity that belongs to me. One I will do everything in my power to not forget. To seal it tight inside the book of her in my head. I toss it on the side of the bed facing the window. The signs of nightfall flash through the small hole from the closed curtains. Standing there naked, my cock slowly dwindling, I notice small amounts of blood on me. I cannot help but smile. She's mine in every way. Not a possession, she's her own woman, and yet the feelings I have for her run extensively through my veins. I clean myself up at the sink in the tiny kitchen then reach for my sweats, tugging them up and over me.

I should call my uncle, pass on the voice mail I received to him. The water is still running. No fucking way she needs to know about this. Especially after what the two of us shared. I've invested way too much of my time, learning every damn thing I can about these motherfuckers. From the time they take a fucking shit to the time they fall asleep in their fancy ass fucking beds. I'm not giving them my time with Anna. Not here. I wish to hell I could say not ever, but the truth is, I can't. I have to tell her something. She's worried and I get it. What my uncle needs to know can't wait.

Therefore, I snatch my phone and find his number. When his voicemail picks up, I leave him the message, telling him what the dumb fuck told me, then let him know to call the room phone if he needs me, praying to god he doesn't. I want him and my aunt to enjoy themselves too. Especially with the shit that went down last night. That bitch is fucking crazy. I can only imagine the state she left those men in. Gutted down to nothing. I cringe when visions of their bodies flash in my mind. She needs to be gone. She's a serious waste of space on this earth. How can one person be evil like she is, have a heart so black you would never be able to see through it? And then there's the one who gave herself to me. A heart so pure it glows without her even trying. I'm one hell of a lucky man.

It pains the hell out of me to know those guys were doing their job, and out of nowhere that cunt slices the shit out of them. Hell, what their families must be going through right now. Pure fucking torture.

Like last night when Anna and I talked briefly about this... I'm pushing that shit from my mind. It will be there for the rest of my life, the guilt, the shame, and the anger. It won't matter if we wipe every single one of them out. Kill them all. The memories will always be there. "Shit." I toss my phone down on the couch.

"You all right out there?" Anna calls out. "More than all right. Trying to decide if I want to dip the strawberries in chocolate or champagne, then lick them from your sweet pussy." It's no lie. I do need to order, and I do want to lick her pussy. Fuck the damn food. I can go without the food, but one taste of her, and I'm at the mercy of needing her to survive.

"Come here, Dilan." I chuckle at her bossiness. I also know if I walk in there and see her in that big tub, we won't be eating any form of sustenance. Well, she won't. I sure the fuck will.

"Good lord, Anna, are you trying to make me have heart failure?" I freeze, my hands gripping the frame to the bathroom door, my eyes bouncing all over this bathroom floor like those tiny bouncy balls you get out of one of those gumball machines from the sight of this naughty little temptress. "Closer," she demands. I study every inch of her spread out across the long vanity in the bathroom. Her body is dripping wet. Her legs are spread open, her fingers playing with her clit. Fuck, for a woman who lost her innocence only a few minutes ago, she sure as hell knows how to play with fire. Fire that shoots straight to my dick.

"Sweet Jesus, Anna." All rationality tells me to go to her, take her finger off of that sweet little nub and replace it with my mouth, but that look of pure female satisfaction on her face as her mouth parts and her head tilts sideways with those damn hazard warning eyes flaring, sends enough sparks straight to my cock, that if I were to take two steps to my right and fall in the bathtub, she would kill me. I'd fucking electrocute.

"You wanted my breasts, come and get them." A shameless smile plays at the corners of her mouth. Her body may have been innocent, but her mind and the way she plays with her pussy sure as hell aren't. This goddess is a handful. I can envision nothing short of pure, blissful bedroom explorations with her. She's a live wire. A man's definition of perfection.

"You're going to play with that sweet pussy while I slide my cock in between your breasts, down your stomach, and back up into your mouth. Don't take your finger off of it. Do you hear me?" She moans instead of answering me, then we stare at each other as I glide my sweats down my legs, grip my cock, and move to stand directly above her.

"Answer me," I demand. "Yes." That barely-there word knocks the damn breath out of me. She gasps, obviously close to a release. "Don't fucking come without me either."

I admire the view once more of her pink, bare pussy as she rubs her clit. The countertop is at a perfect angle for me to skim my cock up her stomach. She groans and arches her back. I gently press her back down, teasing her with my jerky cock across her skin.

"I can't fuck your tits, baby, not sideways like this, but I sure as fuck can stroke him while I rub over the top of this nipple." I bend and pull the taut peak into my mouth. "Oh, my." She squirms. I glance down to make sure she is doing exactly what I told her to do, her finger moving feverishly in circles. "Beautiful," I whisper.

My cock damn near crawling to her tit himself, the minute the tip touches the hard nipple, he jerks, circling the pink flesh while I stroke him vigorously.

"Tell me, Anna. Do you think of me when you touch yourself? Do you wish those were my fingers, or my tongue on you, or better yet, my cock sliding in and out of you?" The devilish smirk on her face tells me she is. I want to hear her say it. "All the time, Dilan. From the first night I met you, I wished it were you." Her words come out huskily, her voice raw and sexy as fuck.

"Me too, baby. Every time I stroked my cock while lying in bed, I fantasized it was you. But god, woman, not a goddamn one of those days or nights compares to the real you." This position may be uncomfortable as hell, but I don't give a fuck. I slant forward, the muscles in my stomach constricting, my balls tightening, ready to shoot my come straight to the tip of my cock. I take her mouth in a wild kiss of pure pleasure, relishing on the way her tongue strokes mine. My hand jerks my cock harder, the need to come all over her tit uncontrollable. Her mouth can suck me later, while I have my tongue inside of her. Right now, those tits are begging for me to come all over them.

"You close? Because I sure as fuck am." I tell her when I pull my mouth from hers and draw my eyes back to the sweet spot between her thighs. "God, yes." She blows out a gasp of air. I bring my free hand up to her neck and close my fingers delicately around her throat, feeling her pulse quicken from my touch.

"Let go." When she bows her back and moans my name, I come all over her tit, marking her in the best territorial way, smearing and spreading my release all over her porcelain skin. Son of a bitch. I could do that again, mark her everywhere. Preferably her sweet ass.

I look at her, this naughty woman, who has my knees damn near buckling from under me. Her face is flush, her mouth is parted open, her wisdom of knowing exactly what she's doing inscribed all over her. Her body may be innocent, but her mind sure the hell isn't. She's as devious as they come. In a damn good way.

Our food arrives about a half hour after our bathroom tryst. Both of us cleaned up. Anna is sitting cross-legged on the couch next to me, while the fire warms the room.

She takes the last bite of her cheeseburger, wipes her mouth with her napkin, and then tosses it onto her empty plate. I know what's coming next. My uncle has already called me, demanding to listen to the voicemail. He wants to hear every word himself. I told him I'd call him back as soon as we finished eating. There was no way around her not hearing my conversation with him.

"Are you going to tell me what's going on?" I'm ready to tell her a small part of it when there's a knock on the door, startling the both of us.

"Anna." It's her mom.

"Coming." Wrapping a blanket around her shoulders, she gets up to answer.

"What are you doing?" Grace saunters in, her eyes protruding when she takes in the messy sight of the room.

"Just finished eating," Anna answers, her voice irritated.

"Hi, Grace." I stand to greet her. Her eyes are flicking from my naked chest to the bed with no comforter. Shit. I love this woman, but if there is any mother who is overly protective of her child, it's her. I understand it's only been the two of them their whole lives, Anna's father always coming and going. For the most part, Anna has always spoken highly of her dad, in spite of him leading a double life.

"I wanted to check on you. I haven't heard from you in a while. I apologize if I interrupted anything." Her eyes are begging me not to do anything to hurt her daughter. I meet her gaze, determined to show her I won't.

"I'm fine, mom. Like I said, we just finished eating."

"I need to go to my uncle," I interrupt and grab my shirt from the floor, along with my tennis shoes.

"Okay. Don't be long," Anna expresses more out of worry than anything else.

"I won't," I say while pulling my shirt over my head, then slip my feet into my shoes and tie them. Snatching my phone off of the table, I walk toward the two women who look so much alike. I kiss Anna on the cheek and smile genuinely at Grace. "See you soon, Dilan." I turn back around and giving Grace an agreeable look.

By the time I make it down the hall and stand in front of the elevator, my phone starts to vibrate in my pocket. Sliding my hand in, I pull it out. It's either Jazmin or Juan. I know it is. Every breath I take is too damn precious for either one of them. My bet is on it being the slut though. My brows scrunch while a devious smile creeps across my mouth. I wait and let the device continue to vibrate in my hand. Stepping into the elevator and pushing the button for my uncle's floor, I lean back when expectedly my phone pings with a voicemail like I knew it would. Rage, followed by an identifiable longing to kill someone slithers up my back. It's the unbearable, shameless urge I had with every punch to my gut when I took hit after hit from Miguel in prison. The only thing holding me back was the yearning to get my ass out of there. Now, out here, no one will give a flying fuck if these fuckers are all wiped off from this earth. Hell, we may even be handed medals from the other crime families. The key to the motherfucking city.

"Fuckers. Even hell is too good for them all," I speak to myself as the elevator comes to a stop. I step off, eager to get this done, to get back to my time with Anna.

"It's a damn battlefield outside of here, Dilan. My men along with those motherfuckers are scattered all over the sidewalks of New York, each one waiting to see who will strike first. And that motherfucker has the nerve to threaten you!" My uncle yells.

"We need to find a way out of here," I tell him.

"The only way out is to fight. They sure as hell don't care if they kill innocent people, but I sure the hell do. Ivan and I will discuss this in the morning. Let me hear what that worthless bitch said." I offer no argument. I do as he requests. When her accent comes through my speakers, I cringe, my stomach tightening.

"Well, hello my pawn. I'm imagining your handsome face right now as you hear my voice. I hope it's shocking. I tried to save you from a painful death. I would have enjoyed the fun we would have had before

I killed you. Now though, I must take matters into my own hands. You see, Dilan, you will never outsmart me. I will always be one step ahead of you and your family. A family who will be destroyed. Don't blink, Dilan, the minute you do, I will be standing in front of you." The line goes dead. When I look up to my uncle, his nostrils are splaying and his throat is bobbing. He is pissed.

"Get Roan, Aidan, and Cain in here. We are preparing for a street war. We attack tomorrow night."

CHAPTER ELEVEN

ANNA

How does one establish a different relationship with the only person who has meant the entire world to you? I turned twenty-four in October. I may be young, but I'm not a child.

I need space when this is all over. It's time for me to move out. I sense her worry. No, I see it when she sighs, her lips quiver, and she treads lightly to sit on the couch.

"I've called you twice, Anna. Both times going straight to voicemail. I began to worry," my mom tells me suspiciously.

"Mom." I plot my words in a manner in which I won't hurt her, but consequently, she has to listen to reason. She cannot be calling all the time. Before the other day with Dilan, I understood why, but god, she must know this isn't healthy for our relationship.

"I'm sorry if I worried you. I thought I made that clear this morning. If there is anything you need to know, I'll tell you, but come on. You of all people know how I feel about him." I point to the door Dilan just left through.

"I know, Annabelle, but hell, this whole situation is because of him. I have every right to worry about my daughter." She does have a right. She always will. I hope to worry someday myself. I sigh, not wanting to hurt her at all. I'm not sure what else I can do or say to make her understand. Her blaming Dilan for this is not right. In fact, it upsets me.

"Mom. We welcomed everyone in this family when we chose to let them help us. Then we decided to stay. You cannot single him out. That is unfair and justifiably wrong. I'm ashamed you would even think of such a thing. You of all people have no right to judge anyone." She's disappointed me, and she knows it. Her shoulders slump forward. Her eyes close. Damn her.

"I won't apologize for loving my child so much I'm scared she'll get hurt," she appeals on a strangled cry.

"I get that, mom. I love you too. Did you see me throw a fit when you started dating Ramsey? No, you didn't. And do you know why? It's because I want you happy. You deserve to be happy. So do I, mom. Dilan makes me happy. Yes, his life is dangerous. But hell, when isn't life dangerous? I care about him. I waited for him, hoping he would come back to me." I point to my chest, my voice rising to a high pleading octave.

"Anna. I'm scared," she admits. "I'm scared too, mom, but I will be damned if I will let people take away my right to be happy, to love someone. Life is too short. I've forgiven him for leaving, it's about time you do too." She says nothing more to me. I give her the space she needs to think about what I said. She knows it's true. The last thing I want to do is hurt my mom. She has to let me go.

"You're right. Just promise me you'll come to me if you need me. I'm... I've never had to share you before. It's rather frightening," she whispers.

"Oh, mom. You won't ever have to share me. I'm your daughter. Besides, I'm not going anywhere." I go to her, my arms travelling around her small frame. She's so pretty. She's devoted her entire life to me. I will always be grateful for her putting me first. It's time she puts herself first for a change. For both of us to live a life full of happiness and love. To have that one person entirely devoted to us. I hate seeing her face distorted in sadness this way.

"Ramsey said the same thing." She retracts from our embrace. "And you're right about all of it, Anna. I know Dilan is a good man. I'm proud of you for defending him, even if it was to me. Your dad would be so proud." Despite her slumped posture, I know she gets it. Her eyes are shining with all the love she has for me.

"I think he would be proud of you too. Now, go get your man. Have fun. And don't worry. After all the crap this family has been through, my guess is no one will be unprepared, mom," I lie through my teeth. The Carlos family are natural born murderers. Disgusting pigs. They know the score as much as Dilan and everyone else does. Blood will be shed. I know it. Dilan doesn't even have to tell me. I can feel it in the depths of my bones. I pray to god it's them who die and not anyone in this family of ours.

I sag onto the bed after she leaves. All I want to do is think about what happened between Dilan and I. The gentle way he was with me, his words soothing as he held me in his arms.

I never knew that engaging in sex would bring out a wild beast in me. Or was aware of how much pleasure my body is capable of experiencing. And god, the look on Dilan's face when he sunk all the way inside of me. I will never forget it. Adoration. Respect. Those same emotions I felt reflecting back at him.

I laugh when I picture his face when he walked into the bathroom. I even astonished myself. He makes me want to do things I've only done in private. I detect so much from him when it comes to sex. Today, his restraints were holding him back. Right now, my pussy appreciates him for that. I'm sore, not so much so that if he were to walk through the door right now, I wouldn't rip those damn sweatpants off and take charge of his massive cock like I own it.

Not only do I want to please him in all kinds of ways, but I want to please myself while watching him take his cock in his hands, stroking the big, beautiful thing, running it all over my breasts. It makes me want to get on the damn internet and seek out sexual desires of men.

"You are a bad woman," I speak to myself.

Instead, I shuffle off the bed, my curious sanities driving me to know more about this Carlos family. I know why he went to see his uncle. I have a horrible feeling shit is going to start, if it hasn't already. Snatching my laptop out of my bag, I settle on the couch, toss a blanket over my legs, turn on my computer, and connect to the free internet.

"Oh my god, no." This cannot be. I know this man. I screech in astonishment when I see Juan Carlos' face plastered all over my screen.

In fact, I know him well. He told me his name was Carlos. I see him almost every day between seven and eight in the morning, when he comes in for an apple muffin and a cup of black coffee. Always to go. He never stays and eats it. What he does do is flirt with me on a daily basis. He's even asked me out on a few occasions. I've always turned him down politely. Our banter back and forth was carefree when I would say no, and he would leave with a smile on his face and say, "Until next time, Anna."

This is not a coincidence at all. He's been coming in for months now. Has he been looking for Dilan? Using me to try and find him? But why? Why would he pretend to be someone he's not? He wanted me as a counter, a bartering chip to get to my family. That has to be it. And he always came in before Deidre came to work. That's because she knows him. I feel sick. "My god. You people will stop at nothing to destroy the lives of others. I won't let it happen. Not ever," I say out loud, even though no one can see or hear me. I jab my finger at his face. The fucking monster.

Until this weekend, I barely even knew who he was. The only time his name was mentioned in any discussion I've had was when Dilan explained to me how he went to prison.

I have to tell someone. Things just don't add up here.

I scroll down, seeing so many photos of him, his sister, and a few mug shots. Page after page shows up on google. These people are take-crime-to-the-extreme type of people. Thank god that since the day I came to this city, I all but gave my heart away to one man. Otherwise who knows where I would be right now, or where any one of us would be. I could be dead.

I hit the first article about them on the page, my eyes scanning and reading.

The Carlos family is one of Mexico's largest drug cartel families. Estimated to be ranking in about three billion dollars a year. They have a greedy market in North and South America. Drugs.

"How can they not get caught?" Anna, you foolish woman. They pay people off the same way the Diamonds and the Solokovs do. But these people are ruthless. Dilan isn't anything like them. I know he's not. I wonder if Alina's family is as brutal as they are. They all seem so well put together, so comfortable to be around. You would never know they deal. I despise the illegal use of drugs. I understand why Alina left all those years ago. Even though her situation had more to do with her ex-boyfriend than anything else. God, I wonder how she dealt with this growing up. Look what greed has driven these people to. It's part of the reason why society is messed up these days. The thought of having poison running through my body, being out of my mind, no control of my actions, makes me want to hurl.

It says both Juan and Jazmin have been arrested twice for murder and drug trafficking. Both times, they were released and the charges were dropped. Not enough evidence. That's such bullshit. They can get off on murder charges, and yet Dilan's drug charges stick when they had everything to do with setting him up. This is exploitation at its finest. Judges and crooked cops. Fuckers. I hate them all. They deserve to die right along with these two and their conglomerate defiance of brain-washed assholes.

My curiosity rises to get a look at that bitch Jazmin again. I hit the back button, then hit images. My eyes are blinded when I look at the two of them. At charity events, the opera, even church. If I didn't hate them so much, I would say they look like any other happy family. Normal.

His hair is cropped shorter than how he wears it now. He has a dark goatee, which, even though I wasn't interested in dating him, did something to my insides whenever he would smile or laugh at something I would say. I thought the man was gorgeous from the first minute I saw him, with his pearly white teeth, dark gleaming eyes. How wrong I was. This man is as ugly and disgusting on the outside as he is on the inside.

I knew Jazmin was stunningly beautiful too, but now that I know so much more about them, they repulse me. Looks don't mean shit when your insides are as black as tar.

I close my laptop, unable to stomach any more, and sink further into the cushions, infuriated. God, what is going on? I hate this for the people I love. The minute Dilan gets back here, he needs to know. This could change everything. Maybe I should call and tell him now.

As if the devil himself has shaken me, I'm startled from my thoughts when the room phone rings, jumping up from my one-woman-rage-party. Anger surges through every fiber of my body. I could kill them all and enjoy watching the blood bleed from their hearts.

"Hello," I speak into the phone as I cradle it to my ear.

"Anna Drexler." I stand frozen when I hear her speak my name. I will never forget her voice. Cold. Callous. Manipulating murderer. My hands are shaking. Whatever the hell she wants or has to say, I will not let fear rule me. Not with the hatred I have for this conniving bitch, who tried to drug Dilan. I decide against telling her I know her brother, and that it's revolting knowing their scam to somehow tie me in with their vendetta may backfire now that I know.

"Jazmin Carlos," I communicate back to her, my mouth tasting like shit from emitting her name.

"I'm impressed, sweet Anna. How kind of you to address me by my name. Either you've done your homework, or Dilan has told you all about me. I'll go with both, especially since you cannot keep your nose clean. It's a deadly shame you had to interrupt my plans. Now, I have the great pleasure of adding you to my list. You lucky woman." My body begins to tremble, my legs wavering to give out. I will show no fear when speaking to this conniving bitch. It doesn't matter if I'm alone or not.

"That's where you're wrong, you fucking bitch. Dilan is my business.

This entire family is. You on the other hand, mean nothing to me. Or to him. Do I detect jealousy along with a threat here, Jazmin?" I articulate strongly.

"You don't have a clue what I'm going to do with you once I have you. And trust me, Anna, I will have you. Once I do, you'll be begging me on your hands and knees to end your life, but I won't. You see, my brother loves blondes. In fact, he wants you for himself. Now, listen very carefully to what I'm about to tell you." She emphasizes her threat in a deadly manner. This is some sick way to play the game twister. It definitely should be titled twisted instead.

"The only thing I'm going to listen to when it comes to you is the last breath you take, you fucking bitch. I'm not afraid of you. You underestimate me. You may be a cold, bitter woman, but I on the other hand, am not. What I am is a woman who will fight for those I care about, so you and your brother can bring it. And you can pass a massage along to your brother. He will never have me," I spew.

"Anna, you have guts, I'll give you that. What you don't have is the knowledge or the power. I do. There's a package outside your door. I suggest you get it. Although, you may want someone with you when you open it. It's not red roses, sweetheart." She hangs up. I stand there, looking at the phone, my mouth hanging open, my fingers gripping it tight to the point I feel it burn in the confines of my palm.

I place it back on the cradle, whipping my head toward the door. So many scenes are gravitating to my brain with what has been sent and what the hell they want with me. This is her way of trying to scare me, or to get back at me for stopping her when I did. No damn way am I opening that door. Fuck no.

I seize my cell from the nightstand and power it on. While I wait for it to power up, I pace the floor, contemplating on whether I should get a hold of Dilan first before I creep to the door to see if there really is something or possibly someone waiting on the other side.

My heart beats rapidly, my eyes blurring from the tears that threaten to fall. I swipe the only one away that escapes. I will not let her get to me like she wants. What could she possibly send me? It has to be some sort of trap for me to open the door. The damn irony of this situation astounds me. She knows who I am. It's visibly clear she's done her investigating about me by her threat about her brother wanting me. Of course she knows, he is her brother after all.

I would rather die than spend one second with that monster.

"Aidan," I whisper frantically into the phone when he answers. "Anna. What's wrong?" I rattle off quickly for him to get down here. I hardly have the chance to change into a pair of leggings and a sweatshirt before the pounding starts at my door. I hesitate with my steps toward the big steel frame, my steps light. I peer through the peephole before opening to make sure it's him.

"Open up, Anna." I unlock and swing the door open, my nerves somewhat calm now that he's here. Aidan's look of concern greets me. I look from him to the floor. There's a box sitting off to the side. His eyes follow mine then travel back to meet my scared gaze.

"Put some shoes on." His nature is alarming. He holds the door open as I move quickly, sliding my feet into a pair of ballet flats. "Where are we going?" When he doesn't answer, my thoughts wander all over the place, my suspicions rising to the highest peak. I become panicky, asking him once again as I grab my keycard and phone.

"Aidan." He bends down, inspecting the outside of the box carefully, without touching the intricate, black, shiny wooden surface. I gulp. I'm unsettled, conflicted about what the contents could be. Then I remember in detail one of the reasons he came to New York was because Calla received a mysterious box, delivered to her at work. "Oh, no. There's a body part in there, isn't there?" I scream, my head struggling to stay clear. I back away, shaking my head. My entire body is trembling.

"Get back in your room now, Anna," he demands as he straightens his body upright. "No. I'm going wherever you are. I'm not staying here by myself." I hardly recognize my voice. It's low. Unsteady.

"Of course you're not staying by yourself. Just calm down. There are other guest here." Calm down? Is he crazy? This is calm. And I don't care about anyone else. My concern is who's in that box.

"I'm sorry Anna. Let's just," He's interrupted by a deep startling voice.

"Is there a problem here, ma'am?" A security guard approaches. His eyes are fixed on me. Somehow, I find my voice to answer him. I tell him no. He looks Aidan over as if he doesn't believe me, as if he's the one who has my mind tumbling down the plush carpet hallway, trailing behind him, when he dismisses us with a glare and walks away. God, people are strange.

"It's me," Aidan clips tightly into the phone. "There's a box outside of Anna's room, similar to the one you described Calla received. And some fucker claiming to be security just approached us. Nametag read Jared. No damn way some fucker is randomly going to be prancing around on the 8th floor. Get someone to find that fucker." His eyes narrow down at me. I know he's searching for my reaction to what he's saying. I'm scared out of my god-blessed mind. I hide it well, though, by narrowing my eyes right back at him. Maybe the guard was the one who put the box here. I don't know. All I do know is I want out of here.

"Motherfucker," I hear bellowing out of Aidan's phone. Cain. His words are short and precise, telling us both to head up to Salvatore's room.

"Let's go." He checks my door to make sure it's locked, pulls his sweatshirt over his head, tosses it over the box, and picks it up. "Fuck," he thunders and plows down the hallway. I'm practically running to keep up with him.

"This is wrong in so many ways, Aidan. And Dilan. If there is someone or something in that box he cares about, it will send him over the edge. He's fighting his guilt as it is," I whisper softly as we make our way to the elevator. There are people milling about. I don't know how much the staff knows here. I'm sure they know something with the type of influence Salvatore and Ivan have. And that guard. What if he was coming after me? Aidan doesn't mention his suspicions; therefore,

I let it go.

"Hit the up button please," he tells me. I do as I'm told, while he stands stoic, all the color slowly draining from his face. I'm about ready to throw more salt into the wound when I tell them I know Juan Carlos. I hate this. I decide against telling Aidan at the moment, choosing to tell them when they're all together. I know this information will surely send Dilan past his limits. It may break him.

I step in and hit the button to the floor he tells me to, saying nothing. It's eerie in this small compartment, knowing there could possibly be the remains of someone we know in that box. It isn't until we step off the elevator, greeted by both Cain and Roan, that I see the alarmed communication they express to one another. They know something they're not telling me. They either know or suspect who it is. My brain races, trying to figure it out. Everyone is here in this hotel. Right down to all of Alina's brothers. I stop. Tears begin to flow down my face. "Anna." Cain grips me by my shoulders.

"It's Jackson, isn't it? He's the only one who isn't here."

"We can't be sure. You let us take care of this. What you need to do before we enter this room is get your shit together. Salvatore is going to want you to tell him everything you know. Then get the fuck out of there and keep yourself occupied. Cecily is on her way to be with you. You stay with her and you keep quiet. Do you get me? Not a word to anyone about this." Cain shakes me gently. Not enough to hurt me, just enough to get his point across. I nod in agreement, knowing exactly what I have to do. When he releases me, I look to Roan. His demeanor is slumped. If this is Jackson, he's going to lose it. I know the two of them have been friends for a long time.

"Why did Jackson leave?" I ask. I need to know why, when all the rest of us are here. If only I would have known that the man I know as Carlos is really Juan, then Jackson would be alive. This is all my fault. I should have paid more attention whenever I heard them talking about Dilan. Instead, I was shattered by him leaving. Every time someone brought up his name, I either left the room or tuned out every word they said.

“He’s a big part of our security. Against my dad’s better judgment, he let him go. The man knows these streets better than anyone. Fuck me,” Roan thrashes, his hands gripping his hair.

“Get in here.” The door swings open to a very angry-looking Salvatore. His eyes sparkle with fury. I swallow back my nerves and walk into the immaculate suite first.

Dilan is perched on a chair in the corner, a beer in his hand. His face is full of dread. He stands when he sees me. I run into his arms and lose it. The fear, the anger, all of my emotions rip out of me. Unexpectedly.

“Hey. None of that. You’re safe, sweetheart.” I sniffle while his soothing hands rub up and down my back. Here I thought he would be freaking out when instead it’s me. This is so wrong. He rubs my back tenderly, resting his chin on top of my head. I want to stay like this forever, but I know we can’t. The quicker I tell them what I know, the faster they can do what they need to. Cain is right in more ways than I will admit right now. I need to be strong. A weak woman has no business standing by a man who leads a dangerous life. I proceed to pull myself together.

The instant I turn around, with so many familiar faces waiting patiently for me, Dilan draws me back, clinging my back to his front. I face both Salvatore and Ivan, and all of these men whose hearts are breaking. That damn box sits on top of the table, taunting every single one of us. I tell them all about my phone call from Jazmin, leaving out the part of knowing Juan. Dilan’s body goes stiff. His arms tighten around me. I choose to let them deal with this blow to their hearts first before I tell them the devil has been stalking me at work.

CHAPTER TWELVE

DILAN

"We'll be in our room if you need us. I will make all the necessary arrangements to have the two of you transferred up to this floor." Cecily's voice is harder than normal, her position showing her years of being by the side of a known killer. Hell, she was one herself. This life is new to Anna, and right now, Cecily is exactly what she needs. Someone to explain to her that if she cares about me as much as I know she does, she has to be strong to be able to survive this kind of shit. Bury it deep. Doesn't mean she can't express her emotions. Or let things pull her under. But she needs to hide it. Keep it buried in a secret spot in the back of her mind and her heart. There's a time and place for letting your emotions become unchecked. To cry and then let the anger set in, only to make you stronger. The time is not here. Fuck, there really is never a good time to be weak or defenseless. Not now anyway.

I'm not worried about her sticking by my side. She's proven her strength by showing up here. By doing the right thing and calling Aidan before she attempted to open that goddamn box.

If I weren't so fucked up about this whole thing my damn self, I would tell her how proud I am of her, but fuck, this shit needs to get moving. They struck first, struck us hard. Now, plans have changed once again.

"Come on. Go with Cecily. As soon as I'm done here, I'll find you, okay?" I fit her body as closely to mine as I can get her. She spilled her guts out. Stood strong when she delivered the conversation she had with Jazmin. That cunt needs to be the first to go. I would love nothing more than to be the one to slice her the fuck up. I don't give a shit if she is a woman. She needs to fucking go.

The door swings wide open, and in walks John with whom I assume is one of Juan's men, and the first candidate to die. He doesn't care about anyone. Just tosses his soldiers into the pit. Kill or die, fuckers. Simple as that. He's notorious for sending his gang of brainless assholes to do his shit work for him. It will be my pleasure to try and get him to talk before John disposes of the man. Stupid fuck.

"Okay. But I need to tell you something else before I leave." Her voice is shaky. Fearful. "Whatever it is, it has to wait, Anna. You need to go now." I tell her the truth. She needs to leave, not bear witness to any of this. "It's important, but first I need to do something."

Despite the vulnerability I hear in her enunciation or the way her pulse is racing beneath my firm fingers that are holding her tight, she stands tall. Then she shocks the shit out of me, out of us all actually, when she moves away from me, my hands dropping to my sides, missing her touch.

"You asshole. You were sent to kill me, weren't you?" She probes a finger into the chest of the fucker whose face had to have looked better ten minutes ago than it does now. He's all kinds of fucked up. I can almost see the heat rising from the top of her head, she is so mad. My once scared little spitfire has turned into a tiny, little devil. My cock has the worst timing. He swings away like the second hand of a clock, hanging fucking free in my sweats, then as if his clock magically strikes midnight, he stands tall. Straight up. Fucker.

"Fuck off, you dumb cunt. I would have killed you quickly. Now when you die, you'll be crying for your fucking boyfriend here to save your ass," he growls. I move. John tightens his hold on both of his hands he has secured behind his back, making him wince slightly.

"You're the only one who's going to die." I stand in front of him. The urge to cut his damn tongue out for even speaking to her has me wishing I had my knife.

"Cecily, please take Anna and go." John cranes his neck to look at his wife.

"Come on, sweetheart." She takes Anna by the hand. Anna briefly shifts her head back to me. I give her a wink. "I'll be fine," I articulate. I have the desperate need to kiss her before she goes, to reassure us both that what I say is true. I'm this close to breaking, worried about who I know in my gut is dead. Her eyes lock with mine. Pleading. I move to stop them. She said she needed to tell me something. I want to know what it is. But I'm halted in my tracks when my uncle grabs my arm, stopping me from going to her. I exhale and close my eyes briefly, getting myself back under control.

The instant the door clicks shut, John slams the fucker down in a chair, then spins it around to face both my uncle and Ivan. I turn around to face this scum, listening to Ivan.

"We don't play games, young man. Therefore, I'm going to ask you one question before John kills you. Regardless if you answer it or not, you're dead. The choice is up to you on whether you want to betray the people who sent you here, knowing damn well you would be caught and die before you do," Ivan drawls his words out precisely and to the point, his accent heavy.

"I'm not telling you shit. Save your question, you Russian fuck." Crossing his arms over his chest, Ivan moves within an inch of this man's bloodied face.

"Like I said, your choice. That's the only choice you have. Now, here's my question. Were you sent here to kill her or anyone in my circle?" He tilts his head, awaiting an answer. The man doesn't speak. Instead, the movement of his head gives him away. His aim is set on Roan.

"I see. You were sent here to take out my son-in-law. To attack us first, in the one place that Juan knows would destroy our stability. Very smart on his part. However, shit for brains," he lifts one finger and pokes him in the middle of his head, "you made your death agonizingly unpleasant for yourself for considering to leave my daughter a widow." Bringing himself up to his normal height, he withdraws a handkerchief from the pocket of his dress pants, wipes his finger clean as if he's been exposed to a deadly plague, and then stuffs the thing into the man's mouth.

"John. I'm going to assume all security cameras are turned off?" Ivan speaks with authority.

"My guess, they've been off for a few hours if this fucker managed to turn them off. I have guys in place. The minute I'm gone with this cocksucker, they will be back on." John grips the piece of shit by his hair and pulls him straight up, while he tries to squirm out of his hold. I laugh. Not a chance in hell is his attempt to get away going to work. Not with John.

"And your plan to get out of here undetected is?" Ivan asks.

"I'm going to shoot this fucker right in the head. Shove him out the back door. Then I'm calling his boss, telling him unless he wants this to become a media circus, he better have this piece of shit's body gone within five minutes." The sound in the room is muted. Even fuckface, who's been trying to plead through the hanky stuffed in his mouth, shuts the fuck up.

"Don't call him until you get back here," my uncle request.

"Come on, motherfucker." John shoves him toward the door. I watch smugly when the door swings open and two of Alina's brothers help the struggling, dead fuck exit him from the room.

How in the hell my uncle and Ivan can make shit happen in a matter of minutes is beyond me. They were both on their phones giving orders as soon as Cain called to tell us what happened with Anna. I clench my hands so tightly, thinking about her and how she must feel, that my digits damn near draw blood.

"This shit ends tonight. No one sleeps, eats, or even takes a goddamn piss until we have demolished them all. Roan?" Ivan directs his attention to my cousin, who's been sitting on the sofa the entire time, his hands over his face, his shoulders slumped in defeat.

He lifts his head. His eyes are bloodshot from crying silently. Goddamn, this fucking guts me, seeing him destroyed like this.

"You don't even have to open the damn thing. I know it's him." Shit, my evaluation of my cousin's emotional state has me going to him. I sit down next to him, guilt ripping my chest in half. I don't know what to say. I do the only thing I can think of. I put my arm around him, letting him know I'm here, silently asking him to forgive me for this.

"This isn't your fault, you know," he tells me. It is, but fuck me if his words don't slice me open even more. The brave fucker. "Yeah, well, for what's it worth, you let me deal with how I feel. My concern is you."

"I'll be fine. It's his woman who's going to need us when we tell her." He's right about that for damn sure.

"Fucking hell." Ivan's tone is stiff. Both of us lurch forward. "Jesus Christ, they are sick." Cain's outburst assaults me like a head-on collision when we approach the now open box. Ivan slams the lid shut before either of us has the chance to see what's inside.

"Let me see it." Roan tries to push past them.

"No, goddamn it, Roan. That box stays sealed." Ivan's face is twisted with anger and disgust.

"Fuck this. I have a right to know if that's him." I can hear the annoyance, frustration, and hurt in his words. I take a deep breath. It's all I can do. I'll be out of line if I demand they let him look inside. I know this. He's not thinking clearly. Hell, he shouldn't even be here.

"It is him and it's his woman too. Is that what you want to hear?" He rotates his entire body to face us. "What?" I watch my cousin unravel, his body damn near crumbling to the fucking floor before Cain grabs him under his arms.

"Why in the hell would they do this shit? She has nothing to do with any of this. Goddamn it, dad. Fuck." Roan jerks out of Cain's hold. This has to be one of the lowest points of any of our lives. I don't want to know what's inside that box, or how the hell they even know it's them for sure, but Roan does.

"Just tell me, damn it. Tell me how you know it's them," he pleads desperately.

Ivan puffs out a large steam of air before he speaks.

"If their matching tattoos of each other's names on their wrists are enough for you, then that's all you need to know."

"Jesus Christ," he mumbles. I've laughed and cried with my cousin our entire lives. Smacked each other around a few times too, but never have I seen him break down like this. It's tough to watch a grown man cry. A strong man who would give his life for you. A man who loves hard. And now, when he looks his dad in the eye, the visibility of him hating even deeper crests across every feature on his frame. From the way he stands to the look of determination. He's pulling his shit together. We fight first, mourn later.

"Don't you dare deny me to kill that cocksucker like you did Royal. He's mine, dad, whether he's the one who killed them or not. That piece of shit is mine." The gaze he had fixed on his dad now travels to all of us standing in this room. Not a single person speaks. If he wants his redemption, he'll get it. Just like I'm going to get my deliverance. No matter how badly I want to be the one to kill Juan myself, I'll give this kill to Roan as long as I'm the one who gets to take out Jazmin.

"Make the call, Ivan," John grunts when he walks back in. He slips off his black leather gloves and shoves them deep into the back pocket of his well-worn jeans. He's changed his shirt over the course of the last ten minutes since he walked out the door with that now dead fuck. Damn, the dude is quick, doesn't fuck around.

"Very well," Ivan slurs in his Russian accent then places his phone on top of the round, wooden coffee table in the middle of the living room, where we all reside. Shit, years ago you would have never seen the Diamond Empire along with the realm of all the Solokovs in one room, but now we're a family. Bonded not only by marriage but respect, loyalty, and honor for one another.

"Ivan Solokov. I've been patiently waiting for someone to call me. Is the Diamond family too upset by their wedding present to call me themselves?" His toying laughter bellows through the phone.

"I would say no, since we're all here, you pussy," I retort.

"Ah. Dilan. Speaking of pussy. How is that stunning, little woman of yours? I'm most assuredly going to have to bathe her for days in disinfectant to get your smell off of her before I fuck her. Tell me, does her ass feel as tight as it looks, because my cock has been hard since the first time I've seen her. She's quite tasty, sí?" He's taunting me. We all know it. I grip my hands together at the nape of my neck before I answer him or wish I had some damn superpower to climb through this phone and slaughter his fucking ass.

My resolve is spitting like embers from a wildfire, ready to blow the hell up at any time. My uncle cuts me off before I'm able to respond, which pisses me the fuck off. I pull my hands away from my neck, every muscle tightening and my anger building. I sit on my hands. Literally. The need to destroy anything, to draw blood, is scratching at my skin like a leech.

"You address Ivan or me. No one else," he strains out, his mouth twisting in a self-conscious smirk.

"What's the fun in that, Salvatore? Let me guess, I'm the guest of honor to the newfound kingdom of the joining of your families?" God, I despise this cocky bastard. Who does he think he is?

"Listen, you motherfucker. This shit ends now. You threw down the gasoline. Now, we're going to light the fucking match. You tell your men to come and pick up the piece of shit who lies dead behind this building, in the gutter out back. Then you and your slut of a sister better stay hidden. I'm coming for you, motherfucker, and when I do, you're going to wish you never stepped foot in this city. I will end you. I will make you suffer, and before I do, you will watch your sister get a bullet right between her eyes." Roan sucks in a deep breath, his chest heaving up and down, darkness like I've never seen in him before darkening his expression.

"Are you finished, Roan? Wait, don't answer that. Take a long, hard look outside. See the bright lights? The busy streets? The millions of people wondering about?" He pauses. "Fuck off," Alina's brother Anton dismisses.

"Very well. Don't look. Let me say this. I'm speaking to each one of you. It seems you all have something to say to me. Your words mean nothing to me. You don't have the upper hand here. I do. You see, out there among all those people are four very important people to you. Or should I say women."

We all look at each other in bewilderment. Two of Alina's brothers snatch out their phones, while I close my eyes, knocking my head back in the chair. He sure has a way with fucking with us. No damn way he has anyone.

"You're bluffing." My uncle leans into the phone. Sweat suddenly appears on his forehead.

"Nice try, Juan. We don't scare that easily. In fact, we don't scare at all. We seek revenge. Now, enough of these games. Prepare for war." Ivan's hand reaches for the phone, I'm assuming to disconnect the call.

That's when we all hear it. The screaming. "Fuck." John draws his gun, aiming it at the phone as if the sound of a shrilling woman is going to take away whatever disgraceful thing they are doing to her.

"Oh, yes. I have your wife, John, even though I didn't want her. She's a persistent woman. Brave, I would say. She hasn't lost her touch. The stupid woman begged me to take her. She'll be the first to die, unless you all do exactly what I tell you."

Every single man in this room remains quiet, unsure of what the hell to do. Cain is damn near ready to explode. Roan's jaw is slacked; the only movement from him is the flaring of his nostrils. John drops his hand, his gun slipping to the floor.

"I see I have your attention now. I'm far from bluffing. I also have your wives, Ivan and Salvatore. And lastly, I have the beautiful Anna." That's when I stand. My heart gives out. My lungs try without succeeding to suck in air in order to breathe. "Don't you touch her." My voice is unable to shred the madness I'm trying to convey. Even I hear the desperation, the weakness, and the yearning need to surrender.

"It's a shame her body will have to be scrubbed, her silky flesh hanging off of her body before I lay a finger on her. By then, she'll be unrecognizable, too disfigured for me to want her, Dilan. It saddens me, because I would love nothing more than to fuck her. To mark her. To make her mine."

"You are one sick bastard." Ivan bends down toward the phone. I'm unable to speak any further. All I have are images in my head of the horrendous things he will do to Anna if we don't find them.

"Not sick, smart. Your wives mean nothing to me. In fact, I should kill them. However, it's not them I want. I want you, Salvatore, Ivan, John, and Dilan. The rest of you, I don't give a shit about. You're too weak to ruin me. So here's what I propose. You have until nine tomorrow morning to find me. To decide if you will trade your lives for you wives. If you don't, then Cecily dies first. And one more thing. My sister is quite torn up about the phone call she received from the prison, regarding the death of Miguel. Which means there will be no trade for the beautiful Anna. It seems my sister wants her a lot more than I do. For some reason, she does not find her appealing the way I do. Maybe I'll change my mind, show her how to be fucked by a real man before I turn her over to Jazmin."

CHAPTER THIRTEEN

ANNA

Something is off. I have no clue how I know this, but I do. I walk clumsily down the vacant hall with Cecily. Our hands are clasped together. My intuition is screaming at me that she knows it too. Whether it's the snowstorm that's happening inside of the room we just left or not knowing when, where, why, or how they are going to strike at us next, I really don't know. All I do know is, something is wrong.

This indescribable nagging hits me worse than anything I've experienced before. It's far worse than what happened several months ago.

It's paranoia more so than a gut instinct. My thoughts are consumed with it. Pressure begins to press down on my chest, making it difficult for me to breathe. Before I have the chance to ask Cecily to stop so I can catch my breath, she comes to a complete stop and brings her hands up to cup my face. "Anna, listen to me. We need to be in the open. There is no doubt in my mind there are more of his people in here. He's smart. I believe he planned all of this ahead of time, knowing damn well we would all be here. Whatever the hell is running through your head, you need to flush it out. I need you with me right now." I feel her motherly touch on my skin, her words trying to penetrate through my foggy smog-filled brain.

"Where are we going?" I ask.

"To the bar," is her response. We don't make it to the bar. In fact, we take a few small, steps, and then everything happens fast. Three men surround us with guns pointed directly at our heads.

"This was easier than we thought. Give her to me," one of them speaks. His face is covered in scars. His teeth are stained. His eyes are dark. "Fuck you. You will have to kill me first," she speaks calmly, quietly, her hand gripping mine tighter. This cannot be happening. My body begins to tremble. The walls feel like they are caving in. Bluntly, I stagger backwards when one of them slams the butt of his gun into the side of my head. I struggle to stand upright, but my legs are giving out. Someone catches me before I hit the ground.

"If you insist. I'm sure the boss will be pleased to know we've killed you." My mind is fighting to stay awake, while my head is pounding the drums in my ears profusely. All I know for sure is we are descending stairs, because my body is being jostled around, bouncing fluently as I hang upside down. Whoever has their hold on me is digging their fingers into the back of my thighs. The warmth of his touch has my stomach convulsing.

"Very nice," I hear a slimy Spanish accent, deep and brooding, and then feel hands gliding, smoothing, palming my ass.

"Get your goddamn hands off of her, Juan." Oh my god. I become alert then. Squirming, screaming to be released from the firm hold keeping me in place on these shoulders. "Feisty. I love it." Vomit is crawling up my throat. I'd give just about anything to be able to hurl the acid in his face. The difficulty to force words out of my mouth has me damn near gagging. The violent hit to my head is making me delirious. His hands on me, touching, feeling places he has no right to explore, make me feel dirty.

"Cecily. Now that you're here, I will find you useful before I slice your throat. Put the other two in the back of the van. And pick this worthless piece of shit up off the ground. These two, though, can come with me." His mark still lingers on my backside after he removes his hands. It's dark. I can't see anything. Not until I'm tossed into the backseat of a car. The smell of leather and cigars is stagnant. Even though my head is pounding and my movements are slow, I scrunch into the farthest corner of the car, away from this dirty man, while I'm shaking and wondering how many of us he has taken. He said the other two. Who could they be? I start crying, frightened for all of us. Images of little Justice and Diesel surface first. If they have Calla or Deidre, then what if they have the babies too? He said two though. There is no way he has the babies. So who is it?

This cannot be happening. My heart is crawling out of my chest. My mom, Alina...he could have any of them.

This out-for-blood psycho has triumphed over our family. He's singlehandedly hit our men with the one and only weakness they have. Their women. He's overpowered us. Taken complete control. Tricked us all.

I am weak from the blow to my head, yet I am determined to not let this man overtake the strength I know I have, to not let him break the love I have inside my chest that is beating out of control out of fear for this entire family. A tank of strength overtakes my fear. I will hide it until I need to use it. To fill these sick sons of bitches full with whatever possesses me to destroy them.

Cecily starts fighting against whoever is trying to shove her in the car, while she tells them exactly what she wants to do with them. "You wanted this, bitch, now get the fuck in there, or I will splatter your brains all over this cement," one of them says. "Fuck you," she spits. I have never seen someone fall so fast to the ground. I'm witnessing from the perched corner of this vehicle that has now become my best friend as she drops him to his knees. I shift away, inching slowly across the seat, my fingers stinging from the cold outside.

"You haven't lost your touch, Cecily." Juan grabs her by her throat. Her eyes stay firm, showing how courageous she is, while I watch in horror as he sucks the life out of her. He lifts her up by the throat, spins her around fast, and slams her head into the brick wall. Then he pulls his gun out and places it to her temple. Another man grips her hands, tying them securely behind her back. He flips her back around while she tries to catch her breath. She's shoved onto the floor of the car, the pain she is in clear on her face, even though her eyes still flicker with anger and resentment.

"Don't you say a word. Nothing. No matter what they do or say, you keep your mouth shut," she whispers while trying to catch her breath. The interior light shows the handprints forming around her neck and a welt forming in the side of her forehead. I close my eyes and scream when I hear a gunshot right outside the door. My neck automatically shifts in the direction of the open door. It's hard not to see a lifeless body being dragged to the back of the vehicle behind us. Obviously the man Cecily took down. His people mean nothing to him.

Juan enters the vehicle beside me with blood splattered all over his fancy suit. He doesn't appear to be affected by this at all. He kicks Cecily repeatedly, her groans scarring, piercing through the vehicle. True to what she asked of me, she says nothing. He must be a man who strives on attacking the weak. Although we aren't weak. We're so much stronger than he realizes. So much better than he will ever be. Any man who strikes a woman, no matter who she is or what she has done, deserves nothing short than to have his balls cut off. What a sick bastard.

"Drive." He shuts the door, smoothens his hair back, and drags me across the seat by my hair. I let out the smallest of whimpers, startled. However, I will show no fear.

Keep your mouth shut, plays over and over in my mind.

"Both of you keep your mouths shut. You will speak when I tell you to. And you will do every damn thing I say." He's calm, which is more frightening than if he were angry. His hands are still wound tightly in my hair. I want to ask him why. Why is he doing this?

He pulls out his phone and stares down at it as if he's anticipating a call. When it rings a few minutes later, I hear him say, "Ivan." I freeze, my gaze falling to the floor. I can barely see my sweet friend, but I can feel her below my feet, feel her body stiffening as well.

It's when he voices his threat, his words describing the things he wants to do to me, when Cecily screams from the floor. She carries on until Juan starts kicking her profusely. I hear bones crunching and small whimpering. And then nothing. I don't even recall him hanging up the phone. My eyes stay trained to the floor.

"She's not dead." His callous way has me trying to jerk out of his hold.

"Oh, no. You will stay right here beside me, dear sweet Anna. The woman who should be mine." My eyes light up with fury. "You," is all I can manage to get past the large lump in my throat. "Sí, beautiful. It is me. Please call me Juan." His Spanish accent is heavier than when he came into the shop. "I hate you. You tricked me. I looked forward to seeing you every day, and now the sight of you makes me sick!" I scream at him.

"Oh, sweet Anna. Don't say things you surely don't mean. It saddens me that I may have to give you up before I have the chance to fuck you properly." My stomach drops. If I didn't know this man was a sick fuck, I would say he truly means what he says.

"You're sick. I would never go for a man like you. You've taken people against their will. Women. Who's in the van?" I try to turn my head around to see if it's following us, but his grip on my hair doesn't allow it.

"You didn't hear my conversation on the phone?" He tries to sound hurt, only it comes out mockingly.

"How could I when you were stomping on my friend?" Even with no blood going to whatever nerve controls my fear, I speak coolly.

"She deserves worse than that for dicing my cousin in the throat back there, forcing me to have to shoot him in the head to take away his suffering." Rage burns through me from the way he talks about her. I couldn't care less if his cousin is dead. I hope every last one of them dies. I've decided I've spoken enough. I keep quiet and take my eyes off of this filth, repressing the things he said about me, the way he spoke about wanting to fuck me, or that he may have to give me up. My guess would be, he's handing me over to his sister.

He releases my hair and shoves me into the corner, where I stare out onto the busy streets, wishing like hell I knew this city better than I do so I could tell where we are going.

Several minutes pass before I hear him on the phone again. My head jerks violently in his direction at the sound of my name.

"You don't come near her until I get what I want, Jazmin. Not a hair on her head is to be touched. Do I make myself clear?" I hear Jazmin telling him to kindly fuck off and to hurry up and get his shit done.

"You know, if I didn't love my sister, or if she weren't the only one I trust besides myself in this world, I would kill her if I knew I could keep you. So I have a plan, Anna. One I think you might agree with." The smell of him makes me sick when he leans closer to me. His confession is lodged in my ear.

I bravely wane my response to him. All kinds of scenes are making a great effort, pushing to the forefront of my mind. Repulsive, vile, and revoltingly images of what his plan could be.

"I'm not interested in your plans. You'll never have me." He laughs then. Viciously.

"Sweet Anna, I will. If you fight me on this, it will make it worse for you. Worse for your friends. Especially for the queens of these two empires, which will crumble with their leaders' wives dead. But if you agree, I will let the two in the other vehicle go. There's no negotiation with Cecily. She's as good as dead already for what she did back there, but you, my sweet little thing, have the power to save the lives of two of your friends. To make both Ivan and Salvatore happy by returning their wives back to them."

I pull away from him as far as I can go. The lights from oncoming cars give me the perfect view of his blazing stare that's scorching my skin. Not in a good way. Not in the way Dilan's look blisters me. Dilan looks at me as if I were a dream come true. As if he had been waiting forever for me, and once we connected, his touch, his words, and the way his skin felt up against mine, his lips soft but firm, controlled my body in every aspect that leads two people to the most powerful emotion known. Love.

This sick fuck looks at me as a possession. A woman who will bend at his command. Who will drop to her knees if he tells her to. There is no way in hell I will become his toy. He's stupider than any creature slithering its way around on this planet if he thinks I'm a woman to submit to him.

"What do I have to do?" I lie. He knows I'm lying too. He spoke moments ago of only trusting Jazmin. Which, he's definitely dumb if he does. She strikes me as a woman who would take him out if he betrayed her. Good, maybe he should, maybe I should listen and think long and hard about whatever he proposes to me. Even if I did agree, he still won't trust me. He knows damn well I would do anything to see no harm come to those women.

I played dumb when he said whom he has taken. He struck in the center of this family, taking the wives of the two most powerful men in this underground world. I almost believe he knows he's fucked up. He's started a war he knows he will lose. I'm not familiar at all with the rules of the underground. One would think though that if a queen is taken under duress, kidnapped, tortured, or whatever the likes this man has planned, that it not only means war, death, or that you have just committed suicide. It means more families will come together to take your entire empire down.

I realize now that this is my winning hand. I'm nobody to the rest of these families, but I'm somebody to my own. They won't give up until they have both Cecily and I back.

"Your beautiful head is spinning. Don't take me for a fool, Anna. I've never wanted a woman like I do you. I will keep you safe. All you have to do is come away with me. Tonight. We can leave now. I can have a plane ready to go within the hour. Just me and you. My sister won't even know where we are. Not until I decide to tell her." He's so damn serious. If I didn't hear him tell me as clear as day a few minutes ago he trusted his sister, I would believe him. He may think I am innocent, but naïve I am not.

"Let me get this straight," I say with persuasion. "You're telling me you would hand over those two, and you and I would what? Run away? You would live your life knowing you would have your sister and my family looking for us. That's the kind of life you're willing to live?" He scoffs at the sincerity of my question. I become more unsettled. How dare this man proposition me, then laugh in my face.

"Anna, you fail to see I know they will come looking for you. There will be fighting, death. My sister will be very angry when she realizes I haven't shown up like we planned. And yes, I will let them go. No harm done."

I tilt my body to face him. He cannot be trusted, and neither can I. We both know it. I have a barter of my own. He can take it or leave it. Well, he can do whatever he wants at the moment. He's the one fully in charge here. He could take me by force. We both know he could.

"They'll kill your sister and you know it. It's bullshit for you to expect me to believe a word you say. You've proven how disloyal you are by throwing her to her death. She can't survive them on her own. You two are a pair." I flinch when his hands come up and cup my face. He's not hard or cold like he was earlier. He's gentle, his thumb tracing the seam of my bottom lip. The vile acid that's been churning in my stomach is daring me to let it erupt and mix with the blood all over his suit.

"Anna. How quick of you to judge me when your family does the same thing I do. They steal, kill, and live off the money from the drugs and guns they sell. What makes the things I do any worse than what they do?" His grip tightens on my chin, forcing me to look at him. To see the determination behind his façade of bullshit. Daring me in an offensive way to answer him.

"Even though all those things you're saying may be true, they are nothing like you. They don't randomly kidnap people, especially innocent women. They don't start a war that they will undeniably lose. And they sure as hell don't betray a single person in their family." I cover his hands with mine and try to pull them away, but my desperate plea for his cold, callous fingers to let go of me only spurs him on more. He reaches for my hair, pulling my head back in a way that has me grunting out my response to his abuse.

"I'm a man who takes what he wants. I want you, Anna Drexler. I want the purity that surrounds you. The fact that you know nothing about the things your so-called family does, fascinates me. You're innocent. You radiate light in the complete darkness of the life I live. I don't expect you to understand any part of it at all. You're a blind fool if you think they don't do the same things I do. Now, I will ask you one more time. Do you want their lives spared? Are you willing to give up your life, your mom, and Dilan for them?" He's so smooth with his words. So right to the point. A single tear runs down my cheek. I may never see my mom, Dilan, or anyone I love again. Unlike him, I'm loyal to a fault. I will not let my family lose the women who help mold them together. They can suffer the loss of only me. They will never give up looking for me. I know they won't. I can only pray they find me before this man takes the only thing I have left. Hope. I have one card left to play. To me, it's the queen of hearts. He better listen and let me win, or I'm folding.

"If you want me, then you will let Cecily go too. That's the only way I will leave with you. Otherwise, I will take my chances on dying by the hands of your sister."

CHAPTER FOURTEEN

DILAN

Silence is an eerie fucker. It seeps into your blood and paralyzes the brain. It consumes your inner thoughts. It fucks you up the ass in a raw way. Silence is deadly. That's how it is for several drawn-out minutes when a dozen or so men stand around, wondering what in the fuck to do, our hearts trapped in thick barbed wire, cutting, slicing us above and below the belt.

This kind of thick silence is killing us all. As we fall into the depths of despair, I allow my thoughts to linger on Anna. On the way she has made me feel since the first time I saw her. On her will to make it on her own, to prove to herself she's worthy. Anna is drenched with love, strength, and trustworthiness. She's an angel. My angel. I'm a damn fool for not reciprocating how I actually felt about her when she told me. Christ. I should have spun her ass around and kissed her like she wanted me to. Like I wanted to when I heard her spill her guts to Deidre. But fuck, no. Instead, I chose to protect her. Look where she is now. She's with the worst kind of man any woman could be with. He's dangerous, manipulating, and a cold-hearted killer.

Anna's life was torn apart when I first met her. Her life at the time was crumbling in every direction. Yet this woman, who had no idea what kind of life she was running to, welcomed us all. Not once judging the shit we do, the way we live, or the means we go about to survive.

Those types of women are rare, women who stand by the side of a criminal, turn their cheek and still love you in a way no one else could. Christ, I need her back. We need them all back.

These are our women. Our foundation. A good woman will have your back, be supportive, and tell you shit you don't want to hear if only to make you see things from their point of view. Fuck.

And now... She's gone. Again, the entire thing is my fault. I should have never come back here. I should have left this shit alone. Learned to go on. But hell, no. I had to seek my revenge. I unwillingly put the lives of the people I love in danger, and now look what the hell I have done. I have all but killed my unt, two other important women in my life, and the woman I love.

It's fucked up as all hell to stand here and admit I love her when god knows what is happening to her right now. I'm the only man who's been inside of her. Completely. She waited for me. She gave her heart to me. I'm in love with her. She's in love with me. I know she is.

I lift my eyes off the goddamn floor of hell when my uncle finally speaks, his words showing his worry. I hunger to let my mind stay with Anna. But it can't. If I want to hold her, to taste her, to tell her I love her, and to hear those sweet words repeated back to me, I need to listen. Need to drive the way I feel about her out of my brain for the time being, but to let it seep deep into my bones, let it drive me in that direction. The direction to kill for her.

"Go get the women and children. They need to be at my house. The Solokov women are welcome there too. I believe once we break the news to each one of them, they will all need each other. My guess is Juan has called off his men from this surrounding area. His threats do not go unanswered. He wants us to find him.

Anton, if you can make sure it's safe for us all to leave, I would appreciate it. Roan and Cain, you handle your wives with care. And Aidan, make sure Deidre is very aware that she is carrying a child she has to worry about. I want them all safe while we meet at the warehouse on 44th. Time isn't on our side. Ivan and I will discuss this.

We will have a plan by the time you all get there."

I can't even speak. Though, I'm not sure what I would say if I could. No one speaks. All I see is a lot of nodding of heads and shoulders slumped forward as if we have already lost. I watch them leave from my position on the sofa, where I now have my hands crossed over my chest, my breathing floating heavily in this room.

Roan pauses in the doorway and turns back to face me, halting both Aidan and Cain along with him.

"I know what the fuck is running through your mind, Dilan. Let it fucking go. You can blame yourself all you want, but this is the last time I'll tell you that no one blames you for this. We're all a little shocked. Stunned to the very fucking core over this shit. One thing you need to know, to hear from me, is this. I can honestly stand here and tell you that if I were you, I would be doing the same thing. Nothing would have stopped me, and I know with every goddamn bone in my body that you wouldn't blame me for a damn bit of it. Pull your head out of your ass. Man the fuck up. I want every one of those women back." I close my eyes and clip the bridge of my nose, exhaling as I do.

"Don't stand there pitying yourself or any one of us, Dilan. We will get through this." My uncle stands directly in front of me. His words are mixing with the ones Roan just spoke, stabbing me with a dull knife into my already wounded heart.

"One thing I hate is repeating myself. But it seems with you I have to. You've always carried this fucked-up world on your shoulders. Just like your cousin, you're a fixer. Determined to do shit on your own in order to protect those you love. Well, goddamn it, sometimes in life we need to ask for help. Even though you didn't, you sure as fuck are getting it. There are things in life that drive us to do things we do not want to do. I know first-hand how these things or people that drive a knife so deep into your gut, twisting the shit out of it until you're damn near bleed dry, can possess your every thought. It damn near killed me to know Royal had a part in putting you away. Why he turned on all of us is irrelevant. He did. He broke the rules and so did the Carlos family.

The situation with Royal has lead up to all of this. My guess is he was jealous of you, like he was of his own brother. He had his filthy hands mingling with Juan's, to attack me where he knew it would hurt me the most. My family." He pauses briefly then continues on, his words pulling me from my gloom of guilt.

"He was my son. For many days and nights after I witnessed him take his last breath, I blamed myself. Then one day, I woke up and told myself I cannot control someone else's actions . I control me. The way I feel. If it weren't this, it would have been something else forcing us to go to war with them. They bring disgrace to all humans. They have no respect for territorial boundaries. They want to rule it all. Someone has to stop them. That someone is us. I love you, Dilan. We all do. I also believe the women, who we all love, will come back to us unharmed. Now, go tell your parents what's going on. Then you need to decide how to break this news to Grace. Thank god she has Ramsey." He lets out a frustrated breath then continues.

"And make sure your dad fully understands he is not a part of this. He will not fight. He needs to stay with your mom. Meet us out front in half an hour. By then, I want the Dilan I know back. I want the man who is prepared to kill for the woman he loves." He sucks in a sharp breath after his long speech that smacks me right across the face. A slap that stings.

"The same goes for me and my family. We care, Dilan. Now, go take care of your parents." Ivan strolls toward me as he speaks, our feet damn near toe-to-toe when he pauses in front of me. His arms settle on my shoulders.

"You're a good man. Trustworthy. This is your fight. We choose to not let you do it alone."

Again, their words snap me to attention, shoot that magical poison into my veins. In this family, killing another for taking the women of a mafia family is one of the worst sins, one of the worst ways to start the next revolution. Killing for the safety of the queens, the princesses, and in my case, my woman, is not a crime. It's a moral necessity. It's a source of survival. We treat them with dignity and have respect for our women. For we as men are nothing without them. I'm tired of blaming this on me, when in truth it should be blamed on those who have committed sins against us. I'm done taking responsibility for this. Am over being a pussy. It's time the real Dilan stands up and takes his place in this mighty powerful family.

"Oh, dear god, Dilan. No." Mom shakes her head when I rely to both her and my dad the stakes of how important it is that they both listen to me.

"I'll stay with everyone. Have you told Grace yet?" my dad comments as I follow them to where my dad helps my mom sit down on the couch. Her sobs create a chaos of emotions inside of me.

"No. I wanted to tell you first. To let you know what needs to be done. I'm going to tell her now." I watch both of my parents' faces take on a warranted downward twist, misfortune and understanding cemented in the way they shift uncomfortably.

"I'll be fine. It's Grace we need to worry about. She survived what happened last time. But this, we all know this is much worse. She's going to need you both. Mom, I need you to be strong for her. Listen to her. Help her in any way you can. We're getting them back. All of them," I stress. She nods and grips my face tenderly. "Of course, I will. I want them all back as much as you do. I can see by the way you look at Anna, by the way you're stepping in and putting her mother's worries to the forefront, that you love her, son. Even though what you're about to do is dangerous and the repercussions are something I won't allow myself to think about, I want to tell you how proud I am of you." Her words come out all rickety and shaken. I know she's telling the truth. It's hard not to miss the concern and worry she has for all of us in the way her trembling fingers try to hold steady.

I would love to stay and make sure they will both be all right, but I have to go. I know my parents well. They have a bond that will never be broken. They will be there for each other as well as everyone else.

"I have to go." I sit down on the coffee table in front of them. Tears continue to fall from my mom's eyes. Even my dad's eyes are glassed over from tears I know will drop the minute I walk out this door.

"You kill them. All of them. And then you come back to us," dad chokes out.

It takes everything I have to finally twist out of my mom's firm hold. I kiss her one last time and hug my dad tightly before I trek down the hall to Grace's room. The sweat running down my back increases with every step I take. I falter outside their door. Laughter rings out from inside. Christ. This is one of the hardest things I have ever done. It ranks up there with when I looked into my parents' broken expressions when the judge bellowed out my prison sentence.

I knock, hollering out my name, letting them know it's me. "What's going on, Dilan? Come in, please." Ramsey strains when he opens the door, while Grace peers at me from behind him.

"Where's Anna?" Her question hammers my already beaten-down chest.

I blow out a large breath. I don't have time to answer all of the questions I see swimming in her nervous eyes. It takes all I have just to tell her this.

"They took her, my aunt, Cecily, and Charlotte," I tell them, my voice small, my phrase right to the point.

"No. Not my baby. Not again. I... I can't go through this again. You all said we would get out of here. That you wouldn't let anything happen to her again. This is your fault. All of you." I close my eyes while I stand there, already numb to the fact that I am the biggest part of this reckoning. This is a mother whose entire life has been built around her only child. A mother who should never have to deal with this kind of shit, not only once, but twice. It's understandably more than any one person should have to take.

"Elizabeth. That's enough. I know you need someone to blame, but you cannot act like this. This is a time when we need to come together. To have faith. Look at the man. Can't you see he's falling apart here?" He turns from her to me. I'll take the blame. I know I deserve it. All of it.

"She has every right to blame me. I'm not going to stand here and defend my actions didn't cause this. What I am going to do is find her. I love her, Grace." She won't look at me. Her hands cover her face as she cries uncontrollably. I get it. She may never forgive me for this.

"Those people are not human. They're wild animals. They will kill her," she rattles off. There isn't a damn thing I can do to convince her they won't or to try and console her. Time is of the essence right now.

"I have to go. My uncle has requested for everyone to go to his house. It's safe and best for everyone." I direct my words at Ramsey instead of Grace. She's disappeared into the suite, her raking sobs burning a hole through my ears.

"Safe?" she screams as she comes back around the corner, piercing me with her tear-stained eyes. Her voice is raw. "There's nowhere safe from you people. You... you're everywhere. I should have never agreed to stay here. I should have told her no. That we would have been better off starting over somewhere else. But no, even though you disappeared and shattered her, she still kept holding on to you. And for what? For you to come back and put her in more danger?"

"We'll leave now. Go do what you have to. I have her." Ramsey places his arms around her. Her hands are balling into fists as she beats her wounded soul onto his chest. I know she doesn't mean what she's saying. But I'd be a liar if didn't admit it doesn't shake me to an inch of losing the little bit of sanity I have left. I go to leave them, her hateful words ticking off like a time bomb down to its final seconds before it blows you the fuck up, crumbles you to a million untraceable pieces. I'm so ready to get the hell out of here.

"Take care of her." I extend my hand out for him to shake. He releases his hold with one arm while holding her securely with the other. The vibes I've gotten from the man since I first met him have been nothing short of sincere. He cares deeply for both Grace and Anna. She will be well taken care of until I return her daughter to her.

"Not a problem. Take care of yourself. Kill the fuckers." He shakes my hand, his hold firm.

"That won't be a problem either," I respond before exiting the room with the weight of the fucking world, my world, on my goddamn shoulders.

By the time I reach the room Anna and I shared, my phone is blowing up with text messages from everyone, saying they are all getting ready to leave.

I can't get myself to look at the bed. My eyes are avoiding it at all costs. I grab everything I can find, both hers and mine, and shove it into my bag and her suitcase. It takes me five minutes tops to cram it all in and exit the room. My heart stays inside that room as the door slams shut behind me. But I'll be goddamned if it stays there. I need my heart to stay alive. To seek revenge. To live. She's everything to me, and a hostage to him. A poker chip he plans to bargain with to try and see how far he can push us to take complete control of all we have. He has no damn clue that every member of our family is worth more than the money we possess. We would give it all up. He fails to see we won't give him jack shit, except to allow him the privilege to dig his own grave right along with his sister's.

CHAPTER FIFTEEN

ANNA

"You drive a hard bargain, Miss Drexler. You see, though, just like you, I do not trust. Perhaps you didn't hear me correctly. Let me rephrase." The way he articulates his words are enough to make me want to jump out of this car and become road kill before he has the damn chance to kill me himself, or turn me over to his cunt of a sister. Either way, it doesn't matter. As long as I can find a way to get away from him. I'll deal with his sister if I have to. In fact, that option is more appealing than his. But I'm given no choice in the matter if I want to save the lives of my family. He can rephrase, repeat until the end of time. I'm not giving in.

"What do I get besides you coming with me? Are you going to give me your body I crave? Are you going to let me bury myself in you? Or will you make me force myself on you?" I am still trembling on this cold leather seat. His tone is colder, harsher than it was a few minutes ago. He's stressing his authority, calling me out, letting me know I have no room to try and barter or play any game with him. Well, fuck him. I'm not a damn quitter. And his threats mean nothing to me. I'm not about to allow this man to break me.

"You wouldn't dare." I don't stand a chance against him. I know this. I'm not going down. Not like this. And not with a man like him.

"I don't want to. I would much rather enjoy you with you coming to me willingly. But do not underestimate me. You may be my saving grace in this world, but I always get what I want, even if I have to take it. Now, I'm running out of time, my patience no longer exists. We have a plane to catch to Columbia. Stop the car," he says on a command, his air warning. And Columbia? That's one of the largest drug capitals of the world. Of course he wants to go there. He will fit right in. Hell, he probably has people there too. Oh god.

Whoever is driving does as he's told. The car comes to a jerking halt. I look around. Darkness is now surrounding us. There is no sign of life anywhere. Where in the hell are we? We haven't been driving that long to be very far away from civilization. Last I looked, we were crossing over a bridge. I gage a glance upfront, checking the dash for a compass. East. We must be either in or near New Jersey.

"What are you doing?" I ask him, freaking the hell out. My god, is he going to kill them here? Dump their bodies?

I begin to thrash in the backseat, crawling to where he is now getting out of the car.

"Stay, goddamn it. Or I will tie you up and shove you in the trunk." His face is burning, his fingers icy cold when he grips my jaw hard then slams the door in my face.

I react quickly. Time is standing still. "Cecily," I call out, shaking her. She doesn't move. Doesn't speak. I place a hand on her chest to check her breathing, and feel her heart fluttering under the tips of my fingers. Thank god she's alive.

"Get her out now." My eyes go wide when two of the men who took us from the hotel swing open the door and grab Cecily by her feet, dragging her out of the car like she means nothing. She means the world to me. I refuse to allow her to be manhandled by these sons of bitches. Her body makes a thumping sound as they dump her lifeless body on the ground.

"Please, Juan, don't do this," I beg. I will give myself to him. I promise him over and over again I will if he won't kill her. My legs are half out of the car. I don't care if he shoves me in the trunk. I need to fight for her. "Stop." He holds his hand up to the man pointing a gun at her form on the ground. I look to him, then over his shoulder where I see the other two ladies standing with black hoods over their heads, their hands and feet shackled together like a small prison train.

"Leave her with them." He says nothing more. His hands are grasping me by my arms as he hoists me up and out of the car.

"You owe me. Don't forget. Now, if you meant what you said, then prove it right now." He pulls my body flush with his. His smell alone makes me sick. My mind wonders what the hell he means by that. He leans into my personal space, his mouth close to brushing mine. He wants me to kiss him. I can't. It's outright impossible to not gag. I feel it rising up, ready to spill all over him. Somehow, I manage to hold it back, the gurgling noises lodged in my throat. My strength is taking over, my determination setting itself free.

"Kiss me," he whispers, his voice low.

"Now, Anna." Oh, no. Kissing is intimate. I've only kissed the man I love, and now it will be tarnished. It's as if he knows the right word in destroying me. He's going to take every gift only Dilan and I have shared with each other away from me. I'm going to be left broken with only memories of one night shared with him. But I have to do it. I close my eyes, feeling his breath sucking me in. All I can do is pretend like it's Dilan I'm kissing. It's the only way I can try and convince him.

When our lips touch, his are warm but nothing like the smooth, sweet caress of Dilan's. My mouth remains closed. I hold back the cringe my body feels raking over me when he darts his tongue out, his taste sour against my lips. This is killing me to have to open my mouth. The second I do, he takes full advantage by swirling his tongue with min. I move my tongue with his, the entire time wishing it were the man I love instead of the man I hate more than anything. He growls, guides me back into the car, and lays me down flat on my back, bringing his body on top of mine. This is too much. His erection is prodding, poking, and driving into my stomach. He assaults my mouth with a vengeance, tasting every bit of me. His hands are holding the back of my head, titling it the way he wants. I continue to pretend he's Dilan. It's the only way I can kiss him. When he removes one of his hands from my head and traces his fingers down my neck, I stop kissing him and open my eyes. His are clouded over. Hungry with lust. Glazed.

"Please," I beg as tears are leaking from my eyes. My shoulders begin to shake. He sighs heavily then brings himself up off of me. I adjust my body somewhat, while he adjusts the bulge in his pants I so desperately want to chop off. I jump when he slams the door behind him. My body is twisted up like a pretzel, half under him.

He doesn't move an inch when I take my feet from underneath him, fixing myself upright, leaning my head against the window. The tears won't stop as we start to drive. All I can do is repeat to myself that I saved everyone's lives, even though they are left on the side of the road; one woman unconscious, the other two left in the darkest of dark and the coldest of cold. Please god, let someone find them. Let them be safe. Let Cecily survive the abuse he inflicted on her. And, please, let them find me.

"Why Columbia?" I dare to ask, desperate to know if my hunch is correct. It's drugs. I know it is. I'm going to be forced to live watching him deal, grow, or whatever the hell he does. Columbia is known for Cocaine.

"I have a home there." His answer is short and clipped.

"Won't that be the first place people will will look for you? Is your sister really that dumb to not know what you're up to?" I glance over at him. I wish I could see his face right now. No, I take that back. I never want to see his face, or the rest of him. He's a disgrace to all humans. The perfect description of evil. I feel him studying me, trying to tear me apart. Dissecting me. Silence travels for miles with us until his low, deep voice crawls up my spine. Creepily.

"She doesn't know about it. I've hidden it from her. From everyone. I've had it for years, planning for the day I could leave, in hopes to find love, Anna. To raise a family there."

I roll my eyes at him, grateful this ignorant asshole cannot see me. Love. If he thinks he will find it with me, he is fucking stupid. I will never love him. And a family? He's all kinds of crazy. This may get me beaten, slapped around, but I'm saying it anyway.

"You expect to have all that with me? I will never love you. Surely, you have to know that." I swing my arm out and smack the leather seat.

"You've kidnapped me. Taken me away from my life. From my mom. From the man I do love. You're out of your goddamn mind if you think I will ever love you. The sight of you makes me sick, Carlos." I am serious. The tension grows thick in the back of this car. I feel his heated stare turn dangerous. But right now, I simply do not care.

I cry out in agony when he grabs my arms and drags me the short distance to him until his face is within an inch of mine.

"Let's get a few things straight, right now. You will never speak of loving another man in front of me. In fact, you can forget about him. You will never see him again. After tonight, he will be dead anyway. And for your mother, I'm sorry about her. I really am. But you belong with me. You're mine now to do with as I please, when I please. And when I tell you to spread your beautiful legs and fuck me, you will. Until then, you will do as I say. Do you understand what I'm telling you now, Anna? You belong to me. And don't ever call me Carlos again. My name is Juan. I've waited a long time to hear you call me by my name. I will wait no longer."

He shoves me back away from him. More tears are threatening to escape. I'm a prisoner. His slave. God, why doesn't he kill me now? Shoot me straight through my heart? He's already dug a hole in my chest. He may as well pull my heart out, end me now before he destroys me for good, leaves me for an empty shell.

"I'll fight you," I whisper from my corner.

"I expect nothing less from you. You wouldn't be the woman I know you are if you didn't." I hate him and the way he sneers his differences of opinion, always having some kind of idiotic comeback to everything I say. He thinks he knows me. Knows the kind of woman I am. He's delirious. I'll find a way to take his life before I let him touch me in the way he wants to. I close my eyes. He may have threatened me to never speak of Dilan again, but he will never clear the man I love from my thoughts. Not ever. His words about him dying grip my throat until I feel like I'm suffocating to death. He's point blank stupid if he thinks Dilan or anyone in my family will give up. They will hunt him down. Rip his heart out of his chest, or I will.

I'm daydreaming of Dilan and how out of his mind he must be right now when I feel fingers trailing down my neck, sweeping my hair off of my face. "We're here, Anna. Time to go." I hate him, hate his sweet and gentle fingers on me. Juan Carlos is like one of those male wild dogs. They like take over, rule, destroy anything that comes near them in their own surroundings. They're evil, territorial creatures, and when they strike, it's right in the throat. They might look handsome and sweet on the outside, but they're untamed, harsh, and unpredictable on the inside. Rapid. And you'd be a fool to trust them.

"Okay, Carlos," I say bitterly. I refuse to call him Juan. He can beat the shit out of me before I give him anything he wants. He leans forward in the seat, his hands dropping away from my face. The thought of him touching me or watching me repulses me. There isn't enough hot water or soap in this world to get his smell off of me.

I laugh inside at my thoughts of comparing him to a dog. Not a cute, little dog you can't wait to get home to cuddle with or greet you at the door the minute you come home. No, he's one who needs to be neutered. Painfully. As I continue to visualize this dog with his deep black, shiny coat, I realize his hair is now slicked back and the motherfucker changed his clothes. When? Must have been while I was lost in thought with Dilan. I sigh. He'll find me. I know he will. I smile inside. Knowing he cleaned himself up while I was thinking of the man he despises so. I would love nothing more than to acknowledge that fact. He doesn't deserve an acknowledgement. He deserves death. I hate him.

"You know," I say, opening the door on my side, completely ignoring his outstretched hand to help me slide across the seat toward him. "For a man who claims to be obsessed or whatever your sick, twisted mind wants with me, you sure do know how to treat a lady," I sneer as I take a step out into the freezing cold. Shivering, I wrap my arms around myself, not bothering to shut the door. Fuck that. His idiot driver can do that.

The wind picks up, whipping my hair all over the place, making chills run through my body.

His smug, nasty self walks behind and around the car. "Move back," he whispers in my ear. My eyes grow wide when he pulls out a gun, opens the front door, and shoots the driver right in the back of his head. "Oh my god. What are you doing?" I back away farther, my head throbbing, racing. "Make this another lesson learned, Anna. Trust no one. He knew where we were going. I'm not leaving any evidence behind. Therefore, he had to die." He snatches my hand, completely ignoring what I said, and tugs me behind him. I'm in shock. Shaking. Scared. The frozen earth below me feels like it's swallowing me up. This is so wrong. Death and destruction are his life. And he's casting me into it.

I look up to the small airplane I see through the blowing snow. My nerves are frayed like the hem on a pair of well-worn jeans with all the fibers falling apart. He's going to bring all he's got to break me down. I know he will. Right now, I don't know what to think. I've gone numb.

"Get in." He pulls me in front of him. I climb the stairs leading into the plane, feeling his eyes on my backside. More chills run through me. Not from the cold, but because I'm now going to be trapped with no means of escape from him at all for hours while we fly to fucking Columbia.

Assaulted by warmth the minute I step into the plane, I make my way to one of the four empty seats and sit down, not saying a word. Dread casts its shadow over me. I'm leaving my life here. My mom, the man I love. Aidan. My entire family. The dam inside my body breaks. Placing my hands over my face, I start to cry. This is far worse than I expected. The not knowing if I will see them again. The pain and suffering they will go through. Will they find me? How much can one person handle? How much is it going to take before I break?

I lift my head when I hear the door close, the latch of the plane securing it in place. His smell is potent, his cologne giving him an air of authority. It's spicy. I hate it. I want Dilan's smell. Natural. Intoxicating. Manly.

"Anna." He towers over me.

"What?" I breathe out rapidly. "I do know how to treat a lady. I will prove it to you once you get over the fact you are never going home. Once you realize you're mine now. And once you learn to care for me like I do for you. I apologize for you being cold. That was rude of me. I'm not oblivious to the fact this is difficult for you. Your world is shattered. You've been taken against your will. And I know you hate me. I don't blame you. However, life will be easier for you, if you learn to deal with it. The things I said about taking you against your will I said out of anger. I knew you would make the right choice, to lose your freedom to spare the lives of your family. That's one of the reasons I'm drawn to you. You're giving, Anna. You have me entranced. You may never understand why." He takes a short gasp of air. My mind is bouncing all over the damn place from his brisk words.

"Buckle up, please." He stands back up. Then he reaches into a compartment above me, retrieving a blanket, and gently places it in my lap.

"We're all set," he says to who I assume is the pilot when he pushes a button on the seat beside him. He's moved to the couch now. I buckle up and turn my face away from him, listening to the gentle hum of the plane while watching the pitch blackness outside, the slight glow from the plane's shadows as we pick up speed and the plane lifts into the air.

All the lights from greater New York are right there. So close and yet out of my reach.

CHAPTER SIXTEEN

DILAN

"How's Grace?" Aidan strides over to my car and helps me retrieve the duffle bags out of my trunk.

"Not good, man." I slam my trunk shut and pick up the other bag. These motherfuckers are heavier than shit. The entire drive over here I beat myself up for not bringing them inside with me. During the wedding, I had no clue that the past few days would be the best days of my life. Now, I wish like fucking hell I would have had these inside with me.

They wouldn't have done me a damn bit of good, though, not when we were ambushed like fucking immature beginners. Everyone had a gun on them. We always do. Like an asshole, I left mine in the glovebox of my car during the wedding. Then shit went down, and I lost myself in Anna. Never thought twice about it. Fucking stupid.

"Let me guess, she blames you." He grabs the door to the warehouse, swinging it wide open. I walk through first with his big ass frame trailing behind me.

"She does. I'm not taking it personally. Anna's her daughter. She has every right to strike out at me."

I turn around the minute he reaches for my arm, halting me to stop.

"We will get them back. All of them." He positions himself directly in front of me. "I know we will, but I'm so sick of this fucking shit, of men who are too weak to take us on. Fucking pussies go after our women. They deserve every goddamn thing they're about to get." He laughs, which has me smiling for the first time in hours.

"Hey. How you holding up?" Roan asks when Cain and him step into the building, followed by just about every damn guy I know. Dozens trail in behind them. All in black, carrying weapons. Looks of purpose, power, and the same pissed-off attitude I have on their faces.

"I'm good. The girls?" Cain shakes his head, a frown creasing across his forehead. "Not good. I hated leaving Calla. When they all pulled away from the hotel, I fucking wanted to kill more than I've ever wanted to before for putting her and everyone else through hell. I'm fucking ready."

I press on with Roan and Aidan, even though guilt seems to try and claw its way through my veins, slithering like a snake after you chop its damn head off. Yeah. I've killed a few live slimy snakes in my lifetime. Now it's time to kill the human kind. They possess the same slimy skin as those reptiles. I hate fucking snakes.

Out of all the women, it doesn't surprise me at all when Roan drones on about how strong and in control Alina is. That woman's honeymoon was destroyed and her mother is kidnapped, and here she is taking care of everyone else.

"I know focusing on everyone else is her way of keeping her mind busy. She never ceases to amaze me." I look down at my bag as I toss it on the table, persistent to get this shit over with. I want my girl back. The desire to tell her how I feel is strong as I listen to these guys carry on about their wives and children. More men join in until Ivan draws our attention by demanding us to join him alongside my uncle where they stand at the end of a long table.

"We have some smart women on our hands. It seems both Anna and Cecily have their phones. Unless this is a trap, they've taken them to New Jersey, which obviously means they are not at his house." He pauses slightly before lifting his gaze to me. There's something pleading in his eyes, both his and my uncle's, as they gaze down to the end of the table where I'm standing, my arms firmly planted across my chest. Whatever the fuck it is, it isn't good. I can tell by the way they both hesitate, as if they're trying to convey what they need to say through their eyes. I sure as fuck am not a goddamn mind reader. I'm ready to share that little tidbit of information when my uncle speaks up.

"We lost Anna's trail about sixty miles east of Newark. Our sources tell us they have no doubt we lost her, because she's in the air. He has her."

My hands close into fists, and I slam them down on the table. I am hunched forward, daring anyone to say a word. The urge to punch something, to gut anything, is raging through me like an angry bull trapped in a space too small for his body.

"Do we know where he took her, dad? And for god's sake, are your resources sure? Jesus Christ!" Roan speaks up. I can't fucking talk. God knows what he will do to her. He is an animal. Only cares about himself and the need to fucking destroy me. For what? I have no goddamn clue.

Christ. I used to lie in my cell for hours, trying to figure out what the hell I ever did to that bastard to have him hate me so much, to make it his life's mission to kill me. The only thing I could come up with always led me back to Royal. But why the hell would they come after me? I mean, fuck, I'm glad they came after me instead of Roan. I would protect him with my life, and he would do the same for me. But fuck me, why her? He's fucking obsessed with her. Any sane person knows an obsession to another human can be dangerous. I know her, there is no way she would have left with him unless she was forced to.

"We're working on tracking the plane. There isn't a damn thing we can do until they find it. It's not an easy task. It takes time. I promise you every source both Ivan and I have is doing everything to track down Anna. What we need to do right now is find the other women and kill anyone who stands in our way." At that exact second, John's phone rings. The knotted cords in his neck relax when he looks at it.

The room is quiet when he answers.

"Cecily." The apprehension in the way he bellows out her name has every single man in this room on high alert. Hearts pounding. Guts wrenching. Waiting.

"Jesus, Charlotte. Slow the fuck down." He pulls the phone from his ear and pushes a button. Her frenzied voice is loud through the speaker of his phone.

"Where's Cecily?" John asks. It's one of the first times I've seen this man look distraught. His chest is heaving up and down. "She's hurt, but she's coherent. In fact, she's bitching up a damn storm, demanding for them to let her go. I'm assuming you're all together, so I'm not going to keep you. It's Anna we need to find. Cecily said she kept drifting in and out of consciousness, but she swears she heard someone mention Columbia. You have to find them." I see Ivan's chest expand at what I assume is relief at hearing his wife's voice.

I stare at a blank spot on the wall. This is an absolute mind fuck. All I heard is he took her. My first reaction is to hop on a damn plane and get to Columbia. To find her before he destroys her or worse. I shake the possibility of him laying a finger on her out of my mind. Listening to Charlotte rattle on about the things he did to both Cecily and Anna, I feel sick when I hear her tell him in a pained voice how Anna bargained with him, sacrificed herself in agreement for him to let the others go. God, she's brave. She made a deal with the devil to save those she loves. I should be proud of her, but knowing the man he is, I know he'll hold her to that promise. We have to get to her before he takes what he wants from her. Or worse yet, kills her. There is no way she won't fight him if he tries to... I won't allow my mind to go there.

"I'm on my way. Do you want to speak with Ivan?" I hear him say before he hands the phone to Ivan, who silences it then places it up to his ear.

"We'll find her, Dilan. Cain, you come with me." John moves his gaze from me to him.

"You got it," he responds.

"He beat the shit out Cecily. Left the three of them alongside a goddamn road. You find that motherfucker and you kill him." Ivan narrows his eyes. He's rigid. Cold.

"What about Jazmin? Where the fuck is she?" I look to Roan. His piercing glare is angered. His pupils turn black when he asks.

"Not with them. I assume she's home. Kill her too. Slice her fucking throat. I don't care how you kill her, just do it." One final glance at his furious eyes sets a fire under my ass.

"Ivan. I'm going with my son. It would make me feel better if you went with John, took a few more men with you in case this is some sort of sick trap he has up his sleeve. We leave nothing unturned. He's unpredictable. Unstable. I want this shit over with now. I'll call the hospital from the car and speak to my wife. Grab every damn weapon you can. Let's get the fuck out of here and kill that bitch before she finds out what the hell her brother has done. He's betrayed her, I know he has. She'll find him if we don't get to her first," my uncle says. His words are determined. Strong. I snatch my already prepared bag off the table, ready to go, while men remove rifles and ammunition out of boxes and shelves.

Ivan, John, and my uncle talk in hushed whispers at the end of the table. It seems we're all on the same page, ready to face what lies ahead. Most of these men have killed more times than I'm aware of. They know the drill, what to do. I hope this cunt is unprepared for her life to end.

"Dilan, Aidan, Roan." John gestures with his hand for us to join them. Without acknowledging them, we move to stand beside them and listen to what they have to say. My breathing becomes uneven when John turns his attention to Roan.

"I've taught you everything I know. You were trained to kill. Use it. Kill every goddamn one of them. Be smart." He pats him on the back. They waste no time in leaving. The door is slamming shut behind them.

"We can handle this, dad. You should go with them. Stay with mom," Roan speaks firm.

"Your mom is fine. If she weren't, I would know and I would go to her. This is just as much my fight as it is all of yours. She knows this. Now, let's go." His voice is confident, brief, and direct.

"I'm calling Alina to fill her in," Roan states as we climb into the back of one of the Suburbans. Hell, there must be five or six of them pulling out of the warehouse, heading for the private estate in Lloyd Harbor. Christ. It's over an hour's drive to reach his damn mansion. Thank fuck it's nestled back in the woods, far enough away that the neighbors won't hear a damn thing.

I stare out the window, vaguely hearing both Aidan and Roan talk to their women, while my uncle sits up front, waiting to be connected to my aunt. I'm not envious like I was before. I'm glad they have it. Found it. Feel it. It makes my blood boil and my teeth grind that some fucker thinks he's going to take away what I found and feel with Anna. Rage. I see rage. My insides roar like a motherfucker.

Grabbing my phone out of my coat pocket, I stare at the photo of Anna I took while she was sleeping peacefully after we made love. A smile is spread across her angelic face. She looks peaceful. "Hang in there, Anna," I whisper. My finger traces over her delicate features. She's one tough woman. If I weren't positive that I loved her before this, I'm damn sure of it now. She was born to be part of this family. Born to fight. Born to survive. She'll come through, I'm sure of it.

"Fuck," Roan cuts out. I lean forward from the backseat, wondering what the fuck is wrong now. "What?" Aidan and I say at the same time. "Alina is calling a doctor for Grace. She's hysterical. They're going to have to sedate her."

"Jesus Christ." Aidan looks from me to Roan. The stress from all of this is wearing heavy on our minds. "It's probably the best for her to be knocked out, especially when she finds out where he's taking her." My uncle turns around from the passenger seat in the front.

"They're not telling her," Roan remarks.

"Good call. You find anything out?" I ask, hoping he understands my meaning. I want to know where Anna is, goddamn it. There's no damn way they can make it in a what I presume is a private plane all the way to Columbia. They have to stop somewhere to refuel or some shit. Hell, I don't fucking know. There has to be a damn way to stop them.

"Making the call now. You three good to shoot and kill on demand?"

"Hell, yes," we all say in unison.

"Good. Let me see what I can find out."

I lean back in my seat and watch the city flash by. My palms start to sweat. None of us have killed a human before. We've come close several times. Especially Roan. He damn near killed his brother. The man who's half responsible for this shit. I know he would have finished it off if my uncle and John hadn't reached him when they did.

When a person is pushed to their limits, they're left no choice but to kill to protect those they love. They do it. They would die for them. I have no intentions of dying anytime soon. Killing, yes. Dying, hell no. I have a life to live with Anna, damn it. One I fully intend on living to the fullest.

I may be a morbid fuck for the barrage of visions rolling through my head like a horror movie of Jazmin slithering away on her belly, covered in blood, gasping and chocking as she tries to escape me. She's not the type of woman to beg for you to save her. Hell, if I were in her shoes, I'd ask to be put out of my misery. Her life is full of hatred and greed. It won't matter what she does in her lifetime, she will never be happy. Things will never be enough for her.

Everyone associated with this underground knows it. She has a web strewn from one corner of the country to the next. She picks and chooses her victims. Some she's killed just because she needed a taste of them; others because they double-crossed her family. Her ways of toying with them are sick. When I said before she cuts off their dicks, I meant it. She's notorious for it. But she slipped up this time. I'm going to make her pay for it all.

"We've got them." Something flickers across my uncle's face when he turns around. It's hard to tell exactly what it is, but for the first time since I found out Anna was taken, I sense a trace of hope.

"Where are they?" I glare at him. "On their way to Cartagena. Seems he has a home down there. The good news is, they're stopping in Miami." I'm not sure I'm following this shit. Roan seems to know, as he lets out the deepest laugh and throws his head back.

"Do you mind sharing what the hell is so funny?" Fucking idiot.

"That's the best thing I've heard since my wife said 'I do'." He somehow manages to get that shit out of his mouth while continuing to laugh.

"You see, Dilan, my cousin Lorenzo lives there. And I guarantee you he'll be waiting at the airport for them. Which means Juan Carlos will be captured." I still don't get it. How the hell are they going to get them in a damn airport?

"How the fuck are they going to ambush him in an airport?" Aidan obviously is thinking the same thing I am.

"It's easy to get someone when they've requested to land on your private landing strip on your private property." No fucking way. It can't be that easy. Juan's too smart for this shit. It's a motherfucking setup again. I know it is.

"I know what you're thinking, Dilan. But trust me on this. They'll get him. I guarantee it. And by the time we're finished here, Lorenzo will have them on one of his planes, heading back here. You'll get your revenge. Most importantly, you'll get Anna back."

He may think that, but something tells me it won't be as easy as he thinks. There's a pot of shit brewing. I can fucking smell it, and it stinks. No. This is all kinds of fucked up. No damn way he will be taken down that easily.

"Tell me you have them on lockdown, Digger." I hear my uncle's quick words when he answers his phone to one of his hitman. "What the fuck do you mean the place is empty? Jesus Christ!" His bark into the phone snaps my attention. I watch him gesture with his hands for Tony to pull off to the side of the road.

"Mother. Fucker. Yeah. Meet you there." He turns, pinning me with a hard stare.

"Jazmin knows her brother was setting her up. She's gone." That's not it though, there's more. Something he's not saying. I know what it is before he spills it out of his mouth.

"Fuck." I slam my fist against the hard plastic of the side panel, the sting and burn shooting up my arm. I glare, the darkness of my eyes scolding.

"She's known his plan all along. She's on that motherfucking plane." I'll bet my goddamn life on it.

CHAPTER SEVENTEEN

ANNA

The only thing comfortable about this entire situation is the soft plush chair on this plane. The thought of being trapped in this tiny vessel with nowhere to go with him frightens me. He could do whatever the hell he wanted to me, and there wouldn't be a damn thing I could do.

I fastened my seatbelt per his instructions the minute we stepped inside, not paying a lick of attention to the fact he sat down right next to me.

As soon as the plane takes off, I close my eyes, wishing I was anywhere but where I'm headed. Dilan. I wish I were with him, his strong muscular arms holding me tight, my head resting on his chest, listening to his heart beat under the palm of my hand while tracing the outlines of his tattoos. My wish carries into a dream that I fight tooth and nail to not succumb to. I give in as I'm hummed to sleep by the strumming of the plane's engines. Or maybe it's because my body is mentally exhausted. Either way, I feel the man I love. I see him vividly and colorfully in my dreams.

His chocolate brown eyes are dark as he thrusts inside my body. "God, Anna. You feel so good. This tight, sweet pussy was made for my cock. Look at the way it takes all of me in. Watch us, Anna. Watch your pussy coat my cock." His voice is deep. His thrusts are deeper.

"Oh my god, Dilan. I need you to fuck me harder," I scream. The need for him to take me hard consumes me. I'm his. I want him to fuck me. To own me. To drive into me hard. I lift my head to watch my body take in his magnificent cock. Stretching me. Opening me up to him. We watch together. Our eyes focusing on the same spot of my pussy. He slams in hard. A moan escapes my mouth. Nothing has felt as good as he does. Nothing ever will.

"You want hard, baby? I'll give you hard." He pulls his cock out, grips me by the hips, and flips me over onto my stomach, then shoves my face into the pillow, jerks my ass in the air, and slides his big cock into my wet pussy. Taking control. "Fuck," he roars as he slams into me the way I want him to. Deep.

"Oh god, yes." My hips buck back into him, which seems to drive him mad. My ass is on display. I would gladly give him that too if he wanted it. I want to give him everything. To please him in any way I can.

The only sounds in the room now are the grunts and groans coming from his mouth as he fucks me hard and fast from behind. My lips are parting; my pussy is quivering. I'm loving every minute of the way he takes domination over my body.

"Is that what you wanted? You want rough, Anna? You want it all, your greedy pussy had me once, and now you can't get enough, can you? I can't get enough of you either. I will never get enough. Every inch of this body belongs to me. No one else. No one will touch you, fuck, or make love to you, only me. I may be fucking you, pounding my cock into your pussy, but Anna, always know this, no matter how I take you, hard, fast, slow, I'm always loving you. I love you, Anna. Now, tell me I'm the only one who will have this pussy. Who will have your heart. Say it!" He slides his hand up my stomach, pinching one of my nipples, tweaking until I'm coming all over him while I scream his name.

"Say it, damn it!" My breast misses him the minute he releases it and grips a hold of my hair, pulling my head back and running his tongue up the side of my neck.

"Fucking say it, Anna." His tantalizing tone has me screaming once

again what he wants me to say. "No one will have me but you. I'm yours."

"I'm yours too, Anna. Always."

I'm awake, and I'm very much aware I'm not in that seat anymore. I'm not dreaming of the man I love. He's not fucking me, making love to me. And I did not tell him I was his. Nor did he tell me he was mine.

I'm handcuffed to a bed. Panic arises; the hair on my arms and neck is standing up. He's watching me. I can feel it. God, no. He cannot take me like this. I cannot have him touching me. I'm Dilan's.

"Why are you doing this?" My voice is barely a whisper. I stare up at the top of the ceiling of the plane. The room is pitch black, but I know he's in here.

"How did you get me in here? Did you drug me?" I say weakly. "Carlos. Answer me, you sick fuck." I lurch forward, only to come to a jerking stop. Shooting pain rockets up my arms. I begin to whimper, until I hear that voice.

"Anna, sweetheart, wrong Carlos." My eyes go wide with fear at the sound of her voice. They blink in a rapidly frantic succession when she flicks on a light. I close them tightly and lie my head back down. This has to be a dream. A nightmare. She cannot be here. Not in my dream with Dilan. This is impossible. I struggle against my restraints, my head whipping around. I need to wake up from this horror-filled hallucination. I try to push off with my feet, but they won't budge. They feel like they're weighted down. Sensationless. I feel nothing.

"You know," I see her moving alongside the bed. The hum of the plane, the power of the force has my ears popping. Fucking shit. We are on the airplane. She is here.

"I can see why my brother and Dilan are infatuated with you, Anna. You really are a very beautiful woman." One slimy finger traces down my cheek. I'm repulsed. Between her and her brother, I will never be clean again. And hell, her voice. It's nasal, nasty, and downright sickening. My skin burns from her touch. I feel it everywhere.

"Fuck you. What did you do to my legs, you fucking bitch?"

Numbness. I feel nothing from the waist down. My god, she is a cold psycho killer who has me trapped in the air.

That finger presses over my mouth. Gently. She shushes me like a baby. Her unabashed eyes are clinging to mine. Then her fingers sprawl out wide, her hand tight across my chin, yanking me to face her, her pointed fingernails digging into my skin.

"How brave of you to sacrifice yourself for your family. That's more than I can say for my brother, wouldn't you agree?" She tilts her head to the side as if she's waiting for me to answer. I say nothing for a minute. Then I let it all loose. The fucking bitch needs to hear it. Whether it sinks into her head full of fucking air or not. Stupid cunt.

"Your brother hates you. All men hate you. You're a cunt, a bitch. You're like a damn rash that won't go away. A piece of fucking shit." If I'm going to die, then by god, I'm going out my way. I'm not shoving my mouth up my ass. Nor am I'm going to lie here and let her try and belittle me or scare me. She can go fuck herself for all I care. I'm sick of people coming along and thinking they can just take and do whatever they want. That the world owes them something. That my family and I owe them. What the hell happened to humanity? To people minding their own damn business? These people make me want to kill them all. Fucking lowlife scum.

"Do you feel better, little girl? Those are some big words coming from a tiny, little thing. Maybe I should show you how much of a bitch I can be." She's so calm. The woman from the other night is long gone. The more I study her, the more I would guess she's on something. Some kind of drug.

"I can't stop you from doing a damn thing, can I? Seems this is the only way you know how to fight, by tying people up or drugging them. Should I be thankful you've managed to accomplish both with me?" I taunt her more.

Her beady, squinted eyes lower down to within an inch of mine. Her face is made up flawlessly. Her nails are scouring through my skin, burning me.

"It's easy to get what you want when you drug someone or something. I hated wasting them on my deceitful brother. But hey, a woman has to do what she has to do. It's a shame Juan drank the last bit of scotch while you were sleeping. Made my plan simple for me really." She brazenly speaks.

I must be a damn good actress, because I notice the very second she does that I'm not afraid of her. I'm afraid of dying. I have my entire life ahead of me. He's searching for me now. They all are. Not a single one of them will stop until they've killed her. She won't be missed. Not by anyone. She's loathed and she knows it.

I should have sold you. That's what I should have done. Made you some man's slave. Had him take you, fuck you, and then turn around and share you with all of his friends. That's what I should have done. Would have made a pretty penny too. Blond hair, big tits. I can change my mind, you know? I can sell you, make you live the rest of your life in hell. Would you like that, Annabelle?" Her tongue darts out, licks up the side of my face. This time, I cannot help but gag and choke. She is repulsive. She draws away from me, her stench lingering in the air. My face feels like someone dripped acid on me. She really is poison.

"Fuck you!" I scream through my gagging. Loud. This bitch is fucked up.

"I've had enough. Shut your trashy mouth. For a beautiful woman, your mouth is filth. Maybe I should shut you up with a bar of soap shoved in your mouth." I roll my eyes. Where does she come up with this shit? I'm more a lady than she will ever be.

"Please do. Rub the soap all over my face before you shove it in my mouth and any other part of me you've touched with your filthy hands. Cleanse me, Jazmin. Although I think I need more than a bar of soap to get the unpleasant smell of you off of me."

"You're a witty bitch, aren't you?" If she didn't have me tied up and half paralyzed, I would show her just how witty I can be by killing her reeking, smelling ass.

I'm about to tell her to fuck off again when she starts in about her brother.

"My brother couldn't have planned this out better for me. He was due to die anyway. Now, I kill you both. And your boyfriend. He'll be dead soon too. They all will. I control my own destiny, Anna. Now, before we land back in New York—" "New York?" I say. What the hell is she talking about?

"Yes. New York. You stupid woman. We've turned back around. I have no desire to go to Columbia, not yet anyway. Maybe once my job here is done, who knows where I'll go. Maybe I'll change my mind about Dilan and take him with me. He does have a glorious cock, doesn't he? Thick. Long. God, you fucked it all up for me. He was the first man I was really looking forward to fucking in a long time. But you. You got in my way. People who get in my way pay dearly." I will not show her how terrified I am of dying. She is psychotic. A sociopath.

"You're delusional. Dilan used you as much as you used him. The only way you can touch a man's cock is by drugging them. Men loathe you, Jazmin. The sight of you makes them sick. You wouldn't believe the way Dilan thanked me with his cock for saving him from you. Now, where's your brother? Did you drug him too? It must be a lonely world for you, knowing that even your own brother hates you so much he left you behind to die." Her eyes turn cunning. The upper half of my body becomes tight. I don't care. I've come this far with defending my family, I will not stop, no matter if she kills me right here. She may think I'm stupid, but she is damn wrong. She's the stupid one. Her plan will fail this time. I can bet my life on it. Well, not really, she may kill me before we land. Though, the more I think about it, the more I know she won't kill me. Not here. These sick people get off on killing people while making the ones they love watch. Their minds are so twisted with jealousy, envy, or whatever gruesome revenge they think needs to be paid. Crazy people do crazy shit. But I know those men. They will stop at nothing to make sure I'm found and that she is good as dead.

"Where's your brother?" I ask again. Surely, he's here somewhere. Oh god. The thought of his dead body right outside this closed door has my stomach rolling. I couldn't care less if he's dead, really. But right now, if what he said to me is true, he's all I've got. "Carlos!" I scream.

I feel the plane taking a nosedive, descending, as she climbs off of me, standing above me, staring, the rage contorting her features into the true nasty wench that she is.

My skin struggles to close up its pores to protect my flesh when her rage turns to pure fury. She moves to the door, opening it wide. There's not a sound coming from out there at all. Good lord, did she kill him? It wouldn't surprise me if she did. I mean, he was basically throwing her into a grave. She outsmarted him and got to him first. I couldn't care less, really, who kills whom. I want them both dead, preferably before she kills me.

She's quick to return, then climbs back on the bed, straddles me at my waist, and dips her head to within an inch of mine again. I'd give anything to be able to vomit all over her.

"You conniving little cunt." Burning bursts through my cheek, streaming its way the side of my face as she openly palm strikes me, my head snapping to the side. I buck hard to get her off of me. I'm blinded by the sting her unexpected blow created. She repeats the same thing on the other side. Only this time harder. The sound of skin slapping splinters throughout the small room. My first instinct is to cry. My face is on fire, but I will never surrender to her brutality. Never let her see satisfaction when I know damn well that is what she wants. She's craving her ability to try and break me. It won't happen. The love I have for to many people is a hell of a lot stronger than the hatred I have for her.

The love they all have for me will overrule whatever the fuck she has planned. She better have a damn army waiting for her when we land. Salvatore and Ivan have resources everywhere; she will never get away with any of this. It wouldn't surprise me in the least if they don't already know where we are. Where we will land. I hope I'm there to witness one of them blow her damn head off.

"You fucking scared bitch." I lurch my head up. "That's all you got?

Don't even bother to answer that. Like I said, the only way you can complete your missions is by drugging people. And do you know why? Because without those drugs, you are nothing but a weak, spineless whore. A woman who is scared to actually fight someone with capabilities of defending themselves. You're weak, Jazmin. Do you hear me? Weak. Pathetic. Are you on drugs now? Are you an addict? A junkie right along with a heartless bitch?"

I've never seen someone turn into a devious monster when my blurred vision slowly returns to normal. She's out of control. Her eyes are livid. Her stone-cold heart is showing how black it is. Her fists attack my face and my chest in a frenzy. She's losing it, and so am I as I sustain blow after blow to the side of my head. My brain is rattling. "Fuck you, you stupid, naïve fucking bitch. You know nothing. You're not of this world, and yet you think you know me." She grabs hold of my hair in a painful grip that has me yelping out, while I'm fighting the worthless fight to have my hands freed.

"I've lived in my worthless brother's shadow for too long. Done all of his dirty work for him, and this is how he pays me back? Oh, no. You are all going to suffer. Every goddamn one of you. Especially you," she seethes.

The plane comes to a sudden halt as it lands. It's obvious by the way Jazmin releases her grip on my hair she had no clue we were close to landing. Her body jerks backward. I scream in what has to be the worst pain I have felt in my life as it zaps up my arms to the tips of my fingers when she grabs a hold of my arm to gain control of her flapping body. Something cracks in my shoulder. My arms are twisting, struggling on their own to support both her and me.

Once the plane slows, she gains control of herself, ignoring my sobs I can no longer hold in. She laughs when she uprights herself, straightens her clothes, and adjusts her sleek ponytail.

"Well, it seems we've landed. Lucky you. For now anyway." She makes her way to the door. My ability to see her is construed. My body is hanging half off the bed. Fatigue mixed with the desire to let myself go, to pass out, to do anything to fight through the sharp throbbing distress my body is going through, hangs on by a sliver. My eyelids droop. The last thing I hear before I succumb to sleep is her heavy breathing, the last thing I smell her overindulged perfume. It's pungent. And her scheming voice when she says,

"Let's see how long it takes lover boy to get here when he sees this?" I see a blinding light in my face. Then I'm out, fading into nothing.

CHAPTER EIGHTEEN

DILAN

Jesus Christ. I mean, what the hell is going to happen next? This hatred and anger I feel towards these motherfuckers is fueled by the second. I'm tired of playing games. I want this shit done. To get out of this maze they have us in. It's like you turn right, thinking you're headed in the right direction, only to come to a dead end. Then you head back the same way, only to find out it wasn't the way you came. Left, right, straight ahead. My head is about ready to fucking explode.

Who knows what the hell is happening on that damn plane. What the hell the two of them are doing to her. Or worse, what Jazmin is doing. That bitch has outscored everyone. She's clever. I'll give her that. Always one spot on the game board ahead of us all. Fucking cunt. She needs to be gone. Dead. Burned like the witch she is. All this time, I wanted to be the one to kill her, now I don't care who does or when. I want her gone. All of them. Prison holds nothing on the hell I'm in right now. I would gladly have Miguel beat me to death repeatedly just to know Anna is safe.

Before I have the chance to retrieve my phone from beside me to stare at her beautiful sleeping form, it lights up next to me on the seat. I glance down at the text from an unknown number.

"Fuck." My pissed-off mood scours through the SUV after picking up my phone and seeing what's on the screen.

Anna. Cuffed to a bed. Small cuts on the side of her face. Her eyes are closed. Hell, what have they done to her?

"Jesus Christ. What now?" Aidan and Roan turn around to face me. I shove the phone over the seat. I can't look at her like that, strapped down to a bed. More than likely drugged. They've obviously beaten her or worse. My stomach coils.

"Sick fucks," Roan remarks. The phone dings again.

"What is it?" I ask, not sure if I want to know.

"It's Jazmin. She said if you want to see Anna, then meet her alone. Here, dad. She is one fucked up bitch." He hands the phone up front. My uncle lets off a slew of swear words, shaking his head in what I know is anger and disgust.

"She's setting up her own death. Surely, she knows you will not show up alone." The vehicle slows, then does a sharp U-turn, while my uncle gives directions to wherever the hell this mess is leading us to.

I listen as he makes several calls, instructing everyone to meet us somewhere in Jersey.

"Jazmin. This is Salvatore Diamond. You will listen carefully to what I'm about to tell you. If you don't, you'll be dead before we get there," he announces, then hooks the phone up to the Bluetooth. Her devilishly laughter erupts throughout the confines of the small space. I cringe.

"I see Dilan doesn't take orders well. I want him. I couldn't care less about you, Salvatore. It was my brother who was obsessed with destroying you. Now, either he comes alone, or I kill his little whore." Her words snap me in half. She knows nothing about the type of person Anna is. The thought of her laying a finger on her has me flying out of my seat, leaning over so I can tell her exactly what I'm going to do to her.

"You won't kill her. That's not your style, Jazmin. You want me to watch you. That's not going to happen. What is going to happen is this. She's going to watch me kill you. The game is over. Lady Luck was never on your side. You'd have to be a lady for that to happen, and you definitely are not one. In fact, nothing has been on your side. Not even your brother from what I gather. It must sting like a bitch to know you've not only been outsmarted but also betrayed. Left to die. Ouch." I cast my gaze over to Aidan, who is biting his damn lip. The fucker is itching to say something.

"You all take me for a fool. As you can tell, I've outwitted my brother. I'm here, aren't I? I have your whore, don't I?" This is stupid. Obviously some sort of trick question. Of course, she has her. The dumb bitch. I grind my teeth. Fist my palms to hold my shit together from her calling Anna a whore. Instead, I let out a boisterous laugh. Her anger seeps through the speakers.

"I'm not sure what you find funny, Dilan. Do you think this is a joke?" Exhaling roughly, I tell her exactly how much of a joke I think this is.

"It's not a joke, it's a pitiful story. One I find intriguing, actually." I'm toying with her, and she hates it. I notice a shadow of a grin curve up Roan's lips out of the corner of my eye.

"Pitiful for whom. You? Your whore is trapped, Dilan. Tied to a bed. Oh, and I almost forgot to tell you the best part. She's paralyzed from the waist down." My eyes boil over in anger. What the fuck did she do to her?

"This conversation is over, Jazmin. This is fair warning. You'll never see us coming. I promise you that." My uncle hits end. My eyes lock on my cousin's. Agony is written all over his face. Who knows better than him the power that a drug can do to you? He witnessed that shit firsthand. Repeatedly.

"She's fucking lying, man. She wants you to panic. To think she has done something to Anna. Don't believe a word that bitch says," Aidan says. It's a risk I'm willing to take that she hasn't hurt her any more than what I saw in the photo. Who the fuck knows with her? My chest physically aches. Christ almighty, this is like one of those crazy ass carnival rides you can't wait to get off of. Spinning out of control. Jerking you one way, and then the other. Fucking shit. When will it stop? When will I find her and get her back? This fucking game is killing me.

I'm done. So fucking done with this.

And where is Juan? Hopefully fucking dead. That sure as hell would make this a lot easier if she polished off her piece-of-shit brother. Then all we have to do is kill her and the army of slaves she more than likely has waiting for us. There is no way Juan's men would turn on him. Not as long as they've worked for him and hell, I can't imagine there isn't a single one of them who can stand that wicked cunt. She's ruthless. How she's lived this long beats the hell out of me. A witch's black cat with nine goddamn lives is what she is. Well, fuck this, her nine lives are over. It's time for her to burn. Sizzle into a scattered mess of charred bones.

"Pull over here. We're walking the rest of the way," my uncle demands. We pull over about a mile up the road from the landing strip. I grab my bag and follow everyone out into the vacant lot. Ivan and everyone else pull in behind us. Roan fills everyone in on what we've learned. When he's done and everyone has seemed to calm down from the news, Ivan delegates. We listen as he instructs everyone to make sure they kill.

"Leave the plane be. Roan and Dilan, get in there. If you're not out with that bitch in five minutes, then we come in after you. I'm done. I want this over with. That bitch is busting our balls, and she needs to go. I've always loved the thrill of stalking my prey, but this bitch I've had enough of. None of us are her goddamn gophers. I want her gone. She has stunk up our city long enough. Let's go."

We walk in the dark. There are no streetlights on the vacant road. Nothing but woods. The pitch blackness drives us forward. About a quarter mile away from where Jazmin said they were, we split up. We all know she has men surrounding her, waiting to strike first. Roan and I dive into the woods, running. Guns drawn. Twigs snapping underneath our feet. This is bound to be a bloodbath. I would be a liar if I didn't say I wasn't nervous. I am. Doesn't stop me from moving forward. My love for Anna outweighs the nerves. It overrides everything. That's how strong I know it is. A bond that will not be severed. Not by the evil that seems to think they can possess it and steal it away.

"Jesus fucking Christ. She has a goddamn army out there." I squat down at the edge of the woods next to Roan, thankful for the foliage of overgrown grass and weeds to shield our body.

"Of course, she does. Knowing her, she promised money she will never deliver, because every single one of them are going to die." Roan laughs deeply but quietly. "You know, I'm not one bit scared to pull this trigger. As sick as it sounds, I'm looking forward to it." I tip my chin in his direction. The playfulness in his attitude changes right along with mine. This day was bound to happen; the day when we would kill. No better day or time than right now.

We see our men then, combing the area like ants searching for that last crumb. Crawling through the tall grass. Undercover. Undetected. Roan and I move, slithering like snakes ready to strike. Like a pack of wolves aiming, converging from every direction. Fuck, the adrenaline pumping through my veins could give me a fucking hard-on. The desire to kill for my woman has me thirsty like a damn vampire for blood. I can feel the energy floating off of Roan the closer we get. The engine in the plane is shut down, however, every exterior light is on to the point it's almost blinding. My uncle was right. She's left these men out here to die. Brought death right to her. She must want to die. To end her miserable life of loneliness.

One of her thugs puts up a hand, silencing everyone. He trains his gun in the direction facing away from us, and fires several shots. I have no damn clue if anyone is shot. I aim my gun and fire. Even from this distance, I watch the idiot who fired first drop his gun and put his hand up to his neck. Blood bubbles out from his wound. He drops to the ground. Roan fires next, nailing one in the head.

It all happens quickly, precisely, as we watch her fucking idiots fall to their deaths one by one. Blood covers the asphalt of the runway, the stench of death filling the cold air. Shots are being fired in every direction.

I force my mind to focus on getting inside of that closed-up plane. Right when I'm ready to run, Roan pulls out his phone and places it to his ear without saying a word.

"Right." His one syllable has me confused.

"Dad said to go. They have us covered. We're going to have to draw her out somehow. You know she won't come out now. She's on a suicide mission. Fucking nuts, man."

"She's not going to come out. I'm going in. I'll blow that damn door open if I have to."

"Well, someone is." He points in the direction of the plane. My brows furrow. "What the fuck?" I whisper confusingly. The door slowly opens. I see no one. Only a soft light reflecting from the inside. I'm going. I need to get in there.

"Dilan, wait!" Roan roars from behind me. I'm not fucking waiting. She's in there. I can feel her, and I'm getting her the hell out of there. I drop my bag and my semi-automatic the minute I pull out a knife and a Barak SP-21 pistol. This fight is far from over. In fact, to me it's only begun.

"Here I am, you fucking bitch. You want me. Come at me, you worthless cunt!" I scream once I reach the plane. I'll keep shouting. She's surrounded by her death, and she knows it.

"Dilan." I hear a low, agonizing, deep moan calling my name from inside the door. I slide my body under the plane until I hear it again. Louder this time. Anguish belting out for my help.

"Juan. Jesus Christ." I watch his body drop, landing a few feet away. His breathing is shallow, labored, and gurgling.

"She's locked in the back bedroom. That's all I know," he croaks out before I watch his conscious body try and suck in the last bit of oxygen he can.

He can die. I don't care.

Hitching myself up on the wheel well, I lean into the door then jack myself up and over, gripping tightly to the frame. I pull myself up, and pull out my gun, unlocking and aiming. I scan the disaster of the inside.

There is blood everywhere. Jesus, she obviously stabbed Juan. More than once by the looks of all the blood. Christ.

I notice a short hallway to the right. She knows I'm coming. I can feel her fear. I pray to god she hasn't done anything more to Anna. I'm not sure what I will do if I kick in this door and Anna's beautiful face isn't the first thing I see. Alive.

I spin, my gun ready to shoot, when I hear someone behind me. It's Roan. Goddamn him. Stupid fucker. I sternly look at him then signal for him to check the cockpit. I don't trust this bitch at all. I know the pilot is dead, but she seems to be full of surprises. Hell, she could have him ready to fire this fucker up and take off, for all I know. She's basically committed suicide by fucking this shit up all to hell. I tuck back around and kick the door open.

"What in the hell?" The scene before me has my blood boiling.

"Hello, Dilan. Nice of you to join us. She bleeds well, don't you think?" Jazmin tilts her head to the side, but me, I cannot take my eyes off of Anna. She is covered in blood. Her clothes are all shredded, half hanging off of her naked body.

My god. What has she done? I take one step forward. The only thing on my mind is getting to Anna, helping her, making sure she's breathing. Then shit happens so fast I'm not sure which way to swing my head. Behind me, where a gun fires, or keep looking forward, where Jazmin lifts a knife in the air over the top of Anna's stomach.

I keep my head forward, because the bullet blows Jazmin's head clean off of her body, her matter splattering everywhere. Fuck, that shit is gross as hell. And quick. Jesus god.

"Fuck. Call an ambulance, dad," I hear Roan yell from behind me. I move then, dropping my gun on the bed and placing my hand to Anna's neck for a pulse. It's light and faint, but she's still breathing.

"Towels! Anything to help stop the bleeding!" I shout at Roan, on edge.

I'm afraid to move her, but god, we have to do something. I race around to the other side of the bed, ignoring the crumpled, dead body on the floor. I lift up the edge of the blanket on the bed, covering Anna's body. I blot. Hell, I have no idea what the fuck to do.

The string connecting my brain to my heart damn near severs as it dangles by a thin shred of hope, tugging fervently to spring back in its rightful place. I've never been so scared in my life.

Roan comes in with a handful of towels. Both of us are working together to stop the bleeding by pressing gently on her wounds. Most of them appear to be surface cuts, yet she's still bleeding everywhere like a stuck pig. And why the hell is she not waking up?

I'm losing control over my mind. Its bleak, black thoughts are taking control. I cannot lose her. Not like this and not to the hands of a vile cunt, whose brains are now splattered all over the place.

"God, no. Anna." Aidan appears at the door, his eyes distraught as he takes in her weakened body. "She's so cold," I mumble. My lips quiver. My heart won't quit pounding like a builder hammering the fuck out of nails. It feels like it's trying to beat its way out of my chest. My thoughts of losing her run like a fast-flowing creek through my shallow mind. Images of her lifeless, dead body flash before my eyes, while I stand here helpless, watching how life performs its next play in this fucked-up downward spiral of a losing battle of self-control.

"I need to see where she's bleeding from, Dilan. You have to move. Hold her hand. Talk to her." Aidan calmly switches positions with me. I drop to the floor, grabbing hold of her icy fingers.

"Baby. I'm so sorry. I love you, Anna. I hope you can hear me. I need you. You're it for me. We haven't even begun, sweetheart. You're a fighter. You fight this. Come back to me." God. I'm not good at this shit. I rattle my words off rapidly. Hopefully, she can hear me.

I hear Roan and Aidan talking, but I have no idea what the hell they are saying. I bring her hand up to my lips, kissing them, mumbling against her skin. I cry. My warm tears sting my face, dripping out onto her fingers.

I look up when I hear the sirens howling in the distance. Tears are flowing freely. I will never forgive myself if anything happens to her. I'll admit that to anyone, whether it makes me a weak man or not. I need her, and I'll be damned if I won't stay by her side the entire time.

"Hey." The paramedics are here. We need to step out and let them get her. "You can ride with them. Dad and Ivan are outside. The cops are here, Dilan. We have to go." Roan places his hand out for me to take. I look at her pale face. Her body is covered with a blanket. I must have numbed out for a minute. Hell, I have no idea. All I know for sure is my cousin saved the woman I love. He killed for me tonight. I'm sure they all did.

I shouldn't be thinking of how quick and easy this all was to kill her, not with Anna lying limp and hurt. I can't help it though. Why in the hell would she bring us here, only to know we would kill her? She's gone. That's all I really care about. Screw the reason why.

It's a bloodbath all over the place. There are dead bodies everywhere. How I missed them before I have no clue. All I really care about now is Anna. I don't even bother to ask if any of our men were killed or injured. Or what the fuck happened to the man who helped start this war. Juan. I hope that fucker is lying here somewhere in the blackest body bag they have. This world will be a much better place without his sister, and paradise if the two of them are gone.

"I'm sorry, sir, but you cannot ride in the back. We need room to move. We're taking her to Saints." He slams the door in my face. I start to protest, only to be drawn back by a firm hand on my shoulder.

"Go. Ivan and I will be there as soon as we can. We have to handle this. Geoffrey should be pulling in with a vehicle any minute now to take you." My uncle grips my shoulder in a firm squeeze, his sympathetic eyes matching his voice.

"Take him, Roan. We've already called Alina. They will be at the hospital as soon as they can. I have a mess on my hands here. Now, go." He releases me with a pat.

I'm numb. The fear of losing her is so strong that bitter tears form in the back of my throat. I hold them in, saying nothing. Hearing nothing. Seeing nothing.

CHAPTER NINETEEN

ANNA

I'm dead. I must be. I feel no pain. I see no dark. I see nothing at all. Hear nothing at all, except the voices in my head. My mom crying. Alina's sweet and calming voice consoling. I hate hearing her cry. She's mourning over me. The only thing I'm thankful for is she won't be alone. She has a man who loves her, who will take good care of her, help her get through this.

I'm drifting, floating toward a blinding light. The strangest sensations migrate through my veins. The light is bright to the point my eyes sting. I squeeze them tight. That's when I hear a deep voice from beside me. Feel my hands wrapped in warmth. My dad welcoming me maybe? No. It can't be. He's in hell for the things he has done. I have to be in heaven. My light is white. Bright. Hell is a combination of red and black. Dark.

"Anna, baby. It's been three days since I've seen your eyes, your smile. Open them, sweetheart." Dilan. He sounds so strange. Almost as if he's struggling to talk. He's hurting, over me. Is he here too? I don't understand any of this.

"Dilan." There's silence. I hear nothing. God, have they gone? Did I imagine hearing them?

"She said my name. She's coming around." What did he say? I'm not dead, or maybe I am and the last thing I remember is the sound of

Dilan's voice.

"It's been five days, for god's sake. They said no brain damage and her cuts were all minor. Why in the hell won't she wake up?" It's Dilan again. God, I could listen to him all day long. Not like this though. Not worried. Not angst-ridden. I want happy Dilan. I swear he said three days before. Now it's been five? Again, can someone please explain to me what in the hell is going on?

"Dilan. She suffered a blunt force to her head. On top of that, she's still in shock. I promise you she will wake up. She needs time." Good, Alina. Keep him calm, and when you're done talking to him, can you please crawl inside my head and help me? I need to talk. I need to see him. I have so much to say. The first being I love him.

My mind reels as flashbacks enter. The abyss of walking on a tightrope, hanging on to that long pole for balance to not scream or show the agony she sent me into while she cut me. God, did she cut me, everywhere. Small, tiny cuts with a knife. Her horrible threats, her destructive words telling me how she was going to ruin my body, mutilate it before Dilan showed up. I remember it all. Every hateful word, every slice across my stomach. And my legs, they still feel numb. My entire body is numb. I'm alive though. I know I am. I need to wake up. I want to know if that woman is dead. If I can live freely now. If Dilan is freed from his past. If his revenge is over.

"My sweet girl. It's been a week, wake up." Mom. She sounds so much better than the last time. She's hopeful. No more crying. Now it's been a week. The days are adding up. It seems my mind has a damn mind of its own, if that makes sense. It won't listen to me as I try and will it to wake. To look my loved ones in the eyes, to make sure everyone is safe.

"Your face is healing. Just a few bruises are left. You have a big knot on your forehead, but that's it. You can wake up now." I'm trying, mom. I miss you.

It's dark. So dark. My eyes blink, water leaking out of them. "Hello." Is that me talking? Good lord, my voice. It's croaky. Rustling. I hear movement from somewhere.

"Anna." I smile in the dark. That deep, velvety voice. "Dilan." My head hurts badly, however, no amount of pain will stop me from turning it toward him. Even though I can't see him, I feel him. Everywhere.

"God, baby. You've given us all quite the scare."

"Sorry." I scrunch up my nose. It hurts like hell to talk. My throat is dry and scratchy.

"Is she dead?" I somehow grate out, praying this is not another dose of the voices I've been hearing for who knows how long now. Please, let this be real.

"Yeah. Let's not talk about that right now. I need to get someone in here to look you over." He lifts my hand. I may have moaned from his moist lips touching my skin. He's real. It's him. I'm awake. "Don't leave me," I say, terrified. "I won't. Not ever. I promise. But I do need to get someone in here. I'll be right back." My body shakes. I'm cold. I want him back. Preferably holding me in his arms, his warmth radiating off of him and slowly spreading across my freezing body.

"Well, Anna. You've been through a lot. I'm glad you're awake. My name is Doctor Hamilton. I'm going to look you over while we talk. I need you to tell me how you're feeling first. And if you have any pain anywhere?" This doctor has the sexiest voice I've ever heard for an older man. Deep, dark, and mysterious. My eyes have adjusted to the bright lights as I watch him read my chart where he stands at the foot of my bed.

I clear my throat. "Just my head. The rest of me is kind of numb." I look from him up to the IV drip.

"And you will be for a few days. I've administered small amounts of morphine through your IV to help with the pain." I'm fully alert now. I have lots of questions, not so much for the doctor though. I need to know what happened. How they rescued me, and what happens now. Are they dead? Are we safe?

"I'm going to slowly put this bed down flat. I'd like to take a look at those cuts on your stomach." He smiles brightly. "Sure." He then lowers the bed. I grimace slightly. Not from pain. From tightness. I feel tight everywhere.

"You're healing well. A few of these have stitches, and you will have some scars. You're a very lucky woman, Anna."

"How many scars?" I'm not a vain woman, but the idea of having to look at the scars every day for the rest of my life to remind me of what she did has me on edge.

"A few dozen at least. But they are small, Anna. Some of them may fade in time." I close my eyes, not quite ready to look at them, when he lifts my hospital gown, proceeding to do his job.

"Is my family here?" I question. "Yes. Your mom and your boyfriend are in the waiting room." God. I can't wait to see them. It was dark when I woke. I'm desperate to see them both.

"Everything looks good. The lump on your head has gone down. If you keep up the good work, eat, and can walk, you should be able to leave here in a few days." Walk? Thank god.

"I'm not paralyzed then? She drugged me." I feel like crying when all the memories surface. The things she said, the things she did.

"Yes, she did. With a muscle relaxant. You're fine, Anna. Trust me." His eyes speak the truth. I'm confused though.

"I don't understand. How was I able to move and feel my upper body but not my lower half?" This doctor radiates confidence as he stands beside my bed, explaining in his doctoral verbiage how my legs were numb, but how the adrenaline pumping through my veins as well as my brain functions made me think I could feel things I possibly did not. It's all so mystifying. All I know for sure is, as I wiggle my toes and bend my knees, I can feel them now.

I should be grateful she either knocked me out or I passed out on my own after she started cutting me, so I wasn't able to watch or hear her when she diced me up more. I hope I never see a knife again in my entire life.

By the time he leaves, letting me know he will be sending someone to my room to help me try and walk, I feel like for the first time since I arrived in New York, I may have a chance at happiness, with Dilan. First though, I need answers before I can begin to think about anything else.

That chance is short-lived by the time I return back from a short walk up and down the floor of the hospital, my mom insisting on helping by pushing the IV alongside of me. We don't have the chance to talk about any of this at all, because the minute I step back into my room, Calla and Stefano are waiting for me. By the looks on their faces, this isn't a visit I'm going to like. Dilan isn't here. I need to know where he is.

"You look great, Anna. Thank god everything turned out okay," Calla tells me. Her eyes say something else though. Everything is not okay, especially with Stefano here. I mean, I know the man, but for him to show up with Calla means something is wrong.

"I feel great. I'll feel even better once I get out of here. Where's Dilan?" I ask, confused.

"We asked him to give us a little privacy. We need to talk about a few things with you. I apologize, Grace, but formalities and all, legally I need you to step out unless Anna confirms it's all right for you to be here." She's in lawyer mode now. This is far from a friendly visit.

"Of course she can stay," I tell her as I make my way back to the bed. My legs are weak and my stomach is tight. Once mom has me situated, I look to the two of them, prompting them with my eyes to let me know what the hell is going on.

"The police need to speak to you. I don't know how much you know about your rescue, but hell, Anna, it wasn't pretty." Stefano brings two chairs next to my bed then sits in one, while Calla sits in the other. Mom is sitting on the other side.

"I have nothing to hide. Juan kidnapped me. Planned on taking me to Columbia. There's not much I remember after getting on that plane, except for what happened with that bitch. Exactly what in the hell is going on? Is someone in trouble?" I keep my attention trained on Calla.

"Yes and no. Which is why we're here. No one has been arrested yet, but with sixteen dead bodies, including Jazmin's, and two families such as ours right in the middle of it, this has spread like crazy. The community wants answers, the cops want convictions, and until Juan wakes up—" I gasp when she says his name. I thought he was dead. Jazmin sure as hell made it sound like he was.

"He's alive. Everyone thought he was dead that night. Unfortunately, he is not," Stefano chimes in.

"I wish he were," I call out. Calla leans in and places her hand over the top of mine. Her expression is full of hope, yet full of dread too.

"Yeah, well, we all do. But to save Ivan, Salvatore, Roan, Aidan, and Dilan's asses from going to prison, we need him. He needs to confess to kidnapping you, Anna, or all five of them are in trouble. Big trouble. That's why we told the cops who demanded to speak to you the minute you were cleared from the doctor to talk, that we would be here when they arrive. The vultures are here. Hell, they've been lurking around for days. They need your statement."

"Bring them in. Those men came to save me, we all know this. I'll tell them everything. Then they can go arrest the man who started it all." It's the least I can do to return the favor to my family and the man I love for saving my life. The best part of this entire situation is knowing that Dilan will finally be able to live his life with the satisfaction of putting the man behind bars who made his life hell. Nothing could please me more.

I'm drained by the time I've talked to the cops. My mom sits quietly beside me, crying when she hears the things I remember. The entire time they questioned me, I felt like I was on trial. The instant I answered one question, they would turn around and ask another. Thank god both Calla and Stefano were here. It didn't matter how many times I told them I had no damn clue what happened when all hell broke loose, or if I witnessed Jazmin being shot, they kept coming at me. Finally, Calla said 'enough'. They knew good and well I was drugged, and cut up, and out of it. I'm not dumb, they were looking for any hole in my story they could find to arrest our men. To put them behind bars. There isn't one, and they damn well know it. Well, there is, they murdered a hell of a lot of people. But the bottom line is, they did it to save me. Every last one of those men and Jazmin can rot in hell.

I remember praying to god that Juan would die. And now, as I sit here, waiting for Dilan after my mom helped clean me up, all I want to do is sleep. I'm exhausted. More out of worry for everyone than anything else. Finally, after arguing with my mom to leave, let me have time with Dilan, she left.

The door creaks open. The moment I see him, my insides flip. Dilan looks as tired as I feel. His brown eyes are fatigued. He looks so worn out.

"Are you going to stand there all night?" A heavy ache grows in my chest, until he finally speaks.

"You look beautiful. I can stand here all night just looking at you, unless there's room in that bed for the both of us." I sure hope he isn't imagining right now what I'm thinking. My body may be battered, but my pussy is aching for him.

His brows quirk up and his lips twitch.

"I would love nothing more than to sink inside of you, Anna. But not here. Not when we have to talk. What I mean by talk is, I want you to come home with me. I need to be the one to take care of you. Plus," his eyes never leave mine when he shuts the door and strides to the side of the bed. I lean into his touch when he places his hand on my cheek, then slopes down to where our mouths are almost touching. "I love you." His expression is tender, warm, and even though we're in a hospital, it's appropriate. Call me a dreamer, because yes, I've dreamed of this moment with Dilan. Many times. And over the course of this entire situation, I began to fear I would never hear him say it, that I wouldn't be able to return it. To tell him we have such a long way to go. So much to learn about each other.

But when fate literally makes two people collide, no matter what the circumstances are, no matter how much time passes by, your heart telling you you've fallen in love takes precedence over everything. Some may guard it, some may throw caution to the wind and live carelessly, go with the flow. Dilan and I haven't had the chance to explore anything outside of being trapped in one place or another. I know with every breath I take, with every fight I've fought, that we were meant to be together.

"I love you too, Dilan." When his lips touch mine, this kiss means so much. It's another first kiss, sending spine-tingling shivers from my neck to my toes. It's deep, emotional, and promising that there is more to come. My hands slide up and around his neck, towing him in closer. I shove the need to cry from an emotional overload deep into the recesses of my mind. I'm done crying.

We deserve to be happy. All of us do. By the time we pull away from each other, our breathing is irrational. My lips are tingling. God, I love kissing him. I will never be tired of it, but really, there is so much we need to talk about. I need to know how he found me, and if the reason behind why he looks so run down has more to do with his worry for me or the fact that the police have been interrogating the hell out of him. Or both.

I adjust my body in the bed and slide over as far as I can go, then roll over on my side. They've reduced my pain meds slightly. Therefore, I hold in the struggle to be comfortable. If he notices, he doesn't say anything as he glides in beside me. Carefully.

"Thank you for finding me. And for killing her," I whisper. "You don't need to thank me. It's my job to protect you and not because I'm being paid to do it. I'm not living my life without you, Anna. No goddamn way. However, it wasn't me who killed her. It was Roan." "Well, at least the bitch is dead," I say. I'm not sure how she died, and I really don't care. Not now anyway. As long as she's gone. That's all I give a shit about.

"What's happening with the police? I told them everything I could. They're persistent." I lean in closer to lay my head on his chest. I need to be close to him.

"They are. They'll do everything they can to try and put as many of us away. Unfortunately, the man who started it all is battling for his life. They could arrest any us of at any time, but with all of us telling the truth, there's not much they can do until he wakes up. We just have to pray he fucking tells the truth himself. He has enough against him by kidnapping all of you to put him away for the rest of his life. The fucker needs to confess. I'm not sure how much more evidence they need. You would think with what happened to you, with the shit they found on that plane, the drugs, and all kinds of shit with Jazmin, they had proof enough we did what we had to do to save you. But we're a crime family, baby, so they'll look for any reason to take us down," he expresses as if he doesn't believe they'll come out unscathed. That they will be arrested. He has doubt. I sense it.

"Dilan. Calla told me how many dead men they found. Surely, they have to see this was all plotted by her. I won't allow them to make this look like a war between families that you started. The evidence is everywhere. We had to stay in a damn hotel, for god's sake, because they threatened us. Roan and Alina didn't go on their honeymoon. Juan has too much against him." I lift my head and tilt it upward to look into his eyes. It's dark, but the glow from the light in the hallway gives off enough for me to see his smile reach all the way to his eyes.

"You amaze me. You know that?" he says with sincerity. "Yeah, well, you amaze me too. We've all been through hell. It's about damn time we bury that hole to hell and start living. I'm sick of it. We deserve to be happy. I'm not about to let Juan or the cops take you or anyone else away from me." I mean it. They may be criminals, but this family does not go out and start a war with others. For the past few years, it's been one thing or another. I'm sure there will be more. It's true what they say about love conquering all. There is so much love in this family. Every single one of us would do whatever it takes to save each other. One way or another, if Juan does pull through this, he better do the right thing. Like Dilan said, he's going down anyway. He started this war; he should be the one to end it. I'll do whatever it takes to make sure he does.

"No one is taking me away from you, or you away from me. Not tonight or ever again," I tell him. If that bastard doesn't tell the truth, I'll find a way to make sure he dies even if I have to kill him myself.

CHAPTER TWENTY

DILAN

Anna is a strong woman. She's positive in a way that makes me love her more, if that's possible. In spite of all she has been through, she lies here, snug in my arms, driven to not let her past interfere with our future. She's mentally tough. A believer. Which is more than I can say for myself right now.

The fucking cops have done all but arrest us. They've been trying to play everyone's testimony against each other. Our stories don't line up. He said this. He said that. It's bullshit and they know it, the way they're trying to break us down, to put all the blame on me. My past record shows I had contact with Juan and his goddamn savages. I couldn't care less if the fucker dies. It sucks hardcore that I need the prick to live. I know him. He will fight this. Lie through his damn teeth. Make up some shit story to try and weasel his fucking way out of this.

I'm so damn tired. Tired of it all.

"Visiting hours are over, Mr. Levy." A nurse opens the door to the room, peeking her head inside.

"I'm not leaving. I just got her back. You may as well shut that door and pretend I'm not in here," I whisper, careful not to wake Anna, who is lying in the crook of my arm.

"Only if you promise to let her rest. She's not completely healed." *Well, no shit, lady,* I want to say. I don't. Instead, I nod and wait for her to shut the damn door.

"She's a fighter and lucky to have you," she says while smiling down at the two of us cramped together in this tiny little hospital bed before shutting the door.

She's right about the fighter part, but wrong about who's lucky. It's me who's the lucky one.

She stirs slightly, her eyes blinking open. God, I want to drown in her. The way she feels up against me, with her sweet smell, there isn't a damn thing I wouldn't do for her.

"Did we wake you?" My fingers start to stroke her hair.

"It's all right. I'd much rather be awake than sleep when I'm with you," she says through a yawn.

"You need to rest, and hell, me sleeping in this bed has to be uncomfortable as hell for you," I tell her but make no attempt to move.

"This is the most comfortable I've been since the last time we slept together. Don't even think about moving. Besides, you heard the doctor. Most of those cuts are almost healed. And I have something else on my mind." I arch a brow when she shifts her leg over mine. Her hand traces down my stomach, past the waistband of my jeans, and cups my dick.

"Anna," I warn. "Dilan. You've spoiled me with this masterpiece. I'm ruined for life. I may be in a sex-starved coma. Now, shut up and let me take care of you. Trust me, I'll let you reciprocate." Fuck me. She slides her hand up and shoves it inside of my pants. My dick is already as hard as frozen cement. The minute her fingers wrap around him, causing him to strain in the confines of my jeans, I reach down and undo the button, lowering the zipper to give her all the room she needs. I'm not going to deny a hand job from her. I couldn't care less where we are.

"Fuck, that feels good. And a sex-starved coma, huh?" I chuckle, but immediately stop when her hand starts pumping my shaft. I'd give anything to watch her crumble and fall apart right now by sliding my fingers into her tight pussy. But I'm afraid to hurt her. "Yes. I'm sure I'm going to need sex every day for the rest of my life." She's damn near panting. I'm damn near close to coming all over my stomach and her hand. I close my eyes, enjoying what she's doing to me. But when I feel her hair on my face and her breath whispering across my skin, my mouth attaches to hers. Hungrily. She moans, and that is my undoing. My digits move to the cheeks of her ass, digging in. I consume the inside of her mouth with my tongue, tasting every bit of her. She tastes like pure fucking innocence, like golden perfection. And this incredible woman pumping my cock like a goddamn expert is mine. Finally with me, where she belongs.

Here she is, cut and bruised, but still wanting to take care of me. God, I love her. Not for this. Even though I would love to be with her right now, sex of any kind was not on my radar. Not until she brought it up. But fuck me, the way she is pumping my cock in her hand has me aching, my balls tightening. My need to come overconsuming every god-blessed thing.

"I'm going to come, Anna. Hard. And I swear to you that when I latch onto your sweet pussy, I'm going to make you beg me to fuck you every day for the rest of your life. And when I do, you'll be left in a sex-*induced* coma. No more sex-starved. I will fuck you, and make love to you, and worship every part of you," I rasp when I release her mouth. And then I come. Christ, do I come.

"I can't believe I just did that," Anna exclaims from her spot beside me in the bathroom. She's washing her hands in the sink, while I'm cleaning my cock and stomach with this damn hard-as-brick, brown paper towel. I feel like I'm running sandpaper over the tip of my cock.

"Yeah, well, you did. You sure your head feels okay?" She turns and gives me a dirty look. "My head is fine. It's other parts of my body that need taking care of."

"Hmm." I grab her bare ass and bury my head in her hair. "I'll take care of all those other body parts. Right now though, you're going to bed." She whimpers but doesn't protest after she dries her hands, and I help guide her to the bed. Once she's settled in, I move to the other side, climb in, and drape the flimsy sheet and pink thin blanket over us.

She settles her head on my chest. My arm wraps around her. I fall asleep soundly. Just like her, the last time I really slept was when she was with me. Right where she's supposed to be.

"Good morning. I love this unkempt beard you have going on, but the clean-shaven Dilan is sexier." She runs her finger down my unshaven jawline and then over my lip. The only time I've left here was to shower in a cheap hotel I rented a room in up the street. My dad went to my apartment and packed clean clothes. There was no way in hell I was traveling very far from here. Not until I knew she was awake and that she was going to be okay. I stretch. My damn back is tight. I'd give anything to be able to take her home today.

"It needs to come off," I tell her truthfully. It's itchy as all fuck. How the hell Roan can stand this all over his face beats the shit out of me.

"You could keep it until I get out of here." I stare into her eyes. They're telling me to shut up. I can feel her warmth pressing against my thigh. Her nipples hardening.

"You're hurt, woman. Are you crazy? The way I'd bury my face into your pussy, you'd be screaming and writhing all over this bed, ripping those stitches out, and then I'd never get you spread out on my bed, where I can really bury my head between your thighs." God, the thought of it has my dick doing a wakeup call. He's blaring like a crazy fucker.

"No. I have a sexy, tatted-up man in bed with me. One I'm crazy about. One who makes my pussy ache, and one whose disheveled and untidy beard could do wild things to ease my ache. So if that makes me crazy, then I guess I am." Fuck. She rubs her sweet, hot cunt up against my thigh. My dick is aching, as much if not more than her pussy. And he got off last night.

"I'll leave it until you're better. Then you can come all over it. Until then, I want you healed, so I can take you home. I don't know about you, but I need my own bed. Preferably with you in it."

"I feel fine. I don't know why I can't leave this damn place." I give her a stern look. Even though she hasn't shown me her wounds, I can feel them taped up through her thin gown.

"You're saying that because you want my tongue and then my cock inside you." I am teasing myself as much as her. God, I'd give anything to be wrapped around her. To show her how much I love her. To take all the shit away from both of us. For it to be just her and I.

"Maybe. But I do feel fine. I can heal at home, with you."

"You can heal at home with me." We both whip our heads in the direction of the door, where Grace stands, not looking very happy at all with seeing me in bed beside her daughter. I care about Grace. She apologized for her reaction when I told her about Anna being taken, until I had to tell her to stop. There was nothing to forgive her for. But this, this I'm not bending on. This is a decision between Anna and I. I'm not asking her to marry me, for Christ sake. I want to take care of her. It's what I do. It's what we both want.

"Dilan, would you mind giving me a few minutes with my daughter, please?" She questions me sternly. I could be a prick and tell her no, that the three of us should talk this out, but Anna speaks up.

"That's a good idea. Do you mind?" She pushes herself up, her face wincing slightly. "Not at all. I'll send the nurse in here on my way out." I kiss her briefly before I get up then snatch my coat off the back of the chair and say goodbye.

I hit the nurse's desk on my way by and let them know she's up and around. I ask them what she can eat and drink. It isn't until I get to my truck that I turn my phone back on and notice I have several missed calls from my uncle and Roan. Shit.

I scrape the snow off of my truck, hop in to warm my hands, and connect the phone to my Bluetooth. Then I hit Roan's number. I'm sure they are both going to tell me the same thing. Either the fucker has died, or he's lied through his teeth. Whatever it is, I sure as hell have a bad feeling it isn't good.

"What's up?" I ask as I back out of my parking spot.

"You must have stayed at the hospital all night with your phone off. How is she? Heard she woke up," he remarks.

"She did. Acts like nothing happened. She's hurting, but fuck, man. She looks good." He exhales with what I know is relief.

"That's great. You holding up okay?"

"I'm good. Something tells me that's not why you're calling. What the fuck is going on, Roan?" I pull into the morning traffic and head toward the hotel. My plan to take a quick shower changes the minute his next words come out of his mouth. "Dad received a phone call. Juan is awake, and he's demanding to see you."

"Jesus Christ. I don't want to talk to that fucker. I can't believe the son of a bitch even survived," I seethe. No damn way am I talking to that motherfucking piece of scum. I'm not a fool. He wants to bait my ass, and he will. There's no telling what he'll say or my reaction to it. He kidnapped the woman I love. All of this is his fault as far as I'm concerned.

"I'm not doing it. Have the cops talked to him yet?" I turn into the parking lot of the hotel. Fuck him. I'm cleaning up and taking care of Anna. He can fuck himself.

"I'm not sure. No one is at this point. All I know is, I want this shit done and over with. This asshole has prolonged my honeymoon long enough." For once, I agree with him. All along, I berated myself with guilt over this situation. It was never my fault. It was always Juan's, and now it needs to come to an end.

"I'm not going. What I am going to do is clean my ass up, go back to the hospital, and take care of what's mine."

I'm in and out the door to my hotel room in twenty-five minutes. I tossed all my clothes in my bag, praying like hell Anna can be discharged tonight or tomorrow. I want normal. To be able to take her out. Show her off. Spoil her in the way she deserves.

Hell, I even managed to trim down some of this shit on my face. No way in hell am I having this coarse hair mark Anna's beautiful skin. At least not if I can help it. Once I have my mouth on her pussy, there's no telling what I will do. I may turn into the primitive Neanderthal I look like. Go all virile on her taste and do exactly what I told her I would do.

Latch the fuck on until she's begging for my cock to replace my tongue. I wanted her before all this happened. Now that's its damn near over, I want her even more. I'm desperate for her.

Twenty minutes later, I'm strolling up to her room. Only to be stopped by her doctor and a police officer. What the hell is going on?

"What the hell do you mean she isn't in her room? Where the fuck is she?" I yell at the doctor then slam the tray holding three cups of coffee on the nurse's station. I'm pissed.

"Mr. Levy. Calm down. There are other patients on this floor, and the use of profanity is not necessary. She's safe." I give her a what-the-hell-do-you-mean-safe look? And if she thinks saying the words hell and fuck are using profanity, she hasn't heard shit if someone doesn't tell me where Anna is and why Brutus The Beefcake is standing here, glaring at me like he wants to beat my ass.

"Dilan. Thank god you're back. I was coming back to get my phone to call you." I turn around to the sound of Grace's voice. She looks scared.

"Is she all right? Did something happen to her?" My voice is panicky. Christ, did she hurt herself from last night and not tell me before I left?

"She's fine. I swear those damn drugs have made her lose her mind though." She stops in front of me to catch her breath.

"Where is she?" Instantly, a heaviness gathers around us like a deathly, destructive storm is about to hit.

"Well. Right after you left, Salvatore and Ivan showed up. Of course, we thought they were here for a friendly visit, you know, to check on her and all. Which they did, by the way. But god, Dilan. That evil man Juan requested to see you both. They took her to see him." What the fuck?

"You have got to be shitting me. Isn't this against protocol or some shit? That bastard kidnapped her. She's a witness, and you all let him see her." I turn to the cop who I still don't understand why in the hell he's even here. Every damn cop around here should be in that room with her.

"Normally it is. The District Attorney, along with Ivan, Salvatore, and two of their lawyers, as well as an FBI agent and Anna, is in that room. They're just waiting for you."

CHAPTER TWENTY-ONE

ANNA

Anger is a healthy response to the way I feel right now. A nurse has wheeled me down the hallway and into the elevator alongside Calla, Salvatore, and Ivan, as well as the DA, a few police officers, and god knows who else, as we now make our way out of the elevator and turn right into a confined area, where a few cops are standing outside a closed door.

I should feel scared, but I don't. What I do feel is anger and resentment towards the man I am about to face. The man who has taken so much away from all of us.

The minute my family showed up in my room, I knew something was up. The looks on their faces told me this was not only a visit to make sure I was doing well, but also a visit to prepare me to see the man behind this door.

Why the hell he wants to see me I have no clue. No one does.

Is he going to lie? And why the hell does he want to see Dilan and I together? This shit is fucked up. Not right at all. Maybe the piece of shit is going to die, and he's finally going to confess on his deathbed. Who the hell knows?

"What the fuck is going on?" My head spins in the direction of Dilan's deep, out-of-breath voice as his long strides bring him closer to us.

“Mr. Levy. You need to calm the hell down before we go in there. Do you get me?” The DA scolds him like a child.

“Fuck that. I’ll calm down when I know what the hell he wants and if the piece of shit tells the goddamn truth.”

“Dilan, please.” Calla stands beside him, placing her hand on his arm. He keeps his focus trained on me, his expression and body easing when he sees I’m okay. I know him. He’s searching to see if I’m in pain.

“I’m fine. Can we get this over with, please? He can’t hurt us anymore.” My hand reaches out to take hold of his.

“You sure?” he questions. I nod.

“Dilan, let’s get this done. We have nothing to hide. Not a damn thing.” Salvatore extends his arm out and grips Dilan in a loving gesture on his shoulder. Then I watch both Ivan and Salvatore extend an unpleasant look in the direction of the DA and the cops. The tension in this hallway has me more nervous than talking to the man in that room.

“Lead the way.” Ivan gestures with his hand toward the door while looking at the DA.

This is so out of the ordinary, the victim having a meeting with the accused. I don’t know what to think, or why in the hell the law would agree to any of this.

The DA steps forward, pushing the door open. All of us follow him inside. I gasp, my eyes dislodging from their sockets, when I see Juan lying in his bed. He’s pale. His eyes are barely making an effort to stay attentive. Wires and machines are everywhere. This man is half dead, and he’s demanding to see us.

“Mr. Carlos.” A man who I assume is a doctor stands next to the bed, leaning over him, his words now soft and low that I cannot hear what he is saying.

“Excuse me. May we get this over with? As you can see, my client is still healing. She needs her rest,” Calla squawks out in her lawyer voice, demanding and ruling.

“I’ll ask the questions here, Mrs. Bexley, not you,” The DA pipes in, demanding, tossing his arrogant authority around like he’s the damn boss. Crooked asshole. He's probably on Juan's payroll. Justice for victims, my ass. I can't stand him. The way he looks down at all of us like we're trash. Like he's hoping to nail us to the wall. He's a damn piece of shit, like the man lying in the bed.

"I beg your pardon," I say, rather rudely, not giving Calla a chance to speak at all.

"Excuse me?" His brows quirk.

"Anna." Salvatore throws me a warning glare along with his stern voice. I ignore them all.

"No. Don't any of you 'Anna' me, or excuse me, or say you're calling the shots here. This man kidnapped me. His vile sister tried to kill me, and you have the nerve to bring me here. To make me face him. I disagree with all of you. It's *me* who has the right to talk, to tell the truth, and it's *your* job," I point at the DA and the cops, "to listen to me. Whatever he has to say is more likely a lie. While all of you have been trying to blame those who saved me from dying, the one to blame for all of this is right there. None of us should even be here." My breathing becomes short as a dozen or so pairs of eyes are glued to me. I don't care. This is my show now. Not anyone else's. I will sit here until this fucker tells the truth.

I stand, all eyes still on me. "Anna, stop." Dilan grabs my arm softly.

"No. That includes you too, Dilan. You all want the truth. Well, here it is."

Bravery consumes me, zings itself out of thin air. Maybe it's because the closer I approach this animal, whose eyes are half-lidded, whose skin is pasty white, and whose hands are cuffed to the bed, the more I realize he is unable to touch me, to feel his slimy hands on me, or hear his threats. Wherever it comes from, I welcome and own it.

It's quiet. Extremely so. The only sounds in this room are the beeping of the monitors and the beating of hearts, wondering what the hell I'm going to say.

I'm surprised no one is stopping me. But why would they? This entire situation of me being anywhere near this man is so far out of protocol with the legal system, I would laugh in their pitiful faces if the freedom of those I love weren't at stake. They need to give answers to the public. Those who want to bring crime off the streets. To feel safe. Well, fuck that shit. The one man they should loathe and be afraid of is right in front of me, looking at me with spite and revenge in his almost dead eyes. He's a fucking fool. Every word he said assaults me in one cold swoosh of air.

How he always wins. Gets what he wants. How he would kill. I'm going to drive this last nail into this self-absorbed son of a bitch's coffin with the one thing he told me to never speak about in his presence. I doubt he will care. He's a liar. A thief. His appearances on the outside makes him seem like a man, when in reality, he is nothing but a lurking, poisonous, shit for brains animal who attacks women. Weak. Asshole. And I want him to die.

He fucking lost. He's lost it all. I really hope when he does die, he rots right alongside his buddy Royal Diamond. They belong together in hell. Burning. Continuously. For these people, who think they can control the lives of others, to kidnap and damn near kill people who have done nothing to them, even the depths of hell are too good. And his sister. Maybe they can make up down there for fucking each other over. Or better yet, they can repeat slaying each other. See who has the upper hand down there. I don't care what hell does to them, as long as they live it. Eternally.

"I'm not going to waste my time telling you what I think of you," I say with acrimony. The sight of him has my knees knocking together. Not out of fear. No way. It's straight up hatred.

"What I am going to say is this. You've lost everything. You're going to die with nothing and no one to give a shit that you're dead. You're all alone, until you meet your sister, who's already rotting." I temporarily halt when he makes an attempt to try and lift his lips into a smile. His nose and forehead pinch, revealing his pain. Good. Let me dig more.

"I hope you die. I really do. Do you know why? Because while you're dead, I will be living my life with Dilan. A real man. A man I love. A man who I will give all of me to freely, and a man who loves me back." If I didn't know better, I would say a flash of sadness sweeps across his face, briefly. An indication that I got to him by saying Dilan's name, a name he told me to never bring up again in his company. Did he honestly think he would ever compare to Dilan? The thought of that makes me sicker than I already am by standing so close to him. By being anywhere near this thing.

"Anna. Listen to me." Soft-spoken, strained words escape his mouth.

"For the last time, Juan, you don't owe them anything." I look up to a man in a black, pinstriped suit. His jet-black hair is slicked back. He looks exactly like a gangster from the 20s. A true crime asshole, who has his shady hands on Juan's shoulder, while his eyes are on me, trying to intimidate. Fuck him too.

"I'm dying, Roger. Let me say what I need to say. I'm halfway to hell anyway," Juan speaks, not once taking his gaze off of me.

I swallow hard, fear flowing through my veins faster than any of the drugs I have been given during my stay here. If he lies, I will kill him and send him the rest of the way to his final destination.

"Whatever it is you have to say, make it quick, Juan. This room smells of trash. The filthy fucking kind," Salvatore informs him.

"Someone put this goddamn bed up. I need to see them all." Immediately, a nurse or an orderly I never noticed before appears by his side, along with a young doctor, whose nametag I caught a glimpse of. Juan cries out when they slowly adjust his bed and body into a position where he can now see everyone in the room. God, the man looks like he could die at any moment. He better say what he needs to and now, damn it.

"I'll confess to nothing, except kidnapping. That evidence is apparent. Besides, I'm dying anyway. I have nothing to lose." He begins to cough. His words are barely audible. He tries to lift his hands to embrace his pain. All we hear is the rattling of the cuffs against the steel frame of the bed.

"Isn't that enough of a confession?" My head whips around, my eyes narrowing on the DA. Surely, it has to be enough to help everyone get off on whatever bogus charges these assholes are trying to pin on my family.

"It is as far as saving you. This information is nothing new to us. What I'm after is an answer as to why I found a dozen dead men, stolen guns, and a dead pilot, along with several other people, dead spread all across my city, Miss Drexler. Men I believe were killed for no reason at all. Other than revenge." This pompous asshole is out of his ever-loving mind. How in the hell he was elected is beyond me.

"You have nothing on us, and you know it. This has to be a fucking joke. Exactly what kind of game are you playing here?" Ivan moves to stand right in front of the DA. I have no clue what the man's name is. He told me, but I sure as hell don't remember anymore. The only name I want to call him is a damn fool. A liar.

"What I'm trying to do is clean my streets. To get rid of the garbage that loiters on every corner. The drugs you sell. The guns you steal. You people control this city, hell, you control half of the damn world, and it's about time someone takes charge and swipes my streets clean."

"Then I suggest you bring in a sweep cleaner, because it doesn't matter what the hell is said in this room. None of it will stick, and you damn well know it. You have nothing on us. Not a crumb. Not a morsel to save the life of a rat. A rat like you. Let me repeat Ivan's question. What kind of game are you playing?" Dilan asks.

"No game, Dilan. I know none of this will stick in court. You're all here on a last wish from Juan. Rest assured, I will find a way to bring all of you down. Every last one of you."

"Good luck," Ivan remarks sarcastically.

"Enough. This isn't a courtroom. This is a hospital. Against my better judgment, I agreed to let you all come in here. Please, take your arguments elsewhere. I have a patient to attend to here."

"A patient? More like a dead man walking. Except the fucker can't walk. He's crawling to his death," Roan responds angrily to the doctor.

"I told you these people care less about me dying than I do. Let them say what they have to say. It doesn't change a fucking thing or the fact they better all watch their backs for the rest of their goddamn lives. I will haunt you. Come for you when you least expect it. This plan of mine may have been mangled up by my crazy sister, but rest assured, I always have a backup plan in place. Always." Juan begins to cough profusely now. His eyes are watering, his expression suffering from the pain he's in. As morbid as it sounds, I would love nothing more than to stand here and watch him gasp and suffer until he takes his last breath. However, the mere sight of him makes my skin burn to a degree that repulses me.

"As you can see, we're all standing here very much alive. Very much a family. Whatever you have in store for us, we welcome it." Dilan takes the steps necessary to reach my side. " If you're done tossing out threats from your fucking grave that we all know will never reach the surface, I'd like to take my lady home." Dilan entwines our hands. His strength is comforting. His touch alone makes me feel safe from Juan's idle threats. I have no doubt he has a second-in-command. Someone who will come after us. If that day comes, we will fight them too. Together, standing strong.

"I have one more thing to say," Juan speaks up. His head is bent, his eyes looking down at our adjoined hands.

"We don't want to hear it. Save it for hell, motherfucker." Dilan tugs lightly on my hand, indicating it's time for us to leave. But I can't move. My feet are rooted to the floor. I know I should leave with the rest of them. I see them walking out of the room out of the corner of my eye. They're all done here. Finished. Why is it that whatever he has to say I feel like I have to hear?

"Anna, let's go. It's over, baby. Let this piece of shit die."

"I may be dying, Dilan, but rest assured, even after my death, I will get my revenge."

"Just like Ivan said. Good luck. Now, go to hell, Juan."

"You make me sick." I yank my hand free and grip the side of the bed. My fingers burn as I twist them around in a tight grip to hold me back from choking the last bit of life out of him.

"It's been one thing after another with you. You have nothing left. You've lost." I bring my face down close to his. I've got one last thing left to say, then he can die.

"It seems Dilan wins the game of revenge. Not you. You set him up. You tried to destroy him for reasons you're too scared to admit. Even on your deathbed. I get it. I really do. You made this too easy. Revenge is bitter; it leaves a bad taste in your mouth. Now that you and your sister are gone, all that's left is your bitterness turning into something sweet. Your death."

CHAPTER TWENTY-TWO

DILAN

I damn near fall into the chair once we reach Anna's room. The thought of having to leave her even for one damn second has me telling the DA to go fuck himself. The lowlife traitor. He'll stop at nothing to try and bring us down. If he were doing his job correctly, legally even, that would be one thing, but he's not. No. We all know how corrupt he is, pretending he cares about the citizens of this city. Fuck him. He's as low as the rest of us. Dirty fucking lawyer. How the hell he was elected beats the shit out of me.

And Juan and his idle threats. Fuck them all. His empire will be burned to the ground before they even make a sliver of an attempt to come after us again. I know my family. They will do whatever it takes to make sure nothing like this happens again. It doesn't matter who tries. I'd give anything to kill him with my bare hands. Drain the last bit of life out of his useless body. Break every bone in his hands for touching Anna. ANY. DAMN. THING.

"I'll be right back," I tell Anna once I have her settled in bed. She looks like an angel, my angel, as she straightens the covers across her legs, her head resting on her pillow, her skin glowing as brightly as the deep colors of the sun.

"Do you think he means what he said? That we will never be safe from his madness?" I give her a sly smile. One that lets her know no.

That we're untouchable at the moment. That everyone will keep their noses clean, staying low for quite some time, until this shit blows over. I won't sugarcoat shit for her though. She needs to always watch her back.

"I have no damn idea. I don't care anymore. All I care about is you and me right now. Danger is a part of our lives, Anna. It is what it is." She looks up to me with those deep blue eyes I could swim in for days, floating peacefully. Suddenly, an idea pops into my head. One I need to talk to everyone about and hope they all agree.

"Go talk to that asswipe. Make sure all of you are clear. My mom should be back with our food anytime." I lean down and lightly brush my lips across hers. My stomach is growling. I'm fucking starving. Thank god Grace was pacing back and forth outside of Juan's room when we left. The minute she saw Anna was okay, she damn near lost it. Good thing all the ladies were standing outside with her. Including Cecily, who I owe so much to for being strong and telling us everything.

"I love you," I tell her. It's the truth. I'm a better man with her.

"I know you do. I love you too. It's over. I choose you. This life. I knew there would be danger along with it. I will always worry about losing you or anyone else, but none of that comes close to walking around for the rest of my life without you in it. I'll always be by your side. No matter what." Her voice is barely a whisper. I lean into her soft hand, her fingers trailing across this scruff on my face. I cannot wait to bury my head between her thighs and watch her come while I fuck her sweet pussy that will only ever be mine with my tongue. I need to get my ass out of here before I actually do it right here.

"We have enough food here to feed this entire floor," my aunt says as they all stroll in, carrying trays and bags, puling me away from this woman who I will never go a day without making sure she knows what she means to me. The aroma damn near does me in. My mom and Grace fuss over Anna. She's going to be fine. She's in good hands until I return. I need to get this shit done. Not only am I starving for food, I'm also starving to get Anna out of here and in a bigger bed. Christ, I want her in a bad way.

"Thanks. Let me meet them. Get this done. Keep her safe," I say as I walk out the door. "Always, Dilan." Cecily looks at me, her eyes saying what our mouths haven't yet. 'Thank you and you're welcome.' God, I love these people. Every one of them.

"Is the fucker dead yet?" My hands begin to anxiously twitch. I need to know if Juan is rotting yet. I ask Roan when I walk into a room on the bottom floor. Looks like a conference room of some sorts. I wonder how the hell anyone managed to get this room. I guess when you're the DA of a big city, you can ask for whatever the hell you want. Lucky for us, he won't be accomplishing his dream to bring us down.

"Haven't heard. Don't care. As long as he dies eventually. Apparently, he's had a few surgeries to try and repair the damage to his lungs. They keep filling up with blood. Hell if I know. Fuck him," Roan speaks honestly. Aidan damn near falls out of his chair from laughing, and the prick of a DA clears his throat, trying to gain our attention. Fuckhead.

"We're here. Get on with it," Ivan commands.

"You all think you're smug, don't you. That you can do whatever the hell you want and get away with it." Every damn one of us shrugs.

"You have nothing on us, and you know it. We did what we had to do to save Anna. You have phone records. The threats from both Jazmin and Juan. They started this. He kidnapped my wife. My family. Damn near ruined my son's wedding. Tried to poison my nephew. You know all this, you son of a bitch, and yet you've kept all of us hanging by a damn sliver of a thread, while we try and put our lives back together, and for what? To make your stinky ass smell better?" My uncle stands and places his hands on the table, leaning in to face the man who for the past few weeks has made our lives hell.

"You may have won this time. But I will bring you down. Every last one of you." This slob of a man snaps his briefcase closed, and without another word, walks out the door. I inhale, welcoming the smell of the antiseptic stench of this hospital. It smells like a rosebush compared to him.

"Well, that's it. Killing those fuckers was a hell of a lot easier than we all thought. One simple mistake is all it takes to destroy. To kill. To seek revenge. They fucked up in a way they will never be able to take back. Let's pray they all rot in the sewers of hell. My family has been through enough. This senseless act of avenging a vendetta against us has other families in an uproar. Ivan and I have assured them all it's over. We will continue to run our businesses the same way we always have. Sticking to our own, minding our ways, and helping out when needed. We will also make sure Juan's threats are just that, threats. And you, my son, I better not see you for a damn month." He shakes his finger in Roan's direction. My uncle speaks loud and clear. He wants him gone. To finally be able to get his honeymoon he rightfully deserves.

"As for the rest of you, get the hell out of here and go to your families. I don't want to see the rest of you for weeks either." He then turns to me, his eyes filled with unshed tears. In all my years, I've rarely seen my uncle like this. We've won. Our vendetta is over.

"Dilan. You take that beautiful, strong woman of yours and get the hell out of here. There are way too many average things in this life. Anna is not one of them. She is brave, loyal, and deserving of you as you are for her. I could not be more proud of you. It's over. Those years you lost will never be replaced, but with a woman like her by your side, they can be forgotten. Peace can now fill your heart." He cups my face as he speaks, his eyes showing me more than what he's saying. I'm choked up. But the hell I've been in isn't over. Not until Juan is dead. My uncle senses it when he stares me down. If this man in front of me can read my mind, he's more of a master manipulator than I've given him credit for. I mean that in the best way possible. I need him to manipulate, to throw his weight around. If anyone can do what my eyes are asking him to, it's him.

He nods, the acknowledgement written clear as day all over him. And I damn near know this will be the sweetest fucking way for me to get my revenge. To deliver all of us from the contamination that has polluted our city for way too long.

"One hour," he leans in and whispers in my ear. I nod. I have one hour, then my hell will be over.

"There you are," I say to my dad the minute I leave my uncle and Ivan. He's leaning up against the wall, his hands in his pockets, with a smile on his face. I haven't had much time to talk to my dad. My focus has been on Anna and this bullshit with the damn DA. I've been mostly talking with both him and my mom on the phone.

I know what he's doing here now and why that smile that resembles mine is written all over him. He's accomplished what I asked him the minute I left Anna's room. Fucking hell. I'm a grown man and I want to throw myself into his arms right now like I did when I was a kid. Thank him for being a great dad. For loving me. For all of it.

"You're taking off tomorrow afternoon. You sure they'll let her out of here by then?" If they don't, I'll explode all over their pasty white lab coats.That's how desperate my desires are to get her alone. It has nothing to do with how much I need to fuck her. It has everything to do with spending time with her. To know every morsel there is to know about the woman I plan on spending my life with.

"She knows her body better than anyone else. She wants out of here." My dad hands me the keys to one of my favorite places in the world, my fingers circling them tight in my hands.

"You're a good man, my son. But you're a dead man if you don't say goodbye to your mother before you go." He chuckles. "I'll call her. Besides, it's only a week. Thanks for this." I look up to him. He snatches me right into his arms. I return his embrace. I love this man who has no idea half the shit I actually do. Well, maybe he does but chooses to let it slide, because no matter what, I'm his son and he's my dad. That's a bond never fucking severed.

"I'm going to go see this woman who has taken over my boy's heart." He places his hand over my chest in his fatherly way. "Tell her I'll be there in a bit. I have a few more things to do before we leave." I stuff the keys in my pocket and squeeze his shoulder. I love this man. He may know that I killed to save the life of the woman I love, but I sure as hell am not about to tell him I'm going to kill a man right now.

"Don't forget your mom," he calls out to me when I start to walk down the hall. I wave a hand in the air, gesturing to him I get it. I need to run to my truck to grab one important item before I take matters in my own hands. Finish this war. Deliver my vengeance.

I nod at the cop standing outside Juan's door, my black leather gloves holding my eager fingers in place. He nods back, opening the door, then shutting it quietly behind me. How quickly money can buy a person off, make them turn that cheek, keep their mouths shut. He's still a motherfucking cop though. If he wants to live to see another day or to spend the money I'm sure he has or will be given, he'll stand out here with his thumb shoved up his ass and pretend he never saw me.

The room is dark, the only lights coming from the monitors on the machines that are keeping this piece of garbage alive. I'm not worried one bit how my uncle has managed to get this done. I don't give a shit either. Slowly, I make my way to the side of his bed. His breathing is shallow. His eyes are closed. I lean into him. His eyes startle open.

"You ready to die, motherfucker?" I whisper. He barely scoffs.

"You may kill me, Dilan, but you underestimate the power I have to make sure you wind up right back in prison." Those winded words don't frighten me anymore. He knows it.

"You underestimate the power of my family. While your dead corpse rots, your flesh falling off of your body until you're nothing but bones in the ground, I'll have my cock inside of Anna. Her lips on mine. My name coming out of her mouth every time I make her come. Every time she tells me she loves me. Every child of mine she gives birth to. Her entire life devoted to me. And then," my hands go around his neck. My mouth goes to the side of his head, so I can whisper in his ear while I suck his last breath into the sterile air of this room.

"I will live my life knowing that I'm the one who killed you." I begin to squeeze. How I wish he had fight left in him to struggle. To fight back. He doesn't. That's the only regret I have about this whole thing. The noises he makes as he tries to struggle for air, I fucking love them. It's morose as fucking hell that my blood rises. My mind drains itself of the pent-up anger, bitterness, and hatred I've had for this man for years. His legs twitch. His hands strangle against the restraints he's cuffed to. "I know the color you're seeing isn't the white light, fucker. It's the red light. The stop sign with a dead fucking end." In less than a minute, I hear him draw his last breath. His body stills. I hold on for as long as I can until the screen shows that beautiful straight line. The green light for me. The motherfucker is dead. And then I'm gone.

My uncle is waiting outside the door. I look at him. There's nothing to be said except get our asses out of here now. That's exactly what we do before the doctors and nurses start running down the hall, screaming their code bullshit to one another. The last thing I hear before the door to the stairway closes is, "He's dead."

"I was beginning to worry about you." Anna sits up in her bed when I walk in. I give her a smile. One of a different kind. One she will never know about. "I had to finish cleaning up some bullshit before I came back." I kiss her. Christ, do I kiss her. Hard. Heavy. Wet.

"Your sandwich is over there." She points to the white bag sitting in the chair. That's how I end my day. Eating and falling asleep in this fucking hospital, where I killed the man who stole my life away from me. Who tried to take the woman I love. Who went to his death with the only secret I will never have an answer to. Why me? Why my family? But none of it matters anymore. I've delivered us from evil.

CHAPTER TWENTY-THREE

ANNA

"Where are we going?" I'm begging Dilan again to tell me where he is taking me. I've been after him all morning while we waited for the nurse to bring in my discharge papers and my pain pills, which I won't take. I don't want them, nor do I need them. I'm fine. Besides, this secret place that Dilan is telling me he is taking me to, has my body humming with excitement.

My mom knows too. It seems everyone does. Except for Roan and Alina. Well, maybe they do, but thank god they finally left last night for their honeymoon. Even though none of this was worth the price of anything, all the pain, anger, and frustration shattered into a million tiny shards of nothing when Dilan's phone went off this morning with a text from Roan.

Our minds woke up when we looked at the selfie of Roan and Alina sitting on the plane, waiting to take off, with a text from Roan saying, "I'm out of here, motherfucker." Both of them had the biggest smiles on their faces. My heart is elated for them. Extremely.

"You make sure you take care of her, Dilan." My mom damn near breaks my eardrums as she screeches loud enough for everyone in the parking lot to hear her.

"Yes, ma'am." Dilan chuckles with his response. He's acting differently. In a good way. Like no burden is on his shoulders anymore.

There's no pain. No anger. I'm done with all of this. I want to leave it all at the doorsteps of this hospital. Yet, somehow I know his mood is lightened because Juan has died. I feel it. Rot, you dirty asshole.

"What are you doing?" I ask in amusement when Dilan literally plucks me from the wheel chair, strides to the already open door of his truck, and places me in the passenger seat. "Taking care of you." He reaches over, grabs the seatbelt, and locks it in place. I roll my eyes. Good lord, just get me out of here.

I'm horny as hell, feisty as fuck, and I'm becoming pissed. Dilan is driving in complete silence, and it's driving me mad.

"Damn it, Dilan, where are we going?" My frustration escalates. I look up and see the signs for JFK airport. What the hell?

"Damn. You make my cock hard when you get mad." He veers down the exit toward the airport.

"Yeah, well, you'll be taking care of the hard cock on your own if you don't tell me. On top of that, I have no clothes. Nothing." I cross my hands over my breasts. I pout and clench my legs together.

"Where we're going, you don't need clothes." His sarcastic mouth gets a brow lift from me, along with a punch in the arm.

"I'm serious. What you do need is in a bag in the backseat. Your mom packed it." I turn around to see two duffle bags stuffed so tight they look like they're breaking at the seams. Lying shithead.

"We're going to the Florida Keys for a week," he finally tells me. "Really?" I uncross my arms and damn near come all over the seat. Warmth. Sun. Sex. Lots of sex.

"Yeah. I need to get the fuck out of here. So do you. I want you all to myself." I'm glad he's not suffering anymore. That no one is. Could all of this really be over? All of us have been through so much. Each and every one of us has had an obstacle, a person who has challenged us, who stood in the way of our lives.

Dilan pulls his truck into a parking spot and shuts it off, then reaches around the back and hands me my purse. "There's a walkway into the airport. Trust me, you will not need that coat." His eyes scan my body.

This is going to be a long flight. Shit. Unhooking my seatbelt, I shrug off my coat. The chill of the frigid air does nothing to cool off my aching pussy. The damn thing is on fire, burning up. It takes five minutes for us to get the bags out of the truck, walk the short distance to the walkway, and make our way to check-in. Memories flood my mind of the one and only time I was on a plane. My life was saved by the man walking beside me. I shove it away. They are gone. All of them. There are no more demons. No more evil. Nothing can stand in our way now, of the happiness we both deserve. My half-brother is gone. Juan and Jazmin are gone. The evil, sinister people who started this all. EVERY. LAST. ONE.

Like I knew it would be, the plane ride is long and torturous. I don't dare look into my seat when I stand up from first class to exit the plane. It's wet, I have no doubt. Dilan made sure of it when he tossed a blanket over the two of us and slid his hand into the waistband of my jeans, playing with my clit, dipping his fingers in and out of my pussy, covering my mouth when I finally exploded all over his fingers. Then, when I came down from my orgasm, I damn near fell apart again when he shoved his fingers in his mouth, licking them clean. God, I cannot wait to climb on his dick and take a long, hard ride.

The turquoise blue waters of the Keys surround us as we drive the short distance to Salvatore's house he owns down here. My mouth gapes open. The description Dilan gave me is nothing compared to the real thing. The driveway is brick. The outside is a mixture of yellow and white. The house is tucked back and barely visible among all the different tropical trees surrounding it. I smell the salty ocean the minute I step out of the convertible Dilan rented for us. My hair whips around in the breeze. I've never seen anything like this before. It's magical. Secluded. He was right. I don't need clothes. I plan on spending as much time as I can letting him fuck and make love to me on every surface possible inside and outside of this house.

"Oh my god. I have never seen anything like this." I inhale the fresh, salty air. My head spins looking at this place. It's remarkable and a damn shame no one lives here year-round. It's almost dark outside, but the lights are on when we enter. The colors magnify with boldness, the bright oranges, gold, and hues of turquoise make every room I enter cheery.

My legs take me to the warm breeze I feel, to the wide open space leading to the deck outside. The sky is a variety of dark pink shades as the sun sets into the water. I feel Dilan behind me as I make my way around the pool, lit up and glistening in its warm depth. I can see all of this later. I want the ocean breeze. The water. The sand between my toes. Moving as fast as my legs will carry me, I duck below a low-hanging branch and kick my tennis shoes off as I walk along the wooden deck to the beach. My t-shirt comes off. My jeans are next. I hop on one foot, anxiously tugging them. My clothes are a trail behind me; even my bra and panties are gone. I'm gloriously naked by the time my feet hit the grainy sand.

Then it hits me. I'm naked on a beach with Dilan. My scars are not healed, but I don't care. I care about nothing right now except the man who slithers his arms around my waist. His heated skin is up against mine, his heavy, thick cock resting along my tailbone.

"I love this idea. You naughty girl." His hand slides down to my wet pussy that's achingly hurting from not having him. I want him. All of him. Those long fingers spread me wide. Gliding. Molding into my wetness.

I pant. I moan. I need.

"Do you still want to be fucked, Anna? Like we talked about on the plane? Do you want to ride my cock out here? Scream my name when I fuck you blind? I have you alone. If your body is up to it, I will fuck every damn hole you want. I will have you crawling back through this sand on your hands and knees. And when I see that tight little ass of yours trying to make your way back inside, I'll fuck you once more. You begged. You asked for it. I'll ask once again. Are you ready to be fucked?" For the love that is holy. I need him to fuck me. Hard. I haven't been able to think of anything else since we left the hospital. My clit has been hard, constantly pulsing, my breasts hypersensitive, and fuck me, this man knows. He continues his assault on my clit and traces teasing circles around my breasts, pinching my nipples to the point of pain. Welcoming pain that zaps to my pussy. The feeling of wanting him to touch me everywhere is overwhelming.

My toes curl in the sand. My ass grinds up against his cock, his heavy breathing over-sensitizing my already scorching neck.

"I'll fuck you first. Then you can fuck me," I say boldly. Twisting out of his arms, I turn around. It's dark out now. I cannot make out his eyes. But I know they're dark. Wanting. Needing.

He drops to his knees in the sand. One lick of his tongue sweeps across my pussy, and that is all it takes to undo me. I shove him back. His body lies flat on the sand. I straddle him, dropping down until I feel him up against my clit. I'm going for a long ride. He's stiff. Solid. Firm. Dilan may think he can outfuck me, but he has another thing coming. Even though this is all new to me, I'm fucking addicted.

"Fuck. If you could see yourself right now. The way your hair is blowing back. The way your lips are parted slightly. And those eyes. You're an animal about to be fed, Anna. Ride me. Fill that tight pussy up and come all over my cock." As an athlete I have never felt sexy. Not until I met Dilan. The thought of exploring everything sexual with him has me going stark-raving mad. I'm powerful. In control. My pussy opens and stretches when I slip him into me, pleasingly expanding to be filled with him. My breathing is shallow as I take him all the way in. My hands are resting on his chest, his hands on my hips. I may have thought I would be the one in control here, but I couldn't be more wrong. He guides me up and down. Fast. Recklessly. Swiftly. His cock slamming into me wantonly. I'm screaming his name. My ass is squeezing, my pelvis tilting, and I'm given the ride of my life, never losing momentum. I up the ante by grinding, shifting, rolling forward and backward, his moans spurring me on, while his hands are tight on my waist.

"Fuck! I'm going to come!" he yells. No one can hear us, and if they do, I really don't care. I come too. Just like Dilan said, he does fuck me until I feel like I can't walk and I need to crawl. I don't crawl though. I spend the entire night under the stars, on the white sands with the man I love.

EPILOGUE

SIX MONTHS LATER

"It's hotter than hell's fucking waiting room down here." I look over to Aidan, whose face is dripping with sweat. I can't help but laugh my ass off right along with Cain and Roan. The ever-dramatic Aidan and his mouth.

"Drink another beer, man, and shut the hell up. In a few months, you'll be bitching about your balls shriveling up when it's snowing back home," Roan bites off.

"Besides, you wouldn't be so damn hot if you didn't have to keep getting up trying to keep Diesel out of the water," Roan says while we all watch Diesel, who's standing next to the chair Aidan is sitting in. His curious, little eyes keep looking out at the ocean, then back to his dad, hoping he looks away for that split second, so he can charge his little ass right back into the water. I love the kid, but Christ, is he a little hellion. The resemblance between father and son is damn near scary. Though, he may look like his dad, but he acts like his mom. The boy is funnier than hell.

"Great, dickhead, now look at my kid." We all crane our necks a little more to look at Diesel, who has his hands shoved down the front of his swimsuit. They boy is smart for his age, that's for damn sure. He pulls his little swim trunks down, turns away from us, and takes a piss in the sand.

"Well, at least he isn't pissing in the water. Be thankful for that," Cain chuckles.

"The only thing I'm thankful for is my wife, who has the patience of a saint and potty-trained him already. Except, he still shits himself. And don't any of you start laughing. It won't be long for you, Roan, since you knocked your wife up on your honeymoon. And Cain, you know all about the shit that comes out of their tiny little asses. That boy shits more than I do."

"Motherfucker. I'm prepared for that shit. We've watched all three of your kids enough that I have this shit nailed, man. Besides, it's the best damn feeling in the world, knowing you have a part of you and the woman you love growing inside of her. I say bring that shit on, bitches." I'm staying the hell out of this. No way in hell I'm letting any of them know the secret Anna told me yesterday. She's pregnant. About six weeks along. Unplanned, but damn, I'm happier than anyone of these motherfuckers, who are sitting by my side with their feet in the ocean and a cold beer in their hands.

We've been here in the Keys for a few days now. Since all the bullshit is over for all of us, things are settling down back home. Our lives are finally normal. Well, as normal as the goddamn mafia can be. I look down to my knuckles, still bruised and scraped all to hell from beating some jackass half to death before Digger blew his motherfucking brains out for thinking he was smart enough to steal some of our guns and sell them on his own. Stupid fuck.

"Why are you so quiet over there, Dilan? The way your woman runs her mouth to mine, I'm surprised she isn't pregnant ten times over." Aidan leans forward and takes a long pull of his beer, that cocky ass grin on his face.

He's right about one thing. She's pregnant, because we can't keep our hands off of each other. Fuck, I love her. She is one naughty little woman. Kinky as hell. I never knew she had it in her. Some of the ideas she comes up with regarding sex have me damn near blowing my load before I'm even inside of her.

"He's quiet, because Anna's pregnant." I snap my neck in Roan's direction, my icy glare sending him the how-the-hell-do-you-know look.

"No fucking way. Congrats, man." Cain stands up and sticks his hand out for me to shake. I grip it tight, pride scoring through my chest. Unlike ass-wipe Aidan, I can't wait to change diapers. Shitty or not.

"Alina told me last night, by the way. Seems Anna will need a good pediatrician once the baby's born. I'm happy for you." He then stands and does the same as Cain. I take his hand in pride as well.

"Well, I'll be a motherfucker. Look at this shit. All of us sitting here with our chests popped out. Kids. Wives." Aidan leans over and takes my hand in his.

The word wives sends another sharp strike of pride along with love to my chest. Last night, right here on this beach, with the moonlight glaring down on us, the stars shining brightly in the sky, Anna and I got married. This was the place she chose. The place where she said was truly the beginning of us. She's right. Even though I was too stupid to see what was right in front of me, while I had my head buried in the sand over my revenge for six months, leaving her behind, my wife waited for me. Forgave me. And now she's carrying my baby. Our lives aren't perfect. Hell, no one's is, but Anna is damn close. Strong. Beautiful. And together, we fit.

"Water. Fucking water." We all strain our heads at Diesel, who takes off like a bat out of hell toward the ocean. Butt ass naked.

"Goddamn it. Where's my wife?" Aidan gets up and runs after his kid, snatching him up right before his son take a nosedive into the ocean.

"Your wife is right here, asshole. And how many times have you four said the "F" word? He sure doesn't hear that from me." There they all are. Finally. Standing there. Every one of them more beautiful than when they left to go shopping. Especially the blond-haired woman whose eyes are trained on me. Her hair is piled on the top of her head. I hate it and love it at the same damn time when she piles all that thick hair on top of her head. My cock gets hard, thinking about unraveling it, then yanking the hell out of it while I fuck her from behind.

Every image from last night soars like a proud American straight to my chest, then travels right to my cock. Anna on her back, her legs wrapped around my waist. Anna riding my cock, her heavy tits bouncing in my hands. Her hair wet. Her pussy clenching me. Her mouth on mine. Right here on this beach. I knew she had a wild streak in her just waiting to come out. For me. That streak is mine.

I take my eyes off of her face briefly to look at her bare stomach, then back to her eyes again. She smirks back at me, knowing damn well what I'm thinking about. You would think we were a couple of teenagers the way we go at it. Anna is one horny woman. And from what Roan has told me over the past few months about Alina, and how much she wants it ever since she got pregnant, my damn cock is like a block of ice. Christ. I'm lucky. It has nothing to do with the sex. It has everything to do with her. My wife.

"Blame Cain. He started throwing the F-bomb around. I told him to knock it off. The asshole won't listen. Just like your kid." Aidan goes to hand Diesel to Deidre, who already has their younger son strapped to her hip.

"Asshole. Asshole. Daddy is an asshole," Diesel starts spewing off in a sing-song voice.

"Woman. I ought to take you over my knee." He looks at her with a smile on his face; she looks at him as if saying 'I dare you to.'

"Those are bad words, Diesel." Alina tries to take him from Aidan, but Diesel lays his head on his dad's shoulder.

"I told you I would beat you when my grandson started swearing." Deidre's mom walks up and takes a still naked Diesel from Aidan, or more like snatches him away from his dad and his foul mouth, while her dad laughs his ass off along with the rest of us. And here come the rest of them. My parents. Roan's parents. Alina's entire family. My new mother-in-law and her now husband Ramsey, who got married a few months ago.

Everyone is down here. Thank god when Anna and I came down here six months ago, I talked her into getting out of bed for one day to go house shopping. We bought a small house down the road. It's not nearly as immaculate as this one of my aunt and uncle's, but it's ours. Still needs some work done to it. That will come in time. This is our vacation spot. A place where we can bring our children. Make memories.

My wife moves to my side, her mother trailing behind her, tears shining in her eyes. Happiness. She told her. Anna needs to go over my knee and have her sweet little ass spanked. We agreed to tell everyone together. It's obvious she couldn't wait.

"Sorry. Mom guessed when I ran to the bathroom and vomited my lunch." She puts her arms around my waist. I know morning sickness is part of the stages of being pregnant, but I hate it. Anything that causes my wife pain, I hate. Even though this is the happiest time of our lives right now, there will never come a day when I want to see her in pain. I trace my finger across one of the few scars on her stomach. A reminder of why it kills me to see her suffer, no matter what the cause. I can only imagine what I'll be like when she gives birth. I'll probably stand there with a gun pointed at the scared-out-of-his-mind doctor, making him or her ease my wife's pain. It will definitely be a woman. No goddamn way another man will ever look at her sweet, tight pussy. That is mine. All mine.

Grace starts bawling, which gets everyone's attention. Her hands fly all over the place while she tries to get whatever it is she's trying to say out of her mouth. Diesel and his words are more understandable than what she's spewing out.

"My little girl is going to have a baby," she finally gets out through her sobs. Christ. There goes our news. I look to my parents. My mom's hands are flying to her mouth. My dad's chest is puffing out. I swear even all the hair on top of his head is standing up with pride.

With a screaming Diesel, who's begging to be let down, because all of Alina's nieces and nephews are in the water playing; a dozen women balling their eyes out; Cain and Calla's shy daughter holding tightly to her dad's hand; men shaking my hands; women placing their hands on my wife's still flat stomach. This is how we spend our time. Bonding. Closeness. A connection made out of the strongest bind there is. Family.

If you thought it was over, you couldn't be more wrong.

More threats. More murder.

One death. One family

Watch for EMPIRE. The series finale. Winter of 2016.

ACKNOWLEDGEMENTS

There are so many people to thank for this book.
First of all always and forever to my husband Tony. Every day is an adventure with you. We laugh, love and dream.
My children. Aaron and Shane. The day I became a mother was the best day of my life. It's a job that I'm proud to say I've successfully mastered.
To my editor Julia Goda. Thank you from the depth of my heart for always coming through for me.
To CP Smith. My formatter. Thank god for you. You my love are a life-savor.
To Sommer Stein. Words don't do your work justice. Again I have a brilliant cover. You amaze me with the talent you have.
To my blog girls. Oh lord. We could spend days going on about the four of us. But let's just say my life is complete now that I have you.
To My BETA readers. Lord only knows what I would be doing if it wasn't for you. You ladies catch the tiniest detail, the simplest mistake and the whoopers. You push me to be better and not one of you are afraid to tell me like it is. That's love right there. That's trust and a friendship that will be carried for the rest of my life.
Eric Battershell. No one will understand the friendship that you and I have. I've found a brother in you.
Lance Jones. I have found a friend in you. Your success has made me very proud. You have come a long way since day one. Keep living the dream.
To all my girls who are constantly posting and pimping my name everywhere. How can I even begin to thank you? You ladies put so much time and effort into what you do and expect nothing in return. You're selfless and it show every day. I would be nothing and nowhere without you.

To every reader, blogger out there. Sweet baby Jesus, you have all welcomed me. Helped me become what I've always wanted to be. You read my stories, you message me with thanks when in reality it should be me thanking you. For without you, where would any of us who write be? Lost, empty and not living a dream. Not doing what we love to do and that is bringing the best stories into your world. Thank you for embracing my work. For the reviews. For the sweet gestures. I adore you.

And lastly. To my sanity, my helper, my friend Helena Rizzuto. I'd have my head buried in the snow by now if it wasn't for you. The ideas you toss my way. The way you jump and have something done before I even ask you about it. The way you've come into my life and pulled those reins tight and took control. I adore you Helena. You are the greatest thing to have stalked me. HA!

Please leave a review for Dilan and Anna when you are done. Those reviews help Authors more than you will know.

Until next time,

Kathy.

Other Books by Kathy Coopmans

The Shelter Me Series

Shelter Me

Rescue Me

Keep Me

The Contrite Duet

Contrite

Reprisal

The Syndicate Series

The Wrath of Cain

The Redemption of Roan

The Absolution of Aidan

Late winter of 2016

The Deliverance of Dilan

Spring of 2016

ICE

FIRE

Books one and two of The Elite Forces Series.

Co-written with Hilary Storm.

Made in the USA
Middletown, DE
10 May 2016